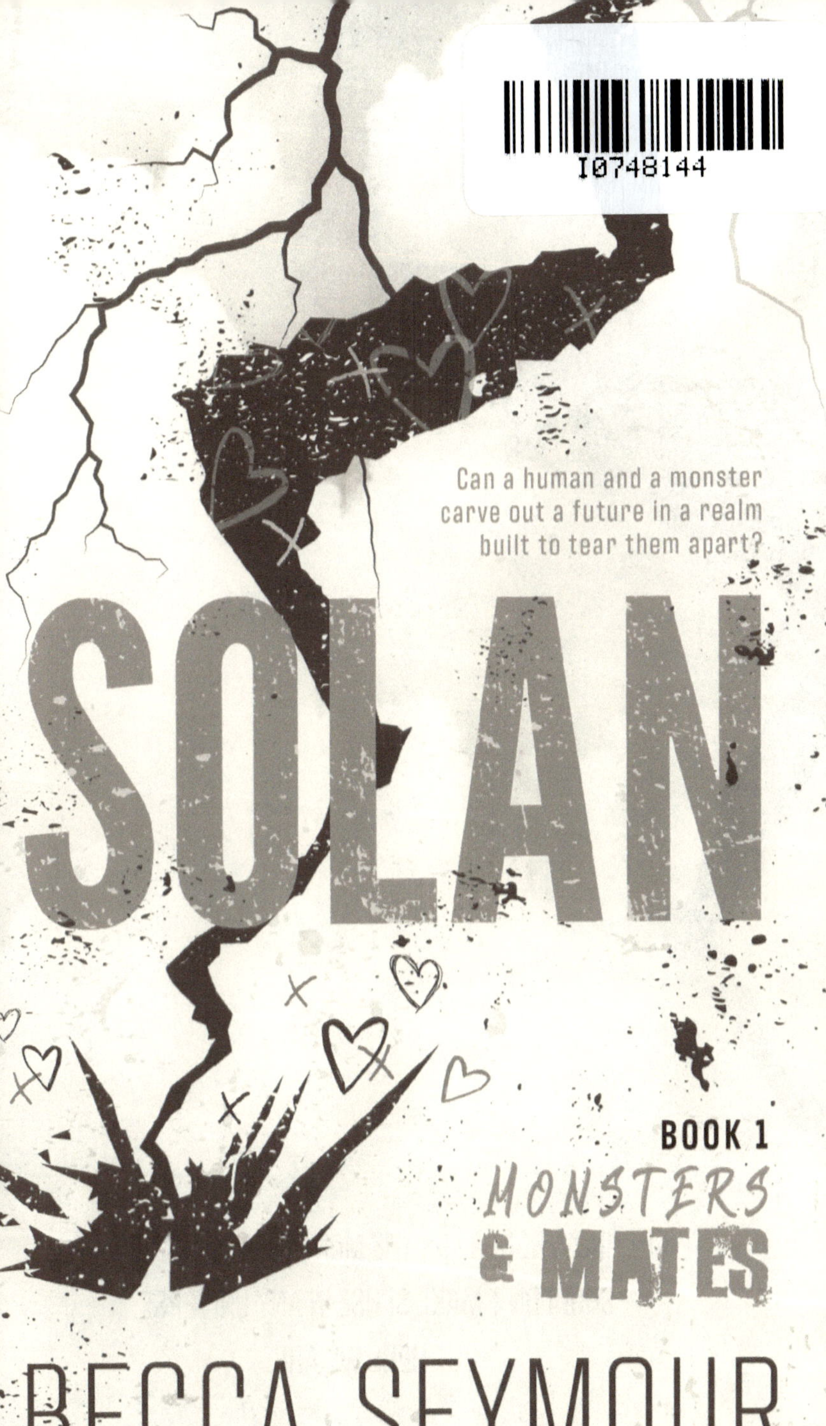

I0748144
Can a human and a monster carve out a future in a realm built to tear them apart?
SOLAN
BOOK 1
MONSTERS & MATES
BECCA SEYMOUR

GETTING A BONER FOR THE MONSTER WHO SAVED US
SHOULDN'T MAKE SENSE IN ANY UNIVERSE.
BUT HERE WE ARE.

SOLAN

BOOK ONE

MONSTERS & MATES

BECCA SEYMOUR

Monsters & Mates

Solan | Kael

Zone Defense

No Take Backs | No More Secrets | No Wrong Moves | No Backing Down

Fast Break

Rules, Schmules! | Facts, Smacts! | Regular Smegular! | Easy, Schmeasy!

True-Blue

Let Me Show You | I've Got You | Becoming Us | Thinking It Over | Always For You | It's Not You | Our First & Last | Next For Us

Outback Boys

Stumble | Bounce | Wobble

Fangs & Felons

Thicker Than Water | Weaker Than Instinct | Brighter Than Fear | Stronger Than Fate | Softer Than Stone

Stand-Alone Contemporary

Not Used To Cute | High Alert | Realigned | Amalgamated | Under the Blazing Stars | Best Kind of Awkward | Tastes Like Sugar

COVER DESIGN: BOOKSMITH DESIGN

EDITORS: HOT TREE™ EDITING

E-BOOK ISBN: 978-1-923252-34-9

PAPERBACK ISBN: 978-1-923252-36-3

CHAPTER
ONE

Sweat draws the flies. After thirty-seven years, you'd think I'd be used to having hundreds of the damn things buzzing in front of my face. Not a chance. They annoy the hell out of me.

A fast flick of my hand in front of my face does virtually nothing to get them to leave me alone.

Taking a steadying breath while trying not to draw one of the annoying insects into my mouth, I lean against the fence, staring out into the distance at the greying sky that has taken on a distinct tinge of green.

The storm's only been brewing for fifteen minutes. It's big and fast, and the hail is likely going to damage the tin roof.

Why the hell did I think it was a good idea for me to come home again?

Sure, I returned out west for my dad, Jack Sr, to help him through his sickness as best as I could before I finally laid him to rest next to the giant bottle tree he loved so much. But that was seven months ago, yet I'm still here.

One hundred and thirty kilometres from sort-of civilisation.

A crash of thunder rends the air, loud enough that the cows in the far-right paddock bolt for the fence line.

With this brewing storm that, honestly, I've never seen anything quite like before, I'm wondering *why* I'm still standing here.

There's a strange orange and red, similar to that of a sunset. The sky is a kaleidoscope of colour as it washes over the dark red dirt. The sky, a stunning wash of vermillion, copper, and desert gold, should be beautiful. But that green and the flashes of lightning set my teeth on edge.

It's enough to have me dragging in a calming breath, thankfully without pulling a flying insect in with—

It's weird. I hold my breath, listening intently, realising that during the past couple of minutes of watching the fast-approaching storm, all the flies have disappeared.

The slowly descending late-afternoon spring sun usually brings with it a chorus of high-pitched buzzing, the song of the cicadas already filling the otherwise quiet space around me by now. But there's nothing.

The birds have already flown away, out of the path of the storm, and even the herd is eerily silent.

The braying of Geralt and Gertie, secure in the barn, has even cut off.

This time of day is usually an in-between time of saying goodbye to a long day of working my old man's six-hundred-acre property—or mine, technically, though it still doesn't feel like it—and taking solace in the peace only the outback can offer.

But then there's this damn storm. It's closer than it was five minutes ago but still sits on the horizon, probably twenty but maybe thirty kilometres away.

And it's just kind of hovering there.

The full display of incredible colours remains awash in the sky as the lightning strikes become more frequent. There's what should be a growl of thunder, but it's a low groan echoing across the flat land before me. A tired, almost-mournful sound reaches where I stand. It lasts ten long seconds, and by the time it ends, my hairs are standing on end and I'm no longer confident the house and the barn are as secure as I thought they were.

It's odd. The whole thing.

The now-posturing storm. The majestic show of lightning. The painful wail tearing through the air.

A crack of sound rocks the very earth between my booted feet. Instinctively, I drop to the ground. The world shifts. Tilts. And doesn't stop moving.

On my hands and knees, I cling to the red dirt as ingrained into my skin as the Australian air is embedded in my lungs. I stare out at the expanding storm. The grey continues to mix with the red and gold, the green growing brighter.

What the ever-loving fuck?

It's like the aurora borealis or even the aurora australis but with its own palette of colour mirroring the outback landscape.

It's also impossible. Here. So far away from, well, anywhere.

With the ground still rumbling under my feet, I use the metal gate to steady myself as I haul my arse off the ground. I don't look away from the mountain of clouds as they stretch and tumble against one another, much like the heaving of ocean waves.

While the storm remains the same distance away,

it stretches across the horizon until I have to physically turn to see how far and wide it spreads.

Eyes wide in fear, I back away from the fence. My house, about two hundred metres behind me, feels far away as the storm clouds continue to extend, the edges seeming to reach for each other, forming a goddamn circle. With me in the bloody middle.

I turn and run, grappling for my phone in my jeans as I race for the house. I manage a glance at the screen, fear slicing into me when no signal is evident.

Not even SOS Calls Only is on display.

Is this what a tornado feels like? Am I going to get sucked up and carried away?

I already live in the land of Aus, and if any walking, talking lions, scarecrows, or tinmen cross my path, they'll be sucking lead.

What I need to do is get the hell out of here.

Hearing Geralt and Gertie, I hesitate, hand on the door.

There's banging coming from the stables. They're freaking the fuck out. And I get it. I'm right there with them.

Fuck.

They're good horses, but trying to get them into the trailer while they lose their shit is going to be a nightmare.

I peer up at the sky, back at where I first saw the storm brewing.

My breath shudders out of me. The edges of the clouds speed towards each other. In no time at all, they're going to touch. The circle will be formed.

While I have no idea what that means, I absolutely know it's nothing good.

"Fuck," I bellow and wrench the flyscreen door open. Half a step inside, I grab the key to my Ford Ranger, turn, and bolt for my truck.

I'm inside in a few heavy exhales, my fingers trembling as I jab at the ignition button.

Nothing.

I press it again, dread curdling my stomach. No lights are on in the dash, and there's zilch coming from the engine.

Gripping the steering wheel, I shake it. Frustration bleeds out of me. "You fucking piece of shit. Fuck."

Think, Jack. Think.

With my pulse racing and my thoughts spiralling, I tumble out of the ute. Right about now, I wish I'd listened to Jeremy. He's a hard-core prepper and would be all over this shit. The man even built a bunker.

Instead, I've got an old Queenslander that's made

out of tin and wood, same as the barn, and an expensive-as-hell Ford Ranger that's worthless.

I'm a few metres away from the barn, heading towards my bike, when silence has me pulling up short.

The growing wind has dropped, and the groaning storm has quietened. All I can hear are my uneven breaths sawing out of me.

Even Geralt and Gertie aren't braying.

I take slow, measured steps to the side of the barn so I can see east—where the storm clouds are meeting. Wide-eyed, I swallow hard. The clouds appear less than ten millimetres away from touching at this distance. I take another breath, and the oxygen is sucked out of my lungs as I fly through the air.

My arms windmill, and any second now, I'm going to be kissing dirt.

I stare up into the once-blue sky, my brain stumbling.

Green.

The green of the Daintree Rainforest.

The sky above my head is fucking green.

I have but a second to process the strangeness before a light fills my vision so bright, I'm unable to see anything. Not the strangeness. Not the usual ochre dirt breaking my fall.

Not my red blood spilling against the soil.

My ears ring. The piercing brightness fades around the edges, narrowing into blackness. The darkness is the only familiar sensation in the changing landscape.

I welcome it.

I DON'T KNOW HOW MUCH TIME HAS PASSED since I was knocked out. All I know for sure is, the back of my head throbs, my coccyx is screaming bloody murder, and it's possible I have a concussion. The latter is the only explanation for the still-green sky above me.

It's a possibility, I suppose, that I'm in a coma. It's a valid reason for the world above me seeming like it's been dipped in the North Queensland rainforest and appearing as a vividly bright canvas textured with varying shades of green.

"Shit me." My fingertips come away damp when I shift my head and touch the tender bump at the back. Red stains my fingers. It's still wet. So either I'm still bleeding or I didn't black out for too long.

I test my limbs. Everything aches, but agony doesn't send sharp stabs of alarm, so that's something. I circle my ankles left, then right, and I release a shaky exhale. Not broken.

It's time to sit up and take real stock. The weird sky above me is a problem I'll solve once I know I can stand without falling on my arse.

I manage to lift myself up and stay upright on my butt, then pick up my worn, dusty Akubra off the ground by my side. The aches are very real, but I think that's all they are: sore bones and muscles. From this position, my childhood home looks untouched from the blast that took me down.

The windows are intact, and the tin roof has the same number of dents from previous hailstorms. It's a relief. Whatever put me on my arse felt like it had the power to demolish the whole building. It's a miracle the old place is still standing—a Queenslander my grandpop built eighty years back.

The panicked braying from the barn has me moving.

I need to check on Geralt and Gertie. That I can hear them is a good sign. Sure, they're distressed—a given considering the storm.

The storm.

The thought makes me slam on the brakes a few metres shy of the closed barn doors.

Where the fuck has the storm gone?

I do a slow 360, then a fast one, which sends a thud of pain through my head. But I don't have the brain space to worry about that.

The dirt beneath my feet remains a familiar deep ochre. The kilometres of barbed-wire fencing—most I rigged up with my dad over the years—are laid out before me, spanning my inherited six-hundred-acre property.

From my property, beyond my cattle, the fences, and the yards, all there usually is to see is the main road, only visible on a still day, about three kilometres away in the south, and my sister and brother-in-law's neighbouring property about four kilometres down the road in the east. Beyond that, there's usually just flat land, red dirt, endless blue skies, and, during the wet season, glorious grass.

Fast, shallow breaths have my shoulders vibrating and my head spinning.

I shake my head, struggling to comprehend what I can see. What's gone.

What the fuck's happened?

The three-kilometre gravel road leading from my property via a two-hundred-metre dirt-track road to the bitumen of the A7 remains intact. Several kilometres out to the left of it, the usual flat plains are gone.

Literally fucking gone.

The ground, where the long grass usually dances in the breeze, hasn't been burnt by the storm—a possibility from the lightning display I witnessed.

I shake my head, struggling to process what I see.

A mountain crouches in the distance. Its peak—impossible to tell how high it is from the ground—is covered in snow. *Snow*. Legit, the first and last time I ever saw snow was on a school trip almost thirty years ago when we visited Canberra. It had been cold—obviously—but disappointingly icy. None of the fluffy stuff good for making snowmen like you see in movies.

It's not just the mountain that is nearly exploding my mind.

To the west, there are buildings. They're too far away for me to tell what kind or how many. All I know is, they shouldn't be there.

"The fuck is happening?" My words catch on a slight breeze that appears. It's warm and surprisingly humid, not carrying the usual dry heat of the outback.

I spin around, looking in the opposite direction, my jaw going slack.

Gut clenching, I've no idea if I'm going to vomit or shit myself. Either is a possibility when, in the distance, I see movement. A cloud of... I swallow hard. Sand. It's fucking sand. Here. Sure, there are deserts and beaches in Australia, but not fucking *here*.

The cloud of sand is heading towards my sister's property.

Even though it looks like a speck from this distance, I can still sense that it's big and fast. It could be an SUV, but my gut tells me it's not.

The moving sand cloud has yet to meet the red dirt I'm so familiar with. It's still several kilometres away.

Either way, my gut's screaming at me to move.

While I'm sure my sister and Derek are at work, not usually finishing till the sun has set at six-ish, Jamie's school bus drove by over an hour ago. He'll be home, doing his chores like the good twelve-year-old kid he is.

Turning on my heel, I race back to my ute, my heart thundering.

Please start.

It doesn't. The battery seems to be dead.

Not wasting time, I rush to the barn while doing a cursory check of my phone, but I already know I'll have no signal. I'm right.

Whatever the blast was must have taken out the

towers. My service is always a little sketchy out here, but I have no doubt that isn't the issue.

When I open the barn doors, Geralt's and Gertie's braying assault me. They're freaked.

"Hey, there." I go straight to Geralt, who's the bigger and noisier of the two. "Shh. It's all okay."

I stroke down his rich brown neck, his hair smooth and familiar. A breath gushes out of me when I do. I'm fucking wrecked, my nerves shot. But I have to pull my head out of my arse and get to Jamie.

"We'll all be okay," I whisper, straightening my spine and willing myself to believe it.

I was brought up here, isolated and battling everything from grassfires to floods to dealing with snake bites. I know I'm made of tougher stuff than this. I need to do better.

Closing my eyes, I take a calming breath. This is the last one I allow myself before I take action and stop having a breakdown. "Get your shit together, Jack."

Geralt nudges my shoulder, and I snap open my eyes.

My dirt bike, quad, and ATV are dead. Even the tractor is fried.

I force steel into my words when I say, "We've got this."

At least I *really* hope Geralt has got this with me.

Rather than cussing up a storm, I put my focus on saddling Geralt.

As I swing myself onto his back, I feel his familiar powerful muscles beneath me, his fifteen hands of chestnut power offering me comfort. He's a stock-horse and has been my steadfast companion for years, yet today even he's skittish.

He whinnies and huffs.

"Come on, boy. We need to get to Jamie."

A snort escapes him, his muscles tensing against my legs as he prepares to move. He's clearly anxious, but he's intelligent and reliable. I have faith that he knows what I need from him.

As we burst from the shelter of the barn into the expanse of rich soil beneath Geralt's hooves, his nervous energy transforms. His strides become purposeful, his movements sure.

With each step, his confidence grows, and thank fuck it does. I can't look away from the changed landscape in the distance and the green-tinged sky that keeps snatching my attention.

Was there a chemical explosion? Maybe radiation is polluting the sky. But what about the buildings? The further I move from my home, it becomes clearer there are shelters of some sort in the distance.

Then there's the goddamn mountain that's appeared like a damned mirage.

Fuck, I'm at the point of believing aliens really do exist.

The first fence is looming, but I know Geralt's got this.

He launches over the barbed-wire fence with such effortless grace, relief barrels into me. He's in control. It feels good. And since I'm the one riding him, I need to suck that shit up and take a page out of his book.

Wind whips around us, but Geralt powers on, his hooves pounding the familiar path towards my sister's property. Urgency gnaws at me, anxiety coursing through my veins.

Jamie's a good kid. He's smart. He's also a country kid. He knows how to handle himself.

He has to be fine.

My reassurances are a mantra in my head as I push Geralt harder, urging him to go faster and cover the distance in record time.

My sister's property grows closer on the horizon, and my heart races, fear and hope battling it out. But the house looks unaffected. So does the barn.

That's a good thing, right?

As we draw closer, the adrenaline in my veins matches the thundering beat of Geralt's hooves.

Movement.

The screen door swings open.

Thank fuck.

Jamie barrels down the steps, his arms pumping fast as his gangly form hits the gravel path.

He's safe.

The weight pressing against my chest eases.

He's unharmed.

"Uncle Jack!" The warm breeze snatches his words and delivers them to me.

His relief mirrors my own, as do his wide eyes.

This kid means the world to me.

In truth, he's the main reason I chose to stay after losing my dad.

"Jamie." On shaking legs, I dismount. "You're okay." I tug him close, embracing him tightly, gratitude flooding me.

He's shaking and gripping me.

Geralt stands by, a comforting presence, his chestnut coat glistening with sweat. Reaching out without releasing Jamie, who takes a long, shuddery breath, I stroke Geralt's mane.

He's done good.

"Hey." I dot a kiss on top of Jamie's dirty-blond

hair, the same colour mine was at his age, but I lost all traces of gold by the time I turned sixteen.

Leaning back, Jamie's wide eyes meet mine.

"You good?" I search his face, trying to see how he really is. His face is flushed, his eyes a little watery, but there are no tear tracks down his cheeks.

He straightens and steps out of my hold but remains close enough to touch.

I do just that and place my palm on his shoulder, squeezing gently.

"I am now. I had to change my undies 'cause I shit myself from that blast. But holy crap, Uncle Jack, what the hell was that?"

Warmth blooms in my chest, humour dislodging some of the fear that's taken root there.

This kid has a mouth on him, which, sensibly, he curbs around his parents.

But not around me.

I swear I'm the best kind of influence on my nephew. Admittedly, Harper doesn't always agree. But this kid's a mini-me. Even his poor folks can't deny that.

"For real," he continues, barely taking a breath, "I fell on my butt."

"Are you hurt?" I cut in before he no doubt continues talking nonstop.

"Bruised." He stops, his eyebrows shooting high as he takes me in. "Bloody hell, you're bleeding."

I touch the back of my head, no longer feeling fresh blood there. "I'm good." I shake my head. "It's stopped." It still hurts like I've been whacked with a piece of two-by-four, but since there's not a pool of blood at my feet and I'm still standing, I figure I'll be okay.

"So, what happened? One minute I was making myself a bowl of cereal, and the next I hit the floor and the air-con went out. I've checked the trip switch, but nothing's working. Ridge hasn't stopped kicking off."

With my panic subsided, I hear Jamie's horse. Ridge does sound like he's going apeshit.

"Is your phone working?"

Jamie shakes his head. "Nope. The internet is down too."

A given, as there's no electricity.

"I tried the Can-Am," he says. "It won't start. I was going to come over, check on you."

Of course he was.

This kid's been brought up knowing how to make a Vegemite sandwich, fix a fence, and ride a bike and a Can-Am. He's also a sure shot with a rifle and can ride a horse even better than I could at his age.

His dad's a good guy—an accountant, if you can believe it.

Which is the reason why my parents shaved off just five acres fifteen years back for them to build a home, knowing that Derek could ride a mower, but beyond that, running a property wasn't his thing.

My dad spent the time teaching Jamie how to live and love the property life, and I did, too, when I visited.

"Let's just settle Ridge, and I'll give Geralt a quick brush down. We'll then figure out what's going on, yeah?"

"Okay." He hesitates, his focus moving beyond me. "And what are we doing about that?"

Fuck. The plume of *sand*—not freaking dirt.

I jolt around and follow his line of sight. Narrowing my gaze, I try to figure out what I'm seeing. It's closer now, but I still can't work out what it is.

"What is that?"

I shake my head. "No idea."

"Are we ignoring the fact that there's sand where Mr Bates's property used to be?"

Why Jamie's so damn calm is beyond me, but my pulse is going berserk. Not only because the plume is likely just seven kilometres out, but before Jamie spoke, I could have pretended I've been hallucinating.

"You see that too?" It's best I double-check.

"Yep. And the giant freakin' mountain. That too."

"Shit."

"And what's up with the green sky?"

I snap my head up, knowing he's doing the same.

It looks more sea green at the moment. Has it changed shade? Maybe the way I'd perceived it earlier was just my head still spinning and struggling to make sense of it.

"Radiation?" It's clear I'm clueless.

"No way is that radiation." My nephew legit scoffs, a sound too light and carefree, considering neither of us knows what the hell is going on.

"How would you know, wise-arse?"

"We did a project on it in science last term. That's not what radiation looks like."

"So, what are you thinking?" I glance at Jamie, my heart squeezing at the contemplative expression forming on his face. God, I love this kid. And thank Christ he's not freaking out.

He shrugs. "It kinda looks like some of the video games I play."

I quirk an eyebrow at him. "Uh-huh. That's helpful."

He shrugs and meets my gaze. "I'm not saying I think we're in a video game, but nothing about this is right."

"True that." He's dead set got it in one. Nothing about this is right.

While our homes are still here, as are part of the road and a section of Liam and Nancy's neighbouring property, beyond that—from the sky to the very ground—nothing is as it should be.

It's like a section of our world's been cut out and stitched into somewhere "other." And just thinking that makes me want to roll my eyes and knock back a bottle of whiskey.

Geralt snorts and paws the ground. I tighten my grip on his reins. He shakes his head, eyes wide, almost frantic.

"Uncle Jack."

The hitch in Jamie's voice captures my attention completely. But his whole focus is on the direction of the plume of sand. I follow his gaze, my heart jolting so hard, my chest feels bruised.

It's no longer a speck I can mistake for an SUV.

"Seriously, what is that?"

At the panic in his voice, the hair on the back of my neck rises. Horror floods my system, but more importantly, I agree with my nephew: What the fuck is that?

"We need to move. Get the saddle on Ridge." I thrust Geralt's reins at Jamie and charge into the barn, knowing I can get Ridge ready for riding faster than my nephew can. "Get the key for the gun safe," I holler as I tug the leather saddle from its mount.

Hearing Jamie moving, I focus on saddling Ridge, my pulse pounding a frantic beat in my ears.

We need to get out of here. Fast.

Whatever the hell that thing is outside, it's not a vehicle.

With shaky hands, I get the saddle fastened and put on the bridle. I can't think about what I saw. If I do, it's likely I'll hesitate. Stumble. Lose my fucking mind.

"Got the keys."

I nod as I secure the reins. "Get your popsy's gun sling." It's one Dad gifted Jamie a few years back even though it would take some time for him to grow into.

"Okay."

After finally securing the stirrup straps, I head to the gun cabinet in the barn and unlock the door. A satchel sits on the floor, one of my dad's that he used to carry ammo when he went mustering—intending to shoot brown snakes and the occasional taipan.

"Here." Jamie passes me the sling as I grab one of the guns.

"Thanks. Take Ridge outside. And grab the water container and make sure it's full. Throw it in one of the rucksacks." I focus on gathering ammo, securing the rifle in its sling, and collecting the saddlebag attachment that carries my sister's shotgun.

I lock the safe back up and look around.

This feels dramatic, reacting this way. Or at least it should.

But deep in my gut, I know something—quite possibly everything—is wrong.

And if what I saw in the distance is real and not my concussed brain freaking me out, getting armed and the hell out of here is simply common sense.

Outside, under the weird sky, Jamie joins me. He passes me a backpack.

"I shoved some jerky and potato chips in there."

I ignore the way his hand trembles and nod, offering a smile I absolutely don't feel. Beyond sheer panic, dread, and knowing I need to protect Jamie, there's little room for anything else.

"Mount up."

He puts on his own pack, pushes his Akubra firmly onto his head, and mounts Ridge. He does so effortlessly, causing pride to swell in my chest.

How the hell he's so calm and keeping his shit together is beyond me.

He saw the same thing I did in the distance.

Yet he's here, kitted out, and looking at me with wide, clear eyes as if I have all the answers.

If only I did.

But for him, I'll bullshit my way through this. There's no other choice.

Securing the shotgun to Geralt, I finally glance in the direction I've been avoiding.

"What's the plan?"

As I stare at the monstrous creature speeding towards us, its horns large and purple, I swallow hard.

What the fuck is our plan?

"We're going to get the hell out of here, head south towards Injune." It's where my sister and brother-in-law work. It's usually a forty-minute drive, so it will take longer than that by horse.

"Do you think it's still there?"

Jamie's question freezes my brain.

Slowly, I glance at him, risking taking my eyes off the creature that I mistook for a vehicle. Understandable, since it really does look to be the size of a big SUV.

I see it in Jamie's worried frown. In the moisture

in his eyes. Beyond the familiar red dirt is a land that we both know is not our own.

If we're right—and I absolutely pray we're not—it's likely that town and the world as we know it has gone. Disappeared.

That or it's been swallowed somehow by the beastly creature who I have no doubt wants to eat our faces off.

Fuck that shit.

"Let's get the hell out of here." I mount Geralt, nod at my nephew to take the lead, and together, we ride on out.

Who knows what we'll find. The important thing is that Jamie's okay and I have a bag full of bullets for the rifle and shells for the shotgun if I need them.

CHAPTER
TWO

FOR OVER HALF AN HOUR, WE'VE RACED OVER the unfamiliar plains. What I thought was sand is more like golden soil over a hard surface. A little like the land at home during a drought.

One thing's for sure, there's nothing remotely familiar about anything surrounding us.

I flick a glance over my shoulder, though the beast is no longer on our tail. It hasn't been for the past ten minutes, but rather than filling me with relief, a ball of dread builds in my gut.

Where the hell is it?

"You think we lost it?"

I'm riding at Jamie's side, so it's easy to flick a glance at him. "Hopefully."

He nods before peering over his own shoulder.

We've slowed the horses. They're calmer, which I hope means they're not sensing whatever creature was chasing after us. The melodic thud of their hooves gives me a moment to think and figure out what to do.

The one thing in our favour is that the sun is no longer setting. It's high in the sky. I think. I can't actually see the blazing ball of fire, but it's bright out.

But still, even if Injune is where it should be, it'll likely take us another six hours or so to get there by horseback. Given that the terrain under the horses' hooves is so unfamiliar, I've got to be smart. That means no pushing them unless our lives depend on it.

The thought turns me cold.

We trek on, Jamie constantly looking around, his eyes wide with wonder.

Ahead, a cluster of arboreal structures resembling a forest emerges like an illusion in the distance. Turning to Jamie, I offer a tentative smile. "Well, kiddo," I say with a light-hearted chuckle that I absolutely don't feel, "looks like we stumbled into the set of a particularly bizarre episode of *Stranger Things*."

He shoots me a dubious glance but manages a small grin in return, adjusting his grip on the reins. "If a gateway opens up overhead, I'm out of here."

I snort. "Sounds like a good plan." I stare back at the forest. "We best head for those trees," I continue, gesturing towards the strange-looking woodland ahead. "It'll be good to get out of the open and take stock."

Just because we can't see the six-legged horned creature in hot pursuit, it doesn't mean it won't catch up.

With a nod at each other, we urge our horses forwards; their hooves kick up strange iridescent dust as we approach the otherworldly forest. The closer we get, the more surreal the vegetation becomes. Towering trees shimmer with hues I've never seen before, and peculiar glowing vines twist and coil around their trunks like pythons crushing their prey.

After trekking further into the cooler canopy of wide leaves and reaching a cluster of boulders, we dismount. I have no idea if it's safe to do so, but my pulse has yet to settle, and I'm pretty sure my blood pressure is sky-high.

"Let's take fifteen minutes, yeah?" I pull out a water flask and hand it to Jamie.

While he takes it with a smile, he doesn't stop peering around. "You think we're okay here?"

I wince and shrug. "I wish I knew, Jamie." I'm not

prepared to lie or offer false promises. "Just take a breath for now, drink, and we'll get on our way."

Nodding, he presses the bottle to his lips. I'm grateful he doesn't push and ask, "Get on our way to *where* exactly?" I press my back to one of the large off-yellow boulders. It's hard against my back, grounding in a way I really need right now.

Beyond Jamie and the horses, the stone behind me is the only thing that feels real.

I've watched enough shows and movies to have a good idea about what could have happened, but it's a struggle to believe any of the possibilities could happen in real life.

Were we sucked into a vortex, abducted by aliens, swallowed into some kind of black hole?

Knowing the truth will maybe help me get my head around what's happening. At least that way, I can try to figure out if we should keep heading east, towards a town I suspect is not there. If not, do we go into survival mode? Maybe find other people?

Humans.

I swallow hard, the blood draining from my face as the word "human" pops into my mind.

"You want a drink?" Jamie holds the bottle out to me.

I reach out to take it, but the movement is

abruptly interrupted by a distant rustling that quickly escalates into a cacophony of crashing foliage.

"Fuck, we've gotta move. Now."

I scramble for the rifle as I latch onto Geralt's reins and put my weight on one foot.

But it's too late.

A ferocious roar rends the air. My whole body jerks as I reach for Jamie, urging him into his saddle.

A loud crunch of something heavy smashing against something hard, and I jolt, gaze snapping in that direction.

It's here.

A deafening crash follows, echoing through the trees, shattering any semblance of safety I may have been foolish enough to believe existed. My heart leaps into my throat even as I manage to get Jamie up. If necessary, I'll make sure he gets out of here. I'll protect him with my life.

Purple horns come into view, emerging from the thick underbrush. They're fucking huge. Monstrous.

"Holy shit," Jamie gasps, and I swallow hard as a creature that's the stuff of nightmares bursts fully into view, its six legs churning up the leaf-littered earth with each thunderous step.

Its grotesque form looms large, dwarfing everything in its path. Three gnarled purple horns jut menacingly from its twisted skull, gleaming with an otherworldly sheen in the dim light. Its eyes, burning with a hunger that makes me close to shitting myself, fix on me.

Fuck, fuck, fuck.

With a primal roar that shakes the ground beneath my feet and has the horses rearing, the creature charges forwards, its intent unmistakable. The bastard thing wants to devour us for a tasty treat. Like hell I'll make it that easy.

With trembling fingers, I raise my rifle, ignoring the onslaught of fear crawling through my veins. I squeeze the trigger, the deafening blast of gunfire echoing through the forest as shot after shot tears through the air.

Each bullet hits its mark.

Fuck, it's not working.

"Uncle Jack."

I cast a glance at Jamie even as I release the final shot in my rifle. He thrusts the shotgun at me. I take it willingly, pushing the rifle into his outstretched hand.

A loud blast from the shotgun, and my heart stumbles when the creature roars louder.

Pain. At least I hope the thing can feel the lead tearing through it.

With each futile shot, it draws closer and closer, its massive form casting a long shadow over me.

I'm going to die. Fuck it all to hell.

"Jamie," I holler, "get out of here."

As the creature closes in, its jaws gape wide in anticipation. I hope the fucker chokes on me.

"Jamie," I shout again, not daring to take my gaze off the creature that's maybe ten metres away.

What the fuck are we doing still standing here?

Fuck. We need to retreat. Need to—

The creature stumbles. I gasp for breath, trying to work out what I'm seeing and what's happening.

A screech in the air and a *thwack* and my lips part, my mouth falling open. It swings its head around, roaring, and another arrow finds purchase in its throat. *The fuck?*

The stumble turns into a crash, and then I gasp as an arrow of fire explodes through the air, hitting the monster with a burst of flames. Its heavy form slams to the ground, creating a silence that leaves my ears ringing.

Three arrows protrude from the creature as flame and smoke curl around it. It's still and, I hope to hell, dead. It's gotta be, right? Flames like that seem like kiln levels of hot.

With ragged breaths, I reach out to Jamie, my shaky hand latching onto his leg.

"What happened?" he whispers.

I dare not take my attention off the purple creature. Who knows if those arrows have killed it or not? Jesus, its brain could be in its arse for all I know.

"Someone did us a solid and took it down." I squint at the arrows, trying to get a better look at them. They don't look like they're made of carbon or even aluminium.

"Who?"

I shake my head and finally risk looking around. "I don't—"

"Come." The gruff voice takes me by surprise. I don't even have enough time to lift my shotgun before the raspy "There will be more. *Klaustras* hunt in packs. That will have been its scout" has me turning in circles, searching for the source.

A flicker of light in the shadows catches my eye. Movement follows, and then I freeze, gawping like a kangaroo who just spotted a dingo wearing a koala costume.

"You and the human child—come with me if you want to live."

A bubble of amusement, completely inappropriate given the situation, clogs my throat. Did he really go all Arnie on me?

"Uncle Jack."

I quickly turn to Jamie, and my humour dissipates. The colour has drained from his face, but fuck if the determination staring back at me doesn't get me to move my arse.

This... person... creature... monster—who knows what the fuck he is, though I am sure it's male—killed the *klaus*-thingy, which is the reason that Jamie and I are still breathing.

"We need to move." He, the monster with pearlescent horns protruding from his head, looks at the destruction the six-legged creature left behind. His muscles tense, and fuck if there aren't a shitload of those muscles on display beneath his deep red skin.

His gaze moves to mine, and I hold my breath. While I have no idea what this guy's species is, he has two eyes, albeit large ones and with no eyebrows or lashes, and he's humanoid—well, he is walking on two legs—and that means I need to make eye contact. I give myself the barest of seconds to meet his gaze and hope to God I can trust him.

Vibrant golden orbs peer back at me. They're beautiful, incandescent. Whether that means he's leading us into a trap or not, who the hell knows. But for now, the odds of us being safer with him are as good a bet as any.

"Okay." I mount Geralt, finding comfort in settling on his saddle. That my horse isn't freaking out and going wild at the red creature's proximity has to mean something, too, right?

"Stay close," I say to Jamie as I get Geralt moving.

We weave carefully through the trees, the almost-fiery strands floating from our rescuer's head a beacon in the diminishing light. He's moving fast, though, and easier than I could through the trees. And even faster than us on the horses.

We weave through strange-shaped plants and foliage and trees that I struggle to make sense of. We do so accompanied by nothing but the sound of our horses' hooves on the sandy ground. I have no idea how long we've been moving, but the "Not far" makes me jolt. His unusually accented words drift behind him, catching on the breeze as we continue to follow. The sound sends a ripple over my skin, goose bumps following in its wake.

"You speak English," I say, my voice rough with nerves when he slows his pace as we reach a point where it's necessary for Jamie and me to dismount. With our feet now on the ground, we're slower.

"Yes" drifts back to me, sending the small hairs on my skin into overdrive, but he doesn't stop pushing through the dense trees.

He doesn't offer more, and even without instruction, I figure he needs us to stay quiet.

A loud thud followed by a crash reaches us. The creature stills and raises his four-fingered hand. Jamie and I stop instantly, our breaths catching, though I rub soothing circles on Geralt's neck, hoping to calm him—or me—while I reach for Jamie's hand. It trembles in mine.

Fear tries to crawl up my throat, and it takes every semblance of control I have to swallow it down. I need to be strong for Jamie. The poor kid's teeth are practically chattering despite his straight back and the way he's lifted his chin.

A gravelled "Wait" has me swallowing hard as I watch the red-skinned creature walk away from us, his footfalls impossibly light for someone his size.

Tension vibrates through my limbs, and I'm tempted to ask where the hell he's going while also feeling the need to plead for him not to abandon us. Out of my depth and beyond confused, I still need to protect Jamie, survive, and not freak out completely. I don't think I can do this alone.

He drifts out of sight, his disappearance somehow making the air around us grow still.

"Uncle—"

"Shh," I whisper softly, squeezing Jamie's hand a little. A crack of a twig has me jerking my head to the left. It's not coming from the way the bow-and-arrow-wielding creature left.

On high alert, I squeeze Jamie's hand once more before gently releasing and slowly reaching for the rifle. Just as I'm about to make contact with the .22, a gruff "Stop" has my head jerking and my breath hitching.

The creature's back, his large eyes studying me intently. Cautiously.

"I heard something," I whisper and nod towards my right.

With a tilt of his head, he keeps his gaze steady on me, but there's a shift in his focus. I have no idea how exactly I know this; maybe it's something to do with his hair taking on a life of its own—almost like tentacles feeling the air around him.

Wide-eyed, I stare at his moving hair. It's like the individual strands are doing a damn dance. Sure, it's mesmerising, but more than that, it's freaky as fuck.

"Why's his hair doing that?" Jamie says, a little louder than a whisper.

Immediately, the strands drop, and the creature snaps his attention to Jamie. I straighten, shifting weight onto my right foot, ready to step in. To do what, exactly, I have no clue, but—

"It was just a *teringth*," he says. At my blank stare, he adds, "A small creature, much like your rabies."

Rabies?

He purses his lips, drawing my attention there as he then stretches them tight, two small fangs revealing themselves. "Not rabies?" He shakes his head. "Small animals that bounce."

"Rabbits," Jamie says.

And fuck me, a wide smile transforms the monster's features. And yeah, he has fangs—twice as long as a human's canines.

I'm sure the last thing I should be thinking is that I like his smile or that the fangs look kinda cute. Jesus, all I can do is blame the knock to my head and the truly fucked-up situation we've landed in.

"Yes, rabbits." He appears thoroughly pleased with himself, sending Jamie a firm nod, his smile still in place. "In *The Last Stand*, the deputy thinks there is a predator, but it is a rabbit. Arnold is not in this scene." He shakes his head forlornly. "Now come. It's safe here. My home. Follow my footsteps."

Honestly, it's a struggle to catch up. What's with

the Arnold Schwarzenegger fixation? I huff out a breath, my brows high. Alrighty then. Into the unknown with the Arnie fan we go.

CHAPTER
THREE

"Uhm...." I eye the array of instruments on the wall, holding Jamie a little tighter to my side. Either I've been a complete pushover and walked into this monster's house—hovel... cave...?—only to have led us to a super bloody demise, or.... I have no idea how to complete that thought.

I can't tell if it's a shrine to a torture chamber or.... Yeah, I've still got nothing.

Movement drags my attention from the razor-sharp equipment. The nameless monster—assuming this creature has a name—moves closer, his golden eyes glinting as he notices me staring at the wall of blades and hooks. His heavy footsteps reverberate in the dim cave, and the array of muscles on display only adds to the sense that, yeah, I may have just walked into a death trap.

But then he speaks, his deep voice rumbling through the air like a crack of thunder—and I absolutely do not jump. "Ah," he says, nodding towards the sharp, gleaming instruments. "You look at my equipment. Yes. It is for farming. And hunting." He says this like it's the most natural thing in the world, but I can't help glancing back at the wall, specifically at a giant scythe that looks like it could decapitate a small car.

Sure, I have a rifle slung over my shoulder, but this looks like next-level *Wolf Creek* shit right here.

"Farming?" I ask, raising an eyebrow. "With... those?"

The giant monster nods solemnly. "Yes. The crops here are... stubborn." He pauses dramatically. "They fight back."

Jamie, bless him, pipes up in the awkward silence. "Cool," he says, his voice small, like he's not entirely sure whether to be impressed or terrified.

"Cool," the creature echoes, nodding sagely, clearly proud of his "tools." "Very cool. In *Predator*, there are many tools for the hunt. I have... learned."

Right. I can't help it—my eyes dart back to the tools. There's a fine line between "learning to hunt" and "preparing for an apocalypse," and this guy's straddling that line like an Olympic gymnast.

Finally, he turns his attention back to us. His expression shifts to something more serious, almost thoughtful. "You wonder... what has happened, yes? To your world?"

I let out a long breath. "Yeah, that would be nice. Any chance you could explain why it feels like we've been sucked into a sci-fi movie?"

"I do not know what sci-fi movie is, but I can tell you what has happened. Of course." He straightens, adopting a stance I can only describe as "heroic." His arms cross over his enormous chest, and he looks down at us as if preparing to deliver a speech worthy of an action movie climax.

He begins gravely, "The dimensions have torn apart and reformed. Worlds once separate now collide, merging, twisting. It is... a cosmic...." He waves a hand in the air as though shooing away some invisible cosmic dust. "How do you say... *clusterfudge*."

"Clusterfudge," I repeat, trying to keep up. "You mean... like a dimensional explosion?"

His already-bright eyes light up. "Yes! Boom! Explosion! Everything goes—" He claps his hands together loudly, making Jamie jump and my heart pound. "Your world, my world, this world, they have... *blended*. Just like in *The Terminator* when machines and humans—"

"—are at war?" I finish, half-dazed by the randomness of his analogy.

"No, no," he says, shaking his head. "When worlds are... entangled. Like when Arnold must stop the nuclear launch by—"

"I don't think that's—" I start to correct him but quickly give up. "Okay, so... what does this mean for us? How do we get back home?"

The creature's face falls slightly, and he shrugs his massive shoulders. "That... I do not know."

I blink. "You don't know?"

"No," he says simply. "It happened before. Many time. I think first twenty-five cycles ago. Just a small sliver of different worlds joining with this one. But do not worry, it will happen again, and I will protect you. I am very skilled. Like Arnold in *Commando*." He flexes his biceps, giving us what I can only assume is his attempt at a reassuring smile, complete with two glinting fangs. "You are safe with me."

Before I can ask how exactly being in a Schwarzenegger movie is supposed to reassure me, Jamie speaks up. "What's your name?"

The creature tilts his head as if confused by the

question before answering in that same dramatic tone. "I am… Solan." He says it like he's revealing the secret identity of a superhero. "You may call me Solan."

I exchange a glance with Jamie, both of us wide-eyed but trying not to let the absurdity of the situation crack us up. It's either that or start rocking in a corner. "All right, Solan," I say slowly. "So, what now? We're just stuck here until the next 'boom' happens?"

Solan nods. "Yes. For now, we survive. Like in *Kindergarten Cop*, we must be prepared for anything."

Jamie stifles a laugh, and I just sigh, rubbing the back of my neck. "Okay, I guess we're along for the ride. At least we've got a bodyguard with big muscles."

Solan's chest swells with pride at the comment. "Yes! Bodyguard, protector… much like Arnold. I will ensure your safety, just like Arnold does for his daughter." He gives Jamie a firm nod. "We are a team now."

Jamie beams up at him. "Cool."

"Cool," Solan repeats with a grin, clearly delighted. "Now, we eat. I shall prepare food, just like in *The Last Stand*."

I exchange another glance with Jamie, and this time, I don't even try to stop the unhinged laugh that bubbles up. I don't even know where to begin with the movie references. Add in my inability to process what he's saying about our worlds merging, and it's likely my only course of action is to ask for hard liquor and a place to crash.

If not for Jamie at my side, I suspect it's exactly what I'd be doing.

"Please. Sit." Solan points to a boulder-like seat. It's covered in some sort of material not dissimilar to reeds.

I urge Jamie over, grateful to sit my arse down before I collapse. My knees are still wobbly, and after the brief, weird description from Solan about what's happened, I need every bit of support I can get.

I glance at Jamie. He's tight to my side, eyes wide and head jerking in every direction as he takes the space in. Curiosity is practically vibrating off him. It's reassuring. I'll take his keen interest above his fear any day.

While I'm relieved, it doesn't stop my thundering heart. It's more than an ache. Any second now, it's likely to burst free, creating a mess on the dust-free floor that looks like it's made from some sort of granite.

As I'm assessing the likelihood of my heart giving out, Solan putters around what's clearly the kitchen area. There's a tap unlike any I've ever seen before made out of black stone. He tugs open what appears to be a heavy rock, revealing an array of items that I suspect are food. The whole time, he's smiling, sending the occasional glance my way with what I'm sure is intended to be a reassuring nod but could possibly be him sizing me up to figure out how much broth to make that'll cover my human form.

After making eye contact, I glance away quickly, my gaze snagging on... the fuck! "That's a TV." I stand and rush over to what is definitely a TV. It's an older style, one from maybe thirty years ago with a large back end but a flatscreen.

Wide-eyed, I turn to Solan. "How've you got a TV?"

A patient smile is already plastered on his face along with a flicker of excitement in his gaze. "Twenty-five cycles ago, a section of your human world replaced a section of this one in Terrafeara."

"Terrafeara?" Well, fuck if that name alone doesn't sound terrifying.

"Yes, Terrafeara is the home of the Glowranth." He pauses the task of preparing food to walk towards me and the TV.

"And the Glowranth is?"

"The dominant species of this world." While his

tone is still a grumble, there's a softening to it, as though he's aware he's got a lot of explaining to do while I try to wrap my head around everything.

I'm still caught on the whole "dominant species" thing and what that implies about Solan. That means he's not a Glowranth, right?

"There is a lot to say. We can talk while the small human watches, yes?" He gestures with a hand towards Jamie, who's paying attention to everything we say.

I know I'm the adult here, but it seems wrong for Jamie to not have as much information as I do.

"Jamie—that's his name. He's my nephew. My—"

"I know 'uncle.' Like Arnold in *The Kid & I*, yes?" His already-bright eyes are practically glowing as he speaks.

I don't have the heart to say I have no idea. Sure, I grew up watching Arnie movies, but I'm not a hardcore fan or anything.

"O-kay...," I drag out. "So, yeah, that's Jamie, and I'm Jack."

I jump when Solan violently thrusts his arm out towards me, flexing his four fingers. Understanding what he wants, I swallow thickly and extend my hand out to him.

As soon as my palm makes contact with Solan's,

the world spins. It's not just warmth that spreads through my body—it's like I've been plugged into a live wire. A surge of heat shoots up my arm, not painful, but intense, almost exhilarating. I gasp, my heart slamming against my chest like a drum.

It feels like my whole body is on fire, and for a second, I'm sure I'm about to disintegrate into ash right here in front of him. But I don't pull away. It's terrifying, yes, but there's something else underneath that fear—something almost... right? I don't even know how to describe it. Like a part of me is waking up that I didn't know existed.

Solan, meanwhile, goes rigid, his eyes widening as if he's just been struck by lightning. For someone built like a tank, the look on his face screams panic. But then, in the blink of an eye, his expression shifts, his features tightening into something neutral, almost forced. He tries to retract his hand, but I can feel the hesitation.

"Ah...." His voice cracks slightly before he clears his throat, then speaks again in that same deep, Arnie-like tone. "You are... strong." The corner of his mouth twitches like he's trying to keep his composure, but his whole body is tense, and his eyes—those bright golden eyes—are almost... frantic. He lets go of my hand a little too quickly and steps back, bumping into the table as he does. "I mean—very strong grip, Jack." He chuckles awkwardly, but there's an edge to it.

I blink, trying to steady my breath. My palm is still tingling, almost throbbing, as if whatever just happened is lingering in my skin. I rub at it absently, my mind reeling. What the hell *was* that?

"Are you okay?"

Jamie's voice cuts through my spiralling thoughts, and I manage a tight nod. "Yeah... yeah, I'm fine," I say, though my voice is shakier than I'd like. "Just... tired."

Solan quickly turns to the food he's been preparing, making a show of chopping some sort of root vegetable with a little too much enthusiasm. "Yes, food! We eat, and we talk, yes?" He gestures towards a crude stone table in the centre of the room. "Sit. I will bring food. Good for strength."

I don't know what's weirder: the fact that I just experienced some kind of fiery body shock or the fact that this hulking creature is acting like nothing's out of the ordinary while he's clearly *not* okay. But I'm still too rattled to figure it out, so I take the seat he offers, pulling Jamie with me.

My palm still burns, and when I glance down, I notice a small cut I hadn't seen before. It must've snagged on something when we were running from that car-sized monster earlier. The skin around it is red-raw, but the heat radiating from it doesn't feel like a normal cut. It feels... alive.

I clench my fist, trying to push the sensation aside as Solan brings over a plate of what looks like cold roasted meat alongside the weird root vegetables. He's still moving with that stiff, too-controlled air, but he's trying to cover it up with forced casualness. I can't help but notice how each of his movements seems hyper-deliberate, like he's focussing way too hard on something.

And how I know that from being in his presence for a smattering of hours is beyond me.

Jamie, oblivious to the tension, digs into the food immediately. "What kind of meat is this?" he asks, his mouth full.

Solan freezes for a second before answering. "It is... *rethog* meat. Very tasty. Like... your chicken." He gives a tight smile, but his eyes flick back to me every couple of seconds, like he's trying to gauge my reaction.

"Right," I mutter, taking a hesitant bite. It's actually pretty good, but my focus keeps drifting back to the monster. There's something about him.... His presence feels different now, more intense, and it's like the air between us is charged. I can't help but notice how his skin glows faintly under the dim light, the way his horns catch the shadows, and that his movements—though controlled—still exude power.

My breath catches in my throat again. Why am I suddenly so hyperaware of him?

"Tell me about this place," I say, mostly to distract myself from the heat still lingering in my palm—and the fact that I feel like I'm being pulled into some strange orbit around Solan. "You said it's called Terrafeara?"

Solan nods, visibly relieved to change the subject. "Yes, Terrafeara," he says, his voice falling into a steady rhythm, as if he's reciting from memory. "It is a land of many species. The Glowranth, they rule here, but there are others—beasts, creatures of all sizes." His eyes flicker towards me, then quickly away. "The merging of worlds... it has brought confusion, chaos. Parts of your world, parts of mine... colliding with Terrafeara... maybe others too. Like *Jingle All the Way* when they fight for the last toy."

"Right," I say, distracted again by the deep timbre of his voice, the way it resonates in the air. It's almost hypnotic.

But then my hand throbs again, the heat spiking, and I can't ignore it any longer. I glance down, and the cut has started to glow faintly. "Uh, Solan...." I lift my palm, showing him the strange light. "What the hell is this?"

For the first time since we sat down, Solan's mask slips. His eyes widen, and there's a flash of something —fear? Worry? Longing? He quickly schools his expression, but it's too late. I saw it.

He leans in, inspecting my palm with more focus than necessary. "Ah... it is... nothing. A small cut. Will heal. Do not worry."

But I can see his jaw tighten, the way his eyes linger on my hand like it's something much more than "nothing." He knows something. He just isn't saying.

Before I can push for more, Jamie says, "Your world? You're not from here either?"

"No." Relief practically pours off him as he gives Jamie his full attention. "This is my home." He indicates the structure we're in. "It once belonged in Pyrima, which is my world. It and some of the forest around us came with me. I left everything and everyone else behind."

Surprise has me sitting up straighter even as sadness penetrates my chest. "And how long have you been here? You said something about twenty-five cycles...?"

He nods, his gaze flicking to mine only briefly before he turns back to Jamie. Discomfort shifts in my gut, which doesn't make a lick of sense. But fuck if it doesn't feel, I don't know, wrong... frustrating, maybe, that he's not looking at me.

I try to shove the weird-arse feelings away and instead concentrate on what really matters: figuring out how Solan's arrival likens to ours and what that means for us.

"I think our moon is all the same... the same pattern. One turn is one cycle."

A cycle is a month?

The heavy thud in my chest hurts, it's that powerful.

"So two years was when it last happened? When you came here?"

A frown dips his large brow. "Two years when a slice of your world merged, yes. I've been here forty cycles. I could find only few remnants of my home." Sadness lingers in his tone, and the thud in my chest picks up speed, creating a fresh ache behind my ribcage. "But there have been more rifts than that. More soon."

Understandably, he's sad, but it's his acceptance... that he seems not content, necessarily, but more resigned that has me shifting, uncomfortable, and fighting not to rub at my chest.

It's best I focus on what he knows. If I start thinking about the fact that he's been stuck here for over three years and fuck knows how many dimensional meltdowns there have been since, I'll be useless to Jamie. I stare once more at the TV. "There's electricity here?"

He perks up a little and nods. "There's a large settlement a quarter of a day's walk from here. They have markets, supplies, goods from this world and others. It is not the same as the power on your Earth with wires underground and in the sky, but wind and water create the power needed. Energy."

So the locals, the "dominant species," know of his existence. He hasn't been gobbled up, plus they have markets, so that has to mean the Glowranth are an intelligent species. At least I hope I'm not bullshitting myself here.

I tilt my head, wondering at his ability to communicate with them as well as me and Jamie. "How do you monsters communicate with them? With us?"

Solan's gaze is on me in an instant. As soon as it is, the air in my chest freezes. The golden hue is so vivid that I struggle to look away. It's only when he blinks and I lose contact for the barest of seconds that I suck in a breath.

"Thraxus."

Right, I asked him a question.

"He is a Glowranth. Many cycles ago... seven of your Earth years, a section of my world was replaced with this one. Thraxus appeared."

My eyes widen. Before I can speak, Jamie says, "This is some crazy shit, Uncle Jack."

A huff of amused agreement escapes me. I reach out, place my hand on his shoulder, and give a gentle, reassuring squeeze. "No argument from me."

Solan studies our interaction. I swear he doesn't seem to miss a thing. The whole time, the strange zap of awareness continues to needle its way through my system.

"And this Thraxus taught you the language here?" I ask, pointedly ignoring the weird sensations flooding me.

"Yes," Solan answers gruffly, pulling his attention away from me and focussing on his drink.

The moment he does, I take a deep inhale. The fresh intake of air helps to settle the vibrations.

"He is a warrior. Taught me how to fight and hunt as well as Glowranthian, the Glowranth language. He is...." He trails off as his gaze snaps back to mine.

What I think is the sound of him clearing his throat follows. "He is bonded to Ignis."

"Bonded as in...?"

"Bonded like Harry and Helen Tasker in *True Lies*." He bobs his head, his hair that appears like dreadlocks—but without the knots—moving with an almost rhythmic flow as he does so.

True Lies. At least it's a movie I remember fairly well. "As in they're married?" I clarify.

"Yes. Ignis is my sister."

Surprise has my brows shooting high. So different species of monsters can be *together* together. And why that's the first thing I properly think about rather than something more pragmatic like how long these merges have been happening is something I'm going to ignore for a while.

That my gaze falls to Solan's deep red lips—a couple of shades darker than his skin—and catch on those two fangs that shouldn't look cute any more than I should be wondering what they'd feel like scraping over my skin is neither here nor there.

"Right." I nod, forcing myself to look away as I gather my thoughts. I settle on: "And English?" I look at the TV again before adding, "And the TV? How do you get images?" I can't imagine him getting a signal out here—you know, in a whole different dimension.

Solan stands. His large form fills my view, reminding me how fucking hot kilts are. Technically, I don't think it's a kilt, but it looks like wide strips of leather that reveal flashes of the hairless red skin covering his muscular thighs.

Without a word, he turns, heading towards a raw-sawn cabinet close to the TV. He pulls open the door and peers over his shoulder at us. "Here."

Jamie immediately jumps up and heads over to Solan while I lean to my side to see what he's showing us.

"Look, Uncle Jack." Jamie holds up two DVDs. "This one says *Conan the Barbarian* and this one is *Twins*."

I glance again at the TV, eyes roaming until I see the bulky compartment underneath the screen. It's a TV/DVD combo. And apparently, the only DVDs Solan has access to are from the Arnold Schwarzenegger catalogue.

Solan saying, "Voran was able to adapt the power source to make the TV work," draws my attention back to him. "Voran is... inventor. He has a store close to the markets. Deals in inter-dimension wares."

"And this is how you learned English?" Honestly, I'm impressed.

As a smile forms, Solan's fangs become more

prominent, and my breath catches. At the sound, Solan's expression turns neutral, and he peers at the DVD in his hand before looking at me again. Some of the shine has dimmed from his golden eyes. I miss seeing the luminescence, but I can breathe easier again.

"Yes, with the movies... and Voran speaks the human tongue, and so do Morvex and Rygor. Rygor is a Shadryn and only passes through every five moon cycles. Morvex is a Sigilari, a rune healer."

A headache is forming behind my right eye. Between the names, the species, the whole Arnie fandom, and, let's not forget, having a nephew to protect in this dimension that has tank-sized monsters—and plants, apparently—that could happily suck on our bone marrow, I'm close to my limit.

What am I going to do? My sister and brother-in-law must be going out of their minds. Panic slices through me, my eyes widening in horror when a new thought hits me. I rush to say, "When the merge happened, our homes and land were brought here."

"That is correct." Solan nods, walking back towards me, a frown appearing above his large eyes, his locks of hair twitching a little.

"What did it replace them with?" I pull my lips

together, flattening them. What will Harper and Derek discover when they head home? Jesus, will they...? I swallow hard, unable to finish that thought, the possibilities too harrowing.

Understanding appears in Solan's features, as does a wince. "Where I found you, it was close to where your world was?"

I draw my brows low. "We'd entered... Terrafeara, yes. Maybe thirty minutes on horseback from our slice of world." I don't even flinch when I speak, despite thinking in terms of worlds or dimensions.

"That is what I thought. Your land is red and brown, yes? Flat?"

Jamie answers, "Ours is, yes. We're in Australia. The Queensland outback. Lots of Earth is blue with the ocean." He's still standing by the DVD cupboard, holding two different Arnie films in his hand.

Solan nods. "Hmm... Australia is mentioned in *Collateral Damage*. But I do not know what it looks like other than the glimpse in the distance where I found you."

Thank Christ he did, but I have more pressing concerns. Specifically, whether my sister is going to need to save herself and whether the police... hell, the damn military can get there in time. "Shit, hold on. That a TV, a fragment of Earth, appeared a couple of years back, does that mean part of Terrafeara has been on Earth all this time?"

Holy shit. It has to be, right? And if so, how has that been kept quiet? The government—of whichever country the exchange happened in—has to be responsible. They must be.

This is some next-level Area 51 shit, but exchange intergalactic aliens with monsters from another dimension.

"Yes. I discovered the TV in a dimensional transfer. I was with a friend."

The ache behind my eye builds right along with the pounding in my ears. "Have you seen more humans here?"

Something flashes on his expression that I can't read before he nods slowly. "Yes. A few times. The last was a female of your species. It was several moon cycles ago." He darts a look at Jamie before staring at me. My gut sinks in understanding.

I don't even question how I know from one hasty glance that the woman is dead. Instead, I focus on what Solan knows about what replaced our strip of land. Sure, Jamie's here, and what we discover, we might not like, but he deserves to know.

Solan's gaze hardens as he retakes his seat, clearly weighing his words before speaking. "It is one of two areas that replaced your land," he says slowly, his voice holding a gravity that makes my spine stiffen. "One is not so dangerous—a radioactively peaceful stretch of Terrafeara. The other... could be a problem."

I force myself to stay calm. He doesn't mean radioactive, right? As in things that are green and will make me grow a third nipple? "Tell me about the first."

Solan nods, his expression relaxing slightly. "The first possibility is an area near the queendom's centre. A well-structured city. Yes, the Glowranth are warriors by nature, but they are also an older society. They've built sprawling cities and, more recently, technology based on other species' developments. But they believe in honour and strength, led by the monarchy... Queen Serresta. They're aware of dimensional rifts and have experienced them long before I arrived. If your land swapped with this area, the Glowranth would not see it as an immediate threat. They would investigate. Diplomacy might even be possible."

I blink, absorbing his words. "So, they wouldn't just... attack Earth?"

"No." Solan's voice is firm. "They are not mindless beasts. The Glowranth know that these shifts occur.

They would assess the situation. It's a society with rules, increasing technology, and understanding. They won't risk war without reason, especially not against another world without knowing its capabilities."

Jamie, still playing with the DVDs, looks up with a curious expression. "So... the monsters have cities like us?"

Solan nods, glancing kindly at him, while I wince a little at the term "monster" we've both been carelessly throwing around. "Yes, Jamie. Different, but yes. Think of towering buildings made of stone and metal, streets that weave through giant fortresses. It's the hub of the queendom. The Glowranth weren't skilled in technology until recently—they have some machines and devices, much like your world, but powered through different means."

Jamie grins. "Like magic?"

Solan chuckles softly. "In a sense, yes. Though to them, it's more like advanced energy manipulation."

I let out a breath, feeling a glimmer of relief. "Okay, so if it's near their"—I hesitate over the next word—"queendom's centre, we might not be in immediate danger."

"But...." Solan's expression darkens again, and my

relief fades. "There is a second possibility. One that is far more concerting."

I swallow hard, assuming he means *concerning*. "What's the other option?"

Solan's gaze flickers, his eyes turning sharp. "The second area your land might have merged with is a Glowranth training facility. It is a place where the royal heirs are sent to train under the head of the royal guard. It's isolated, deep in the wilds, and used for intense combat training. The heirs who will one day rule Terrafeara are expected to be battle hardened. It's a harsh place where they learn to fight and survive."

My chest tightens as I consider the implications. "So, if that training facility merged with my section of the world, then a royal heir and their guard are on Earth?"

"One of them, yes," Solan confirms, his voice grim. "If that is the case, the guard would view your land's sudden appearance as a direct threat. They are isolated from the larger society, which means there would be no time for diplomacy. The guard is fiercely protective of the heir, and they wouldn't hesitate to act."

I shake my head, trying to grasp the reality of it

all. "So, the mo—species here wouldn't know what happened to the heir?"

Solan's expression turns serious. "The Glowranth," he says. "Exactly. They would search for answers. If they discover the section of your world that contains your land, they might suspect interlopers and see you and Jamie as possible threats. The royal guard could use you to try and reopen the dimensional pathways to retrieve their heir."

Panic rises in my chest. Is that even possible? And if so, from the concern radiating off Solan, it doesn't sound like it's a good thing. "So, it's essential we figure out which part of Terrafeara has merged with Earth. If it's the training facility, we could be in serious danger."

"Yes," Solan agrees. "Once we find out, we will know if you and Jamie may become targets. The royal guard would stop at nothing to find their heir, and you could be caught in the crossfire."

I glance at Jamie, who's obliviously inspecting the DVDs. The thought of him being used as leverage sends a chill down my spine. "We need to come up with a plan."

Solan nods, his golden eyes steady on me. "First, we'll need to get some rest. Tomorrow, we will return to the location where your home appeared in this dimension. From there, I'll be able to know which part is missing. We'll figurine out whether we're dealing with a peaceful section of land outside of the city or the training facility."

I nod, determination settling in, barely even drawing my brows together anymore at the occasional incorrect English word he uses. "All right, let's do that. But we have to be careful. If we're near the royal heir's training ground, we could be walking into another dangerous situation, right?"

Solan's expression softens a fraction, the tension in his posture easing. "I will protect you both. You have my word."

I manage a strained smile, though my thoughts are still racing. A part of me had been clinging to the hope that this dimensional merge could somehow be undone quickly or that we could figure out how to survive here. But the thought of a monster royal heir and their guard seeing Earth as an enemy? That changes everything.

As I guide Jamie towards a sleeping area, I can't shake the feeling of impending danger. I am absolutely not cut out for this level of action.

Tomorrow could reveal whether we have allies or

adversaries in this strange, monstrous world. Whatever the outcome, I'll do anything to keep Jamie safe.
I just hope my family on Earth can keep themselves
out of harm's way too.

CHAPTER
FOUR

I wake with Jamie's elbow jabbing into my cheek. He's always been a damn wriggle monster, rarely keeping still. *Monster.* The thought freezes the breath in my lungs. It takes five long seconds before I can exhale and draw in another breath. Another five as I tentatively peer around the sectioned-off part of the cave where we rested our heads.

The eyes that I half expected to see homed in on me are not there even though the sense of being watched was what first dragged me from my sleep. I inhale a little shakily, focussing on my surroundings.

The stone walls are smooth, interrupted by the occasional shelf cut into the hard surface. All are covered in the soft green light of devices dotted around the room. Before we slept, Solan explained that a gentle wave of a hand in front of any of the devices could brighten or dim them. A lot like sensors on Earth.

But with no wiring or batteries in sight, it's not electricity as I know it powering them.

A sound beyond the open archway sends my heart skittering. It's a soft scrape and what's definitely a noise coming from him. Solan. Jamie's still sleeping soundly, so I stand, the fluttering in my chest increasing as I make my way outside of the room and into a larger living space.

It's brighter out here, a brilliant beam of green light entering from a skylight of sorts. Because yeah, I didn't imagine that the skies are green in Terrafeara.

I spot Solan immediately. Broad shoulders are showcased by leather bands of some kind of halter, not doing a thing to conceal his defined muscles. Said muscles are thick and in slightly different positions than a human's, but there's enough similarity between his body and the genetic makeup of mine— at least on the surface—that makes his form familiar somehow.

It's the only explanation I have for why, despite the pounding of my heart increasing, I'm not shit scared of the monster's form before me. Sure, Solan is physically intimidating, and I still have no clue why his hair—though I'm not sure it's technically hair like I know it—practically dances and moves like it—they?—have a life of their own.

Despite my galloping pulse, I stay stock-still as I watch Solan. In one hand, he grips a carrying device, something between a woven basket and a backpack. In the other, he holds the bow and arrow he so expertly used yesterday.

Whether it's the short inhale that garners his attention or something else, I have no idea, but his body turns rigid even as his deep red strands flow like they're feeling the air around him. "Jack."

The gruff tone sends goose bumps skittering across my skin. It's the turn of his head, his gaze locking with mine, that sends my mouth outback dry.

Somewhere between his tone and the intensity in his stare, I feel fully snared. Legit feel trapped with barely the ability to take a breath. Add in the errant thought of him being criminally hot—I have no idea what it says about me that my dick is rock-hard and pressing uncomfortably against my zip—and I begin to believe I do have a concussion from yesterday's explosion.

Though, was it technically an explosion that ripped the dimensions apart?

"You managed to sleep?"

His question cuts through the cotton wool filling my brain, and I immediately nod, fighting hard not to adjust myself. "Yeah, thanks. Jamie's still asleep. Are you ready for us to leave?" Because that's all that should be on my brain: getting back to my property and figuring out how fucked we are.

"It would be best to leave. The *chalka* birds have yet to rise, and the day is not yet hot. The sooner we discover the location of the rift, the sooner we can make preparations."

I balk, his words sounding far too doomsday-prepper-like for my ears. I have no choice but to trust him, which is not as hard as I think it should be. But what the fuck do I know? It's not like I've been in this situation before.

"Okay, I'll wake Jamie." I turn on my heels, but Solan saying my name stops me. I ignore the gooseflesh peppering my skin and turn back to him, my eyebrow raised. Yep, nothing to see here, folks. I'm not in any way affected by how my name sounded on his lips.

"It will likely be dangerous. The *klaustras* found you by the merge point, yes?"

I blanch just thinking about the monstrous beast. "Yes." I nod.

"The boy child, Jamie—it would be safe if he did not come."

The hairs on my arms shoot straight up, an argument on the tip of my tongue.

Solan's remarkably humanlike hand gesture as he tries to placate me has me pausing. "I would struggle to leave him behind, too, if he were of my blood. But he is not fully grown, correct?"

My nod is stilted.

"The *klaustras* pack will be alert, have found their dead by now." Solan studies me carefully, his expression soft, each roughly spoken word of English deliberate. "Their senses are unlike any others' in Terrafeara," Solan continues, his voice low, laced with a careful warning. "*Klaustras* are highly evolved to hunt, especially the young. If they catch Jamie's true scent, they will pursue him relentlessly. Their hunger for youths' flesh is... instinctive. They won't stop until they taste it or I've killed them all."

The breath catches in my throat. My body turns rigid, fighting the instinct to shout that no one, no *thing*, is going to lay a finger on Jamie. Solan watches me with that soft intensity as though he understands exactly what I'm feeling.

"Back in my world, I used to be a hunter," Solan

explains, his eyes catching the green light spilling from above.

He was a hunter? A tendril of fear unfurls in my gut. Something tells me he's not talking about hunting for wild dogs or fresh meat. Questions burn on my tongue, but I swallow them away.

Do I really want to know what exactly he means?

"But the creatures here... they're different. Relentless." He pauses, glancing towards the dark mouth of the cave, in the direction of his small valley. "And they will be many."

The weight of his words sinks in, nearly stealing my breath.

Solan continues, keeping his voice steady and assured, a promise of safety underlying each word, "Jamie will be protected here. This home is secure, concealed from sight, and guarded by sensory triggers. I will activate the alert myself—nothing will step foot within this boundary without my knowing. My home has strong scents to keep creatures away from my territory."

I rub the back of my neck, my mind reeling. Leaving Jamie here goes against every instinct I have. It's unnatural, every part of me screaming that my place is by his side. But Solan's right. Bringing Jamie could mean him ending up face-to-face with the kind of creatures that crawl out of nightmares.

"Do you promise?" I ask, the words escaping me before I can stop them. "Do you promise he'll be safe?"

Solan nods, his gaze unwavering. "He will be."

My heart beats fast as I try to reconcile the overwhelming urge to protect with the truth that sometimes protection is choosing the harder path. Jamie will be safest here.

A soft sound from behind catches my attention, and I turn to see Jamie standing in the archway, his eyes bleary, but clearly he's heard more than enough. He's clutching the shotgun, knuckles white around the handle, his face set in reluctant determination.

He sighs, the weight of everything visible in his expression. "I'll stay," he says reluctantly. "But I'm keeping the shotgun."

The faintest hint of a smile tugs at the corner of Solan's mouth. "It is a good weapon. Keep it close."

We pack up in silence, checking our gear and arming ourselves. Every movement feels too loud, too final. I give Jamie one last once-over, then draw him into a fierce hug, knowing he understands more than I'd like him to. He'll be safe. And that has to be enough.

As I pull away, I meet his gaze, giving his shoulder a squeeze. "I'll be back before you know it."

He nods, his bravado holding steady. Then, with a deep breath, I mount Geralt, his muscles tense beneath me, and turn to follow the monster who's taken it upon himself to protect us. As we ride out of the valley, I can feel Jamie watching, his gaze like a tether pulling at me as we vanish into the distance.

IT'S IMPOSSIBLE NOT TO WHIP MY HEAD around, trying to take everything in. Yesterday, the whole journey had been shrouded in fear. Am I still afraid? I barely hold back my snort as I even think that. I'm fucking terrified. Scared for Jamie, and for me, at the very idea of not getting home.

I'm also petrified of what we're going to find the closer to my property we get.

Considering all that, it's easier to focus on the unusual trees, the banks of purple flowers that look like a cross between a lily and a Venus flytrap. That alone tells me it's likely to bite my face off if I get any closer.

Solan jogs at my side, something I'm becoming more

accustomed to. After he saved us and we fled together, there's little doubt Solan's speed and endurance are beyond that of human capabilities. Honestly, that Solan can hold a conversation while Geralt is likely doing twenty kilometres per hour is impressive.

Solan jogs easily alongside me, his movements so smooth that he barely seems winded. During the past thirty minutes, he's been peppering me with questions about Earth, clearly fact-checking bits and pieces of what he's learned from Arnold Schwarzenegger characters. The unexpected quiz is oddly comforting, distracting me from the gut-churning fear and keeping my mind away from the twisted, gnarled plants flanking our path.

"Is it true that all Earth males are expected to be able to bench... what was it... at least a hundred pounds?" he asks suddenly, breaking me from my thoughts.

I blink at him, nearly missing the humour sparkling in his golden eyes. "Uh, no. Not all of us can lift half our own body weight, actually. But, uh, some do to stay strong and fit." I can't help a smile as he absorbs this, apparently genuinely surprised.

We continue in silence for a few more steps, only for Solan to throw out "And this thing... called a 'toaster'—is it really used to, what did they say... prevent food from becoming 'sad'?"

"Wait, what?" I laugh, nearly choking. "A toaster? No, it's... it's just for making toast. Like heating up bread. It has nothing to do with sad food."

His brow furrows, and he shoots me a sceptical look as though I'm pulling his leg. "Strange. You Earth humans have peculiar gadgets. But I like the idea of not making food sad."

Another chuckle escapes me. As it does, his red strands dance in a way that has nothing to do with the breeze or his running. They're too controlled, like there's almost a pattern to them. It's on the tip of my tongue to ask him about it, but a flash of familiar scenery has me stopping and clamping my lips together.

On the horizon is rich, red earth as well as a cluster of gum trees that are as familiar to me as the land itself.

Just as I'm about to instruct Geralt to pick up his pace, Solan's "Wait" stops me in my tracks. Literally. He comes to a halt, taking Geralt's reins as he does so. Geralt barely makes a peep as he pauses from his steady run. Not that I'm surprised about my horse's easy acceptance. Beyond a sniff of Solan's large four-digit hand when I introduced them, Geralt has been weirdly at ease with the red-skinned Pyronox—something else I've discovered on this journey: his species name.

And yes, I have so many questions that I'm determined to get answers to—when I'm not wondering if I'm going to have to run—or fight—for my survival in the next half hour.

"What is it? Is something wrong?" I scan the area with narrowed eyes, alert and hesitant even as longing urges me forwards to once more feel the Aussie soil beneath my feet. But I need to be smart. That means I need to listen to Solan and follow his lead.

The Pyronox is a hunter, for crying out loud. The closest thing to hunting I've experienced is battling a few brown snakes who've slithered into the house over the years and putting down a few roos who've got themselves tangled in barbed wire.

When Solan doesn't respond, I cast him a glance. His focus is to the west of the property—where the edge of my sister's fence line touches Terrafeara.

Mountains are set back way in the distance, their outline barely visible. Closer to where we stand—but honestly, I'm struggling to process the distance with how alien and... *wrong* everything feels—is what's clearly a hub for civilisation.

It doesn't, however, look like a city, let alone a queendom with a castle or palace. That is, unless I'm greatly overestimating the scale with my expectations.

And if it's not the centre of the queendom....

Fuck it all to hell.

"What is that?" I ask, despite my mouth drying out, pretty damn sure I know what it is.

"The royal training ground."

I twist my lips and gnaw on the flesh, only stopping when I realise Solan is peering at me, his eyes zeroed in on what I'm doing. His golden eyes flash in what I'm sure as shit is awareness, turning distinctly darker. I release my lip and dart my tongue out, struggling to catch my breath.

The fuck is happening?

Several heartbeats pass, and a trickle of sweat rolls down my neck. It's only then that Solan looks away and I remember how to function.

I gulp in air and will it to clear my brain and the battering of emotions in reaction to getting caught up in Solan's gaze. That shit just isn't right. In all honesty, I'm close to freaking out.

But that's the last thing I have time for.

"So, the training ground," I finally manage to say. "If it's there, that means everything is okay, right?" I don't dull down the hope in my voice. "The royal heir and whoever else won't have been sucked in, and the royal guard won't be on the warpath… right?"

My lungs freeze as I wait for his response. From the tensing of his jaw, whatever he's considering doesn't seem like it's something I'm going to want to hear.

"Maybe."

My breath saws out of me. "And that means…?"

"The training grounds span a large section of this area. It's rare that I travel out this far, so I am not completely sure."

I wait as he pauses, his focus still intent before he brings out what looks to be a spyglass. It appears to be made out of some kind of dark metal polished to a dull shine, with intricately carved markings running the length of it. The craftsmanship is incredible—simple yet elegant. I'm almost mesmerised by the way his fingers—broad, strange yet oddly graceful—wrap around it as he raises the device to his eye.

The quiet stretches between us, broken only by the distant chirping of a creature and the rustling of plants that look suspiciously carnivorous. Solan's still as a statue, eye pressed to the spyglass as he observes the horizon.

After what feels like an eternity, he finally lowers

the device, his jaw tightening. Unease stirs in my gut. Sure, Solan saved my bacon yesterday, but he's been so positive—heck, jovial, even—since we met that the shift threatens to take my breath away.

"There is movement near the structure," he says, his voice low and clipped. "Guards, I think. Perhaps checking for disturbances from the rift."

I swallow hard, the hope I'd been clinging to shrinking. "Does that mean they know something's off?" At his quizzical look, I clarify, "That something is wrong?"

"Possibly," he says, meeting my eyes. "But it's also common for the royal guard to conduct training exercises here. The area is secured so they can patrol and practice without interruption. It's best if we don't assume the worst just yet."

There's something unspoken behind his words that makes me shiver. He knows I'm terrified that I left Jamie on his own, but he also understands what we're risking by going any closer without a plan. And how the fuck is it when he's talking about something so bloody ominous, his diction sounds so damn perfect? What's up with that?

"Okay," I say, nodding, even though my nerves are twisted up like barbed wire. "But they're not going to miss the appearance of a sliver of my world right next to their facility, right?"

Solan grimaces, but it's more a quiet acknowledgment than outright fear. "No, they won't miss it," he says. "If they haven't fully checked the area yet, they will soon."

We continue our slow, careful trek along the edge of the familiar fence line until we pass it and are once more away from the merge point. A new fence line of sorts comes into view. There's a strange, iridescent shimmer, almost like an oil slick, coating the metal.

As we edge closer to the base, we come across a cluster of boulders. They're blank and shimmer as though granite. I dismount, asking, "Should we leave Geralt here?" I'm already feeling exposed, but on horseback, it's definitely going to be more difficult to keep cover.

"Yes, here."

When Solan presses his hand over the rock, I'm baffled at first, caught between confusion and curiosity. It's a rough stone, pockmarked and dull, nothing about it standing out from the dozens of other rocks and boulders littering the area. But the moment his hand makes contact, something remarkable happens. A faint shimmer rises in the air around his palm, warping the rock's surface. It's like the mirage that dances on the horizon in the outback heat, only here it's coming directly from *him*.

I gape, barely able to process what I'm seeing. The rock under Solan's hand softens, almost as if it's becoming clay. The surface shifts, its gritty texture melting ever so slightly until it twists upwards, forming a looped shape. The entire process takes seconds, but it feels like watching hours of erosion condensed into a moment. My brain stumbles to catch up—rocks don't bend or shape themselves. Not like this. Not with just a touch.

"Wait, what did you just...?" I fumble, blinking at him. "Did you... are you—did you heat the rock?"

Solan's eyes flash with a hint of amusement as he watches my reaction. "Yes. Heat manipulation is a skill my kind are born with," he says, voice calm, as if casually discussing the weather. "Pyronox like me use heat for all manner of things, though it's mostly practical. We're not made to walk through flames," he adds, maybe to reassure me. "It's more about control. Like this." He lifts his hand, and I notice how the stone has taken on a perfect, solid shape—a makeshift hook embedded in the rock itself.

A surge of questions bubble to the surface. "So... you're telling me you just reshape rock by touch? And you don't get burned? Can you, I don't know, melt metal and other stuff too?"

He chuckles, a low sound that seems to vibrate through the very ground we're standing on. "We can, though it depends on what we're working with. Some Pyronox focus their ability to manipulate hotter or harder substances, but most of us only learn to use it with what we need, like tools, barriers, or"—he gestures at the rock—"simple things like this."

My thoughts whirl as I loop Geralt's reins around the hook. The makeshift tie-off is strong and solid, and the way Solan manipulated it so effortlessly was like watching someone bend time itself, skipping the slow process of shaping and eroding rock.

Awe for him fills my chest, even as my mind races with possibilities. "So... you're, like, walking furnaces? This heat power—you just *have* it?"

Solan's lips quirk in a grin, though his expression turns thoughtful. "Not quite furnaces, but yes, our bodies produce and control heat to a degree that we can direct it outwards. It's a skill that grows with time, as natural to us as breathing. We don't think of it as unusual."

I shake my head, almost laughing at his understatement. "Well, it's a hell of a lot more unusual than toast."

A smile tilts his lips, revealing those fangs, and once again, I can't help but wonder what they would feel like dragging across my skin. Fuck, I need to prioritise. Being turned on at all, let alone by a monster species, is hardly what I should be focussing on.

Though, maybe in this world, I'm the monster.

I clear my throat and look towards the distant buildings. Without a word, which I'm grateful for, Solan starts moving, leading me carefully around the boulders and towards a tree line. There's an element of cover here as we—okay, *I*—stumble over branches.

Then I see it. A figure moving in the distance.

We both stop and scramble to the ground, where Solan immediately uses the spyglass.

"Here," he says, passing it to me after a few seconds.

Grateful, I take it and look through the spyglass, the view before me zooming in and coming into sharp focus. My heart leaps, only to freeze in my chest as I recognise that it's some other kind of creature entirely.

"Is that a Glowranth?" I whisper. We're a good distance away, but after witnessing Solan's ability, there's no saying that the home species doesn't have super hearing or something.

"Yes."

The creature—the *Glowranth*—is humanoid but definitely... other. But fuck if the creature doesn't look like something a kid would create at school when drawing the monsters hidden away in their closet.

Tall and slender, with sinewy limbs covered in smooth, dark blue skin that glistens faintly in the greenish light, the Glowranth stands on two legs. Its hands have three fingers, each one tipped with a slight, almost-clawlike curve, which it flexes with each movement. A faint bioluminescent glow runs along the ridges of its arms and neck, casting it in an eerie light. As it moves, the light shifts and pulses, reflecting.... Hell, it could be emotions or something for all I know.

What shocks me even more is what the monster has with it. Gertie stands beside the Glowranth, halter secured with some sort of twisted metal rein that appears both crude and functional. The horse looks, well, calm, even, but the fact that this Glowranth has it means something deeply unsettling —they've reached the rift point, found my home— and likely my sister's—and investigated.

Solan's tense stance confirms that I'm not alone in feeling this dread.

"Who... *what* are they doing?" I whisper, barely daring to breathe.

He squints, watching the Glowranth as it leads the horse somewhere. "He doesn't look like he's a part of the royal guard. Maybe he lives in the surrounds."

A sound breaks my focus, and I glance back towards the handful of small structures on the training grounds where several heavily armoured figures now stride into view. Their heights rival Solan's, their builds solid and imposing. Each one is dressed in layers of protective armour, dark metallic with flashes of orange—a clear uniform. The leader wears a tall helm marked with jagged symbols that stand out like scars against the dull metal. They're speaking loudly, their language strange, guttural, with a cadence that sends shivers down my spine.

Despite their bulk, they appear to be the same species as the Glowranth with the horse. Considering humans vary in shape, size, and colour, it makes sense that individuals within a species aren't identical.

"They're part of the royal guard," Solan says, answering my unspoken question. He focusses, lips tightening as he listens intently. "They're questioning the Glowranth with the horse, asking about the appearance of... foreign creatures and the changes in the land."

My pulse races. "So, they know? They know something's wrong?"

"They suspect," he says grimly, gaze still fixed on the scene. "But for now, they're probing for answers. They're asking the Glowranth if he's seen anything unusual, any signs of intruders... which he'll report."

"And anything about the heir?" Obviously, any Glowranth going missing and appearing in my dimension isn't ideal, but it being the royal heir seems like it would be seriously bad news.

I pass him the spyglass, and after a beat, he shakes his head. "No one seems alarmed."

"Do you know what the heir looks like?" I ask.

"Yes." He glances at me. "I've met him, and I can't see him now."

"So that means he could just be tucked away in one of those buildings or something?"

"That's a possibility," he agrees. Solan turns his head sharply to the left. "Look."

I follow his direction, zeroing in on the cluster of Glowranth all in full armour. It appears like they're organising themselves to head out of the compound. That can't be good.

From the way Solan tenses at my side, I suspect

he's come to the same conclusion. Tension radiates from him. We're so close, I feel the tightness. I also feel a blast of heat when his grip on the spyglass tightens.

"What's—"

"We have to move."

Before I can process his words, he's up, his heated hand landing on my arm as he drags me up with him.

"Come quickly." He's hauling me back the way we came, his palm drifting to mine, our pace no longer slow and steady.

I struggle to keep my footing but sprint beside him, his unwavering grip still on my hand. "Did they see us?" My question is barely discernible beneath how heavily I'm panting. The loud pounding in my ears doesn't help.

"Yes. They looked right at me." Gravel fills his voice, a whisper of a growl barely being held back.

"Fuck." I pump my arms, losing Solan's grip. He jerks his head my way, concern etched in his gaze, but he doesn't reach out to me again. "And we can't simply stop for a chat? Let them know I'm here and everything's cool?"

He's shaking his head before I finish. "Not wise."

"But the Glowranth accepted you, right?" I push, ignoring the branch that smacks into my face. It stings, and I feel a trickle of blood, but I keep pumping my arms.

"Yes, but that was after weeks of negotiation and a promise," Solan says, his words clipped as we navigate through the thick brush. "The Glowranth don't tolerate outsiders—they capture them and take them to the queendom's epicentre. Those with gifts are expected to serve the realm, offering skills, whatever they can, for the betterment of society."

I'm jolted, and a flare of anger heats in my chest. "You're telling me this *now*?"

Solan doesn't miss a beat, glancing at me as if he expected my reaction. "It's... complicated."

I press on, disbelief edging my voice. "This whole society just... grabs people to use them?"

Solan's shoulders tense, and he avoids my gaze as he continues, "The Glowranth believe every gift, every skill, should serve the whole. Outsiders are seen as opportunities, not individuals." He finally looks at me, a shadowed glint in his golden eyes. "They assume anyone strange to the realm has abilities they can use. They're taken, studied, and trained if they're found useful."

"So, how are *you* not in their ranks?" The frustration bubbles up even as I push forwards, my breathing turning ragged. He clearly knows a lot more than he's let on. Hell, he's a firestarter or some shit. How can *that* be a gift not being manipulated by the realm?

Solan sighs, pressing his lips together as though weighing how much to say. "My brother-in-law, who was caught in the rift with my world, is the son of Harith, the chief merchant in Myra's Crossing. When our worlds merged again and I told him who I was, he called on a favour with the realm—a one-time pardon. The queen granted me my freedom on one condition: that I support Myra's Crossing, make it prosper."

I process that, frowning. "And that's how you've avoided being captured?"

Solan nods. "In a way, yes. I've been useful to the realm by proxy. My brother-in-law's family is influential enough to protect me so long as I stay within their territory and aid them however I can. As long as Myra's Crossing thrives, I'm safe. But that safety doesn't extend to... everyone." He gives me a look that's loaded with implication.

I swallow my irritation, doing my best to keep my focus. He'd kept this from me, yes, but it had kept him alive—and by extension kept us from being hunted sooner. Still, the weight of it sits heavily between us, his obligation to the town and his tentative freedom hanging by a thread.

"So that's why you're helping me?" I ask, my voice low as we keep moving. "Because you know what they'd do to me?"

He hesitates briefly, and the skin around his large eyes pinches. "Yes," he replies, his expression shifting. "You'd be taken to the queendom, interrogated. If they deemed you useful, they'd put you to work. And if they didn't...." He trails off, the silence a grim indication of what happens to those who don't fit neatly into the Glowranth's plans.

I grit my teeth, nodding. For now, my questions will have to wait.

CHAPTER
FIVE

The heavy pounding of hooves echoes in my brain. Geralt has been racing flat out for at least twenty minutes while Solan keeps pace. Sweat soaks my shirt and plasters my hair to my forehead. The hammering of my heart is so intense, it's difficult to register where we're going or what we're going to do.

I don't even know if we're heading in the direction of Solan's, where I hope Jamie is safe inside the thick walls of rock.

Geralt shakes his head. He's almost done. Such a fast-paced run, especially after the exertion of yesterday, is more than he's used to.

I risk a glance over my shoulder, not seeing anything but trees and jagged rocks. "Is it safe to slow down?" I holler, hoping the wind doesn't steal my words and carry them to the guards in pursuit.

How has this become my life? How did the thought of my words carrying into the distance become a fear so terrifying that it threatens to make me numb?

Solan's intense gaze is on me in an instant, ensnaring me. The moment gives me barely a reprieve, a minuscule distraction, but then he parts his lips and says, "Head to the grove of silver drungas."

I follow his line of sight and spot towering spikey silver stalks that look a little like bamboo. They're slimmer, though, and covered in thorns I absolutely don't want to get close to even as I steer Geralt in that direction.

We remain silent as we reach the copse of drungas, and I finally ease back on the reins, slowing Geralt down when Solan reduces his pace. Without the wind blasting my face, I inhale deeply. It's shaky, and fuck if it doesn't remind me of the time when I was twelve and was out on a muster with my dad and Uncle Dirk and had been responsible for riding to the nearest ranch for help when Uncle Dirk broke his leg and collarbone.

Until this moment—hell, the past forty-eight

hours—that had been the most frightened I'd ever been. There's nothing like an interdimensional clusterfuck to remind you that you're only human and nothing can prepare you for shit being this insane.

"Can you breathe okay?" Solan's gruff concern has fresh goose bumps springing to life while I jerk my attention to him, taking in his expression. His whole body is rigid, his hands clenched at his sides, a couple of his digits twitching.

The motion reminds me of what it felt like when he held my hand. In fairness, he gripped the fuck out of it and tugged hard as we ran as if a pack of... well, like a goddamn army was after us. But now, it's easy to recall the sensation. Which is weird, right? That I can remember the touch of his skin. The flare of heat before it cooled and seemed to match mine, feeling almost like his body was an extension of my own.

Yeah, definitely strange as fuck.

A rough whine-like sound grumbles out of Solan. I widen my eyes at the noise. He sounds distressed, and from the force of his gaze, it takes me barely a second to register that I've been staring at the palm of my hand. I didn't even realise I'd lifted it.

"Yeah." I clear my throat, returning my hand to the reins. "I can breathe okay. Geralt needed a break."

I have no issue using my horse as an excuse for my meltdown.

Solan's gaze remains fixed on me, and even in the heavy silence, the intensity of it anchors me more than I care to admit. His brow furrows slightly, and he nods, accepting my explanation about Geralt's exhaustion. He continues to study me before he bobs his head and focusses on the path ahead. For a few tense moments, we catch our breaths in the shade of the towering silver drungas. We're shielded from prying eyes, but their spikes feel like a warning of their own.

Without another word, Solan gestures for us to follow him eastwards, skirting around a thick copse of low-hanging branches. The relentless gallop slows to a quiet but steady jog, allowing Geralt some relief and my pulse to calm. My mind's still swirling—fear and adrenaline mixing in a potent cocktail that keeps me from asking more questions. But Solan keeps glancing my way, waiting.

Finally, I give in, forcing my breathing to even out. "What's the plan?" I ask. "Where are we going?"

His gaze sharpens as if the question grounds him. "East first. Then we'll double back, avoid the merge point entirely. After that, we'll follow a path the guards don't often patrol." He glances over his shoulder, ensuring we're not followed. "But first, we're going to see my brother-in-law's father."

"The chief merchant?" I ask, recalling what he told me earlier.

Solan's lips tilt upwards just slightly. "That's right. To Myra's Crossing. His store is like a Schwarzenegger safe house. Not exactly impenetrable, but he's got enough muscle to keep most people from poking their noses in. And enough hiding spots should they be needed."

The comment catches me off-guard, and I laugh, partly because of the absurdity of Schwarzenegger even existing in this world and partly because I could use the levity. Solan's chuckle is rich and low, a warm rumble that has me grinning despite myself.

"All right, fine. If we're heading to your Arnie's stronghold, do I need to do anything? Like... blend in?"

He grins wider at that, glancing at me with that playful spark that feels like a lifeline right now. "Yes," he says with mock severity. "We're going to make you as inconspicuous as possible. And that's where the flowers come in."

He stops at a break in the trees where a trickling stream runs over a rocky bed, the water glistening under the sun. Blooms that are a bright almost neon blue cluster along the stream, their five-petalled heads stretching towards the light.

"These flowers can be used to make dye," he explains, kneeling by the stream to gather a handful, while I make sure Geralt drinks. "It should help you blend in better once we get to the market town."

Wiping the sweat off my brow, I push off my dusty Akubra. "So, what? We just... rub the petals on my face and call it good?"

He grins, shaking his head as he begins to crush the petals into a thick paste with water. "It's not quite that easy. Hold still." He glances at my shirt, nodding. "You'll need to remove that. It's the only way the dye will cover evenly."

My pulse quickens, though I tell myself it's from adrenaline alone. I pull my shirt over my head and glance up to find Solan staring at me, his own cheeks a slight shade darker than normal. For a moment, we're both frozen in place, tension humming in the air between us, thick as molasses.

"All right," I murmur, swallowing hard, "just get on with it."

He dips his hands into the paste, then spreads a warm layer of blue across my shoulders and down my arms, his touch careful, almost reverent. His fingers move smoothly, but each pass over my skin leaves a tingling trail of warmth that makes it hard to breathe. Every now and then, I sneak a glance at him, his focus so intent on the task, it's almost disconcerting.

Unable to help myself, I blurt, "Is that... your tongue?" He's still focussed on the dye, but when his lips part slightly, I catch a glimpse of a long, slender tongue, dark and slightly forked.

He raises an eyebrow, glancing at me with amusement flickering in his gaze. "Curious, are we?"

"What?" I flush. "I mean, I didn't know if... uh, if monsters, uhm... different species, you know, use it the same way we do."

He chuckles softly, though there's something intense in his gaze. "My species may be different, but we experience... closeness... in our own ways."

As he says this, his hair flickers, the tendrils seeming to float, almost reaching, like they have a life of their own. They undulate subtly in time with his breathing, reacting to something beyond my understanding. It's enough to distract me that he immediately responded to my interest in context to "closeness" rather than tasting food.

"What's going on with that?" I ask, gesturing to the strands. "It's... your hair... it's like it's responding to me?"

"Not just you," he says quickly. "These aren't

exactly hair, not in the way you understand. They're —" He hesitates, the tips of the strands curling as if considering how to explain. "—a part of my sensory system. A kind of living flame, in a way. They react to my surroundings, to people... and yes, to emotions."

"Emotions?" I whisper, transfixed by the gentle, flickering movements. The bright strands sway and shift, a physical embodiment of whatever emotions he's trying to contain. "So, they respond to what you're feeling?"

His voice drops, quiet, almost vulnerable. "They do. And they're sensitive, in more ways than one."

"And... if someone were to touch them?" I ask, my curiosity piqued. "Would it hurt?"

He considers my question, his gaze softening as he watches me. "For a human, it would. They carry a heat that can burn on contact. My species has to learn to control it. It's part of becoming fully grown."

"Has anyone ever...?" I start but pause, feeling my own cheeks heat. Because yeah, asking the guy if damage is caused when he's fucking and things get out of control, resulting in someone gripping his hair, is definitely *not* what I should be thinking, let alone asking. But screw it. Focussing on this gets my mind off other shit. "Like, do they... interact with your emotions like that? If you feel out of control?"

He holds my gaze, a beat of silence stretching between us. "They can," he says slowly, and it's crystal clear he's read between the lines. "For us, there's... a bond. A mate. One person who's like a second soul." He clears his throat, looking down at the dye as he continues applying it to my shoulders. "When the connection forms, it's a link deeper than anything else. Physical, biological... emotional."

I can't look away from him, my mind racing with questions I can barely find the words to ask. "A mate... like... a soul bond?" That's a thing, right? In books, in movies? And bloody hell, in real life, too, apparently.

He nods. "It's rare. But when it happens, it's as if every part of us, from those 'tendrils' to our emotions, is in tune with that other person. It's... consuming. And no part of me—my flames—could ever hurt my mate. It's physically impossible. I would rather my heart and soul perish before I hurt them."

His voice is soft, but the emotion there is real, raw in a way that makes me ache. I want to know more, to ask if he's ever experienced anything like that, if there's someone out there who's felt that connection with him. But before I can find the words, his hands glide down my arms, his touch lingering just a moment too long.

The final bit of dye applied, he releases me, pulling back to give me space. "There," he says, voice low. "You're ready."

I'm almost disappointed when his touch is gone, replaced only by the cool weight of the blue dye on my skin. But the air between us is electric, charged with an unspoken pull neither of us seems able—or willing—to break.

Who am I kidding? My dick is hard, and not even my confusion can get it to behave.

He doesn't say anything, and neither do I. But as we gather ourselves, preparing to head back into the wilderness, I can't shake the thought that maybe this strange connection, this intensity, isn't so one-sided after all.

It's not something I should be thinking about. But the very idea of "mates" constantly swirls in my thoughts even as we draw closer to the market town.

It's obvious we're almost there. What's also worryingly obvious is, I don't have a clue what I'm doing.

I've spent a good portion of my time talking to cattle and living in my own bubble. The sight before me is the result of a thick, sharp needle that's exploded it well and truly.

How the hell do I "blend in" when surrounding me are more and more varying shades of blue monsters? I'm doing a stellar impression of a dying fish, but it's impossible not to gawp. And if I carry on, I'm going to give myself away.

We're on foot, having stashed Geralt away from prying eyes. A cloth of sorts covers my head and part of my face. Another is wrapped around my jeans, much like a sarong. Honestly, when Solan dressed me, I was more than a little dubious, but the further we walk into the hustle and bustle of the town, the greater variety of species I see.

Not that there are many compared to the number of Glowranth.

The Glowranth is definitely the dominant species —obviously being born in this world will do that. But after spotting at least five different types of creatures, it's clear that rifts have been happening more regularly than I thought. That or some of the dimensional merges happened in built-up areas and resulted in a huge population growth.

Solan remains close, his familiar heat a steady presence, which sounds crazy, considering it's only been a day since the world showed me its arse, so nothing should be feeling "steady." As we walk, several Glowranth and almost every other species dart their attention Solan's way. The majority offer a barely perceptible up-nod. It would be easy to miss,

I'm sure, but since I'm wide-eyed and not being subtle, I notice every single one.

But it's the sometimes-wide-eyed looks of fear that capture my attention, closely followed by the terrified monster scuttling off. Two go as far as doing an about-turn and bolting down the closest alley.

"Does everyone know you?" I say quietly, fully aware speaking English in the bustling streets is likely to cause more heads to turn. The buildings around us are mostly single-storey. They're brightly coloured in various shades of the rainbow. Another time, I'd be joking about preparing for a Pride parade and feeling right at home. But I'm certain that's not what's going on here.

While market-type stalls are visible, they're staggered apart with storefronts separating them, and smaller side streets break off from the large open walkway that's clearly the main path. With the increasing number of monsters around me, I can only imagine how sprawling this place is. It's nothing like the outback towns I'm used to.

I side-eye Solan when he doesn't respond, my hidden brows shooting high when his strands react in a gentle wave.

He's embarrassed. Fuck knows how, exactly, I'm so sure, but without a doubt, he is.

"What is it? Are you some kind of celebrity or something?" I'm only half-joking. But if he is, I'm not sure how long I can get away with blending in. It's the few legit terrified expressions I'd caught, though, that make me suspect that he's far from holding some sort of celebrity status.

After the briefest of hesitations, he shoots a glance my way. "No," he answers gruffly, his voice quiet as he steps to the side, his palm touching my back and sending a bolt of awareness to every nerve ending. He guides me away from something blue and sticky on the ground and then drops his hand.

Inhaling a ragged breath, I pretend like the storefront selling some sort of metallic-looking pot is the most interesting thing in the world. It's safer than chasing Solan's touch while wanting to race back to Jamie and hide somewhere until another freak explosion happens.

Yeah, talk about mixed fucking feelings.

I'm dancing between hating the sensation of contemplating all these bullshit thoughts and feeling so incredibly grateful that Solan was the one to come to our rescue.

Maybe that's all this is: gratitude. Getting a boner for the monster who saved us shouldn't make sense in any universe. But here we are.

Solan saying, "I have a role here. It is why I am known," makes me jump. He'd been quiet for so long, moving with sure, certain movements through the increasingly busy streets, it was easy to forget I'd asked a question. After his "No," I hadn't expected anything else.

I angle my face to peer up at him, meeting his eyes briefly before he looks ahead. "And what's your role?" I keep my voice even despite a flurry of nerves waking up in my gut. That Solan's being evasive is obvious.

Nothing he's done has made me doubt him or his intentions, but I've made more than one decision over the years that's ended up biting me on the arse. And sure, I might like the idea of Solan scraping his sharp fangs over my skin a little too much, but it's not sensible to put my complete faith in him.

So why the fuck does even thinking that I can't trust him implicitly send a slither of wrongness dancing up my spine?

"Solan?" I push, keeping my voice quiet but threading as much of a demand through it as I can.

His throat moves in a swallow, tugging my attention there, and I follow its path. I dart my gaze back to his face as he turns it my way, hauls me to the side, and pauses.

Nerves send a shiver down my spine, causing a fresh outbreak of goose bumps.

But fuck if he doesn't look equally as nervous.

His gaze searches mine, the flash of his fangs appearing as one pinches against his bottom lip. He parts his lips, his voice a deep cadence as he says, "I'm... I'm the *Kelvarra*." Despite the hesitation that preceded his statement, he manages to keep his voice steady. The unfamiliar word rolls off his tongue with an almost-reverent weight, but it leaves me blinking in confusion.

"The what now?" I ask, leaning closer to ensure I've heard him correctly.

"The *Kelvarra*," he repeats, his gaze shifting away from mine to scan the bustling street. A couple of Glowranth pause mid-stride, their eyes darting between us before they hurry on. Solan doesn't seem to notice—or maybe he does and chooses not to care. "It's... a title. A role given to me by the town's *Harethrin*. You might call her a mayor or governor, though she serves the sovereign state."

My confusion deepens. "Okay, so what does a *Kelvarra* do, exactly?"

His jaw tightens, and the strands of his sensory "hair" ripple faintly, betraying his discomfort. "I am this town's protector," he says, his voice low enough that I have to strain to hear him over the clamour of the market. "When someone or a creature threatens the borders, when something unnatural breaches the safety of Myra's Crossing, I am called upon to eliminate the threat."

That part makes sense. He saved me and Jamie, after all. His accuracy was true and deadly. But there's something more in his tone, a gravity that tells me he hasn't shared the whole truth yet.

"And?" I press, my voice quieter now, coaxing rather than demanding. "That's not all, is it?"

Solan exhales through his nose, his head tilting downwards as if the weight of what he's about to say has become too much. "No," he admits. "I am also… the executioner. When the queen's law must be upheld and punishment delivered, it falls to me to carry it out."

I stagger back a step, my chest tightening as I process his words. The picture of Solan I've built in my mind—gentle, compassionate, with those sparks of humour that keep me grounded—is suddenly painted over with shades of violence and death.

An executioner.

My throat feels dry. "You kill people," I say, the words blunt and unpolished as they tumble out of my mouth.

His sharp intake of breath makes me flinch. His gaze meets mine, and for the first time, there's something like shame simmering beneath his glowing eyes. "Only when there is no other choice," he says firmly. "Only when the *Harethrin* decrees it necessary to uphold order. The *Kelvarra* must serve the town and its people. I do what is required to keep them safe."

The bustling street seems to fade around us as the implications settle in. Fear prickles at the edges of my mind, but it's not for me—it's for him. I've seen how others look at him, with that blend of respect and terror. I can only imagine what it must feel like to carry that burden.

"How long?" I ask, my voice softer now. "How long have you been doing this?"

"Since the rift," he answers. "The *Harethrin* saw my... abilities and deemed me fit for the role. It was all Harith—my brother-in-law's father—could arrange to keep me from being sent to the queen's domain. He... he called in every favour he could to ensure I remained here."

The weight of his words hits me square in the chest. Solan isn't some coldhearted killer revelling in his power. He's a monster caught between survival and duty, forced into a role he didn't choose but one he fulfills with unwavering resolve.

"And the monsters here?" I ask, glancing at the retreating figures who give him such a wide berth. "Do they respect you? Fear you?"

His lips press into a thin line, the tendrils of his sensory hair flickering faintly. "Both," he says after a pause. "Many respect what I do because it keeps their families safe. But there are those who fear the *Kelvarra,* who see only the death I bring and not the lives I save."

I open my mouth to respond, but nothing comes out. What can I even say to that? My gut churns with the knowledge of what he's endured—what he's *still* enduring—but more than anything, I'm grateful. Grateful that Solan is here, by my side, using that lethal precision to protect me and Jamie. Grateful that despite everything, he's not some heartless monster.

"You're not what I expected," I finally say, my voice trembling with the weight of my emotions. "You've been through all of that, and you still... you still care. About these monsters. About me."

His gaze snaps to mine, surprise appearing in his glowing eyes. For a moment, the hardened exterior he wears so well seems to crack, revealing a vulnerable core beneath. "Of course I care," he says softly. "If I didn't, I would have become the very thing I'm meant to protect against. I couldn't let that happen."

The sincerity in his words sends a lump to my throat, and I nod, swallowing it down. "I'm glad you're on my side," I say, my voice firmer now. "Grateful as hell for it, actually."

A faint smile tugs at the corner of his mouth. "Always," he promises, and the single word feels like an anchor in the storm of uncertainty swirling around us.

I don't press him further as we continue through the market. I need time to process everything he's just shared, but one thing remains crystal clear: No matter how dangerous Solan's past—or his role as the *Kelvarra*—might make him, there's not a single doubt in my mind that I'm safer with him than anywhere else in this fractured world.

CHAPTER
SIX

AFTER ANOTHER FIFTEEN MINUTES OR SO OF heading through the market, it becomes more and more obvious that everyone else navigating the crowds is being jostled and having to squeeze through. But not us. It's like Solan has an invisible shield or something around him, one that repels and creates a path for us.

Not gonna lie, it's kind of cool in an "I'm really trying not to freak out" way. And to be honest, I'm tired of that reaction, of being scared and running on fumes. It's a version of myself that I don't recognise. I'm not a fan at all.

Life has taught me to take the shit thrown my way on the chin—that's if I can't dodge it first. My dad was a firm believer in standing up and taking action. He was incredible that way. Sure, he could be a miserable old coot, too, especially when times on the property were tough, but he persevered. He didn't constantly question and tie himself up in knots. He simply dealt with his lot the best way he could.

It's the reminder I need to stop questioning every-thing. Admittedly, I suspect Dad never experienced anything like this, but with worry being my constant, it's time to shake it off. I've never worked well under a cloud of stress.

"So," I start, determined to win this internal battle I have going on, "you think Harith will be able to help in some way?"

Solan side-eyes me and nods once before returning his full focus to the path ahead, his subtle scan of the crowd continuing. It's something he's been doing nonstop since we entered the town. "Yes, Jack," he responds, my name a low grumble that tightens my gut. "Information travels fast in Terrafeara, but even more so in Myra's Crossing."

"Any reason for that?" I'm curious about... well, everything. Sure, Solan's managed to magic or some shit his found TV to work, but nothing else about the place screams technology or even hints at it that I recognise. Though I do recall Solan saying something about the cities having technology. What I didn't think to ask was what kind.

"Dracodines."

I tug my brows low. *Dracodines*? Am I supposed to know what that is?

As I part my lips to ask, he gently presses two of his large fingers against my chin, tilting my head slightly so I'm looking up at the rooftops. "Look," he says softly, and I do, but I can barely concentrate on anything but his touch. It burns, a searing heat that should cause me pain. All it does is send goose bumps erupting on my skin and draw my breaths from me unevenly.

The creatures are birdlike in as much as they have wings. They're a similar size to a seagull, but beyond having feathers on their two wings, that's where the similarity ends. Rather than a beak, the *Dracodines* have long, sharp snouts that curve slightly downwards, resembling scaled talons. Their heads are covered in small, smooth scales that glint faintly in the sunlight, giving them an otherworldly sheen. Their wings, while feathered, have a distinct leathery texture near the base, and their talons—hooked and razor-sharp—grip the rooftops with ease.

But it's their eyes that grab my attention, making my breath hitch. Each orb is a swirling mix of colours, shifting constantly as though liquid fire flows just beneath the surface. They seem too intelligent, too perceptive, like they're not just looking but seeing everything, dissecting it, cataloguing it. The sight sends a shiver racing down my spine.

"They look...." I hesitate, searching for the right word. "Intense."

Solan nods, his gaze flicking to one of the perched *Dracodines* before returning to our path. "They are. *Dracodines* are used to send messages across long distances. They mimic entire sentences perfectly, word for word, tone and all."

"Like parrots?"

A faint chuckle rumbles from him, the sound warm despite the tense set of his shoulders. "Parrots? Perhaps. But more useful and far more dangerous."

I glance back up at the *Dracodine*, and it tilts its head, almost as if it's acknowledging my attention. The movement is unnerving, far too deliberate. "Dangerous how?" I ask, lowering my voice instinctively.

"They're often used to spy," Solan replies, his tone clipped as his eyes dart to the rooftops again. "The queen and her sovereignty, rival towns, even private individuals can train them to record conversations and carry them back to their owners. In some regions, they're considered the ultimate tool for intelligence gathering."

The *Dracodine* flutters its wings once, and I swear its swirling gaze sharpens on me for a heartbeat before it shifts to scan the crowd below. "And nobody notices these things eavesdropping?" I ask, my voice tinged with disbelief.

Solan smirks faintly but doesn't take his eyes off our surroundings. "They're common enough here that most don't give them a second thought. But that's the trick, isn't it? Something seen too often becomes invisible."

I frown, studying the creature. Its talons flex briefly, and the subtle glint of something metallic catches my eye. "Wait—do they wear... jewellery?"

Solan shakes his head. "Not jewellery. Those are message cylinders. They're attached to their legs to carry written missives."

"Efficient," I murmur, though I can't help but feel unsettled by the thought of these creatures flying around with recorded voices or secret messages strapped to them.

"It is," Solan agrees, his tone darker now. "But don't trust a *Dracodine* just because it carries a message. If someone gets their hands on one, they can tamper with what it delivers."

I stare at the creature for a moment longer before finally tearing my gaze away. "That's... terrifying."

Solan offers a small nod, his expression grim. "It should be. In the wrong hands, they can be weapons. In the right hands, tools. In either case, always be on the lookout for them."

His words linger in my mind as we continue through the bustling streets. I cast one last glance at the *Dracodine* before it spreads its wings, the feathers flashing iridescent in the light, and takes flight with a single powerful leap. It vanishes into the sky, but its piercing, all-seeing gaze stays with me long after it's gone.

"We're here." Solan's voice is low. He flashes me a glance, his focus intent. Worry appears in his eyes, blatant enough that my chest tightens. If Solan is concerned, is he expecting something to go wrong?

Before I returned to the outback to support Dad and take over the family farm full-time, I'd spent years in Brisbane. Time working on the ranch, both growing up and since going back home, meant I had no choice but to work and think independently, think fast on my feet. When mustering especially. Sure, I had seasonal workers to support me, but that meant I had additional responsibility. Decisions could mean the difference between life and death. Okay, that sounds a little more dramatic than it likely is, but ranching life could be dangerous.

Before returning to the outback, I'd worked as a firefighter in Brisbane. Fires don't wait for you to figure things out. You make decisions fast—whether it's kicking down a door or deciding which way to direct your crew to keep them safe. And it's not just about the fire itself; it's the people.

You learn to read panic in someone's eyes or hear it in their voice. Not everyone reacts logically when their world is literally burning around them. That's where reading the room becomes as important as knowing how to handle a hose or an axe.

But it was my time as a firefighter that really taught me the significance of thinking fast and staying on my feet. Not only that—the skill of noticing the tiniest details in the heat of the moment and acting without hesitation.

I shake off the creeping unease and glance at Solan. "Should I be worried?" I ask, trying to keep my tone light.

His lips twitch—a faint smile or grimace, I can't tell. "No," he says, but the way his hair ripples in an almost-imperceptible wave tells me he's not as confident as his words suggest.

Reading a situation is one thing. Reading a

monster with sentient hair? That is a whole new challenge.

Solan pushes open the heavy door, and I follow him inside, stepping into a building that smells of something earthy and slightly spicy, like freshly cut wood and warm pepper. The walls are crafted from a material that looks like wood but shimmers faintly, catching the light with an almost-metallic sheen. It's larger inside than I'd expected. The space is open, high ceilings arching overhead, with beams that stretch across like the ribs of a great beast.

To my surprise, it feels more like an office than a store. A long counter with polished surfaces stands at the far end, and scattered throughout are desks, some piled with neatly stacked parchment, others with odd contraptions I can't even begin to identify. This isn't just a merchant's shop—it's some kind of hub for activity, far more organised and official than the dusty, ramshackle trading posts I'd imagined.

A smaller creature—not a Glowranth—sits to one side, perched on a stool that seems slightly too large for its compact frame. Its skin is a mottled mix of blue and green, textured like tree bark, and its three round eyes blink in unsettling succession. Those eyes keep darting towards me, curious but not hostile. My hackles don't rise, and I let myself relax. It's clearly wary, though I can't tell if it's because of me specifically or just their general behaviour.

Solan strides towards them, his gait confident but not rushed. His voice takes on the rhythmic cadence I've heard while walking through the township, speaking in the language I assume belongs to the Glowranth. It flows smoothly, musical but with sharp edges, like the hum of a song interrupted by snaps of static.

The small monster nods rapidly, its gaze flickering to me, then back to Solan. I watch their exchange, trying to piece together the meaning from their tones and expressions. The smaller monster looks unsure, then placated, though its wide-eyed glances my way don't stop.

After a brief exchange, Solan gestures for me to follow him into a back room. I trail behind, stepping into a quieter space that smells faintly of ink and some kind of herbal musk. The walls are lined with shelves stuffed with parchment-like books, their covers worn and their edges uneven. The floor is a patchwork of mismatched rugs that are soft underfoot.

Behind a low desk sits someone who I assume is the chief merchant, and immediately, I know this isn't your average shopkeeper. He's a Glowranth, his luminous, iridescent skin casting a faint, warm glow that shifts subtly with each breath he takes, like sunlight refracting through a thin veil of mist. The surface of his skin shimmers with faint hues of gold and violet, as if alive with its own energy. He's engrossed in writing, long, sharp fingers moving deftly across a sheet of parchment, the fluid motion as precise as it is practiced.

The merchant looks up as we enter. His gaze locks on Solan first and then shifts to me. A flicker of recognition flashes in his intelligent eyes, his expression sharpening. The curve of his lips hints at a smile, though it's tempered by something serious.

His gaze travels over me, and I know immediately that my disguise isn't fooling him. I resist the urge to fidget, instead standing as straight as I can, though my insides twist with nerves.

"Solan," the merchant greets, his voice deep and smooth, but there's an urgency in his tone as he continues in the Glowranth language. The two exchange words quickly, their voices quiet but intense. I can't understand what they're saying, but the merchant's eyes widen briefly as he takes me in again, his expression shifting from cautious to concerned. Then, surprisingly, something softer takes its place.

The merchant leans back in his chair, his skin shimmering like moonlight rippling over a smooth dam, and switches to rough but comprehensible English. "You are welcome," he says, his tone surprisingly warm. "I am Harith. We felt the shift but had not yet heard where it took place. There is news that the Prince Aelith is missing... as is his bodyguard." He tilts his head slightly, watching my reaction.

Panic seeps through me at his words, threatening to buckle my knees. Harith leans forwards, his face darkening. "The royal guard searches. It is... not good."

My chest tightens as worry flares. "I left my nephew behind... at Solan's," I blurt, my voice cracking. "He's just a kid. I didn't have a choice. Is he in danger?" Even as I say the words, I want to go back in time. What the fuck was I thinking, leaving him alone in this strange world? Fuck.

Harith's expression hardens instantly, and dread clenches my stomach like a vice.

"They will care," he says grimly. "A human child linked to the shift? The royal guard will take him to the queen without hesitation. They will assess his skills, determine how he can serve society. See what he knows about the prince."

My heart pounds. "He's twelve," I snap, panic

sharpening my tone. "What skills? All he does is eat, fart, and tell jokes so bad, they make you want to crawl under a rock. Sure, he can ride and shoot better than most adults, but he's a *kid*."

Harith doesn't flinch. "They will not see a child. They will see potential. And potential is something they do not waste." His gaze flicks to Solan, who stands stiff, his face carved from stone but his worry glaringly clear.

"No," Solan says firmly, stepping closer to me. His deep voice is steady, a stark contrast to my fraying nerves. "Jamie is smart. He will endure."

My throat tightens, and Solan reaches out, cupping the back of my neck with his broad hand. The warmth of his palm seeps into me, anchoring me in the moment. I close my eyes for a beat, pulling in a deep breath that does little to calm me.

"Going back isn't safe," Harith says. "The royal guard will expect it. You would be walking into their trap."

"We need a plan," I say, the tremor in my voice betraying my fear. We were meant to be heading back today to be with him. He can't be left alone. My eyes dart to Solan while my brain becomes overloaded with questions. The most pressing is *why* will the royal guard be expecting it? It doesn't make a lick of sense. What I say instead is "Jamie's capable." Fierce resolve settles in my chest. Anything else is too dangerous. Too debilitating. "He could ride a horse before he could tie his laces. He could shoot a rifle before he could spell *complicated.* But he's still just a kid." The last words spill out unbidden. Fuck.

Solan's grip tightens slightly, and his hair ripples like a flame with renewed access to oxygen. "We will find a way," he says, his voice unyielding. The sheer conviction in his words grounds me more than his touch.

Harith nods slowly, his expression clouded with thought. "There are... contacts I can reach out to. Those who might help. But it will take time. For now, you must stay hidden." He glances between us before fixing Solan with a pointed look. "And you, Solan.... You know what is required."

Solan's jaw flexes, his entire frame going rigid. "I know."

I look between them, unease churning in my gut. "What? What does that mean?"

"We protect you," Solan says, his tone like iron, his eyes taking on a glowing sheen, a testament to the fire beneath. "No matter the cost."

CHAPTER
SEVEN

I don't like the plan. In fact, I bloody hate it.

Letting some random monster go to Solan's to find and fetch Jamie is not something I can get on board with. "He's *my* responsibility," I grit out for likely the hundredth time since we've been led to a room that will be ours while we stay here. And just like the other ninety-nine times, Solan stares down at me with nothing but patience and understanding.

"I understand, but this is safer for Jamie."

Struth, when he puts it like that, I'm the dickhead. With my jaw still tense, I grumble, "I don't like anything about this plan."

"I know."

The arsehole, who is absolutely not an arsehole—

but I need to believe he is in this moment so that guilt doesn't eat me alive—reaches for me and grips the back of my neck.

Every time he does that, I almost melt, my muscles immediately relaxing. It's at complete odds with the desire that unfurls in my gut. It's not the time or the place, not when I'm going to have to trust monsters to protect my nephew.

"Tahrionne is strong. A protector. He can also be trusted. He will take Calythra with him, another young one similar to Jamie. Your nephew will be safe."

I reluctantly nod, understanding the plan despite my fear.

Tahrionne has been given my watch—something my sister had got engraved for my thirtieth birthday from Jamie. *Time spent as an uncle is time well cherished.* Needless to say, my sister knew what she was doing—reminding me that I had a family out west and that Brisbane was just a pit stop. But the watch is intended to reassure Jamie that I'm the one who sent them to protect him.

While Tahrionne can't speak English well—or at all—Calythra can. He's also a warrior in training, and from what I could gather, he's more of a teenager than another child. Should they be stopped—though

Harith reassures me Tahrionne is the master of stealth and covering his tracks, so it'll be unlikely— they'll say Jamie, like Calythra, is Tahrionne's apprentice.

"Can I meet him? See?" Discomfort settles in my chest. Calythra isn't a show pony, but I'm trusting these monsters with Jamie. And fuck if he's not the single most important person in my world. I love him fiercely. I already met Tahrionne, and while he looked appropriately menacing, his eyes were filled with a kindness that made me instinctively trust him.

"Of course," Harith answers. He's stayed out of the conversation, allowing Solan to take the reins and offer me reassurance and comfort. He leaves the room with a nod while I wait, body vibrating with tension that's likely going to buckle my knees.

"I hate this," I whisper, more to myself than anything, but Solan hears, his palm that's still on my neck shifting slightly as he draws one of his large fingers up and down the column of my neck, passing over my pulse with each swipe.

"What do you hate, Jack?" Concern pulses from him, a hint of a tone that manages to let me know if I told him and he could fix any of my pain, he'd do so in a heartbeat.

I've long since passed questioning the calming

power he has over me or the way he lights up my body. All I find now is comfort rather than questions. Too much has happened and too much is at stake for me to waste time hemming and hawing over my reaction to the large red monster who offers me reassurance that simply feels right. Natural.

"Feeling so out of control. Feeling inept." I meet his golden gaze. "Relying solely on you while giving you nothing in return."

His gentle stroking stops, just for one beat, before he starts it up again. This time he steps closer—so close, I have to angle my neck to peer up at him. Bloody hell, this close, his scent wraps around me like the fragrance of the first drops of rain on parched earth, fresh and intoxicating. My breath stutters, and I feel that ridiculous pull again—the one that makes me want to close the space between us, to touch him, to *taste* him. My stomach flips, and I swallow hard, forcing myself to look away, but it's no use. His golden eyes seem to tug me back, grounding me and scattering my thoughts all at once.

"You give me more than you realise," Solan says, his voice low and rich like the promise of safety in the middle of chaos.

I laugh softly, bitterly. "Like what? A headache?"

His lips twitch, not quite a smile, but close.

"Trust. Hope. A reason." His hand tightens slightly on my neck, a gentle squeeze that makes my pulse jump. "You are more than you think, Jack. To me. To Jamie. To yourself."

The intensity in his gaze makes me dizzy, and I suddenly feel like the air between us is charged, heavy with something I can't quite name. My heart pounds as his eyes drop—*to my mouth.*

I can't move. Hell, I'm not sure I *want* to move. My breath catches as he leans down so close, I can feel the heat radiating from him, his lips almost brushing mine—

"Am I interrupting?"

The voice snaps through the moment like a whip, and I stumble back a step, heat flooding my face. Solan's hand falls away slowly, but his gaze lingers, his expression unreadable.

Harith strides back in, Calythra—I assume—following close behind. My stomach knots at the sight of the new monster.

Calythra's young—definitely a teenager in human terms—but there's a confidence in his posture that's unnerving. His features are humanoid but ethereal, his skin so white, it's nearly translucent, veins barely visible beneath the surface. His eyes are a startling, vivid blue, impossibly large and framed by thick lashes.

"Jack," Harith says, his tone formal, "this is Calythra."

Calythra's grin widens. "G'day," he says, and I blink, startled by the pitch-perfect Australian accent.

I narrow my eyes, wondering how the hell he's mirrored my accent so perfectly. "You're taking the piss."

"Not at all," he says, still grinning, his voice a perfect mimic of my own cadence. "Thought I'd give it a go. Figured you might feel more at ease hearing something familiar."

I'm torn between being impressed and annoyed. "That's... unsettling."

"Good," he replies cheerfully. "Keeps you on your toes."

Before I can reply, something startling happens—his skin begins to shift. The pale, translucent white darkens, deepening to the same iridescent red as Solan's. The change is fluid, mesmerising, like watching liquid fire ripple under his skin.

"Pretty neat, eh?" Calythra says, holding his arms out to show off the transformation. His expression is light, playful, and there's an undeniable pride in his tone.

My breath catches as he steps closer, extending a hand towards me. I hesitate, and he chuckles, his tone somehow both amused and patient. "Relax, mate. I'm not going to hurt you. Look." He presses his hand to his own chest, and the colour spreads like water on blotting paper before returning to normal.

Tentatively, I extend my arm. His touch is warm, not uncomfortably so, but the change is immediate. My skin flushes red where his fingers make contact, the vivid hue spreading outwards until my entire forearm matches his.

"What the hell?" I pull back instinctively, staring wide-eyed at my arm.

Calythra laughs, a light, airy sound. "Magic, mate. Or close enough."

"It's not magic," Solan says, his voice calm but firm. "It's a biological adaptation unique to Calythra's species. His body can mimic his surroundings, and he can share that ability with others temporarily."

"Temporarily?" I glance between them, still unsettled by the sight of my own red skin.

Calythra nods. "It'll fade. Could make it last longer if I wanted to, but that takes effort. Don't worry, *mate*, you're not stuck like that."

Sure enough, as I watch, the colour begins to fade, my skin returning to its normal tone. His own skin shifts back to its original translucent state, the change just as seamless as before.

I glance at Solan. "This is who you're sending to protect Jamie?"

"I'm flattered you're sceptical," Calythra says, his grin widening again. "Don't let the looks fool you. I might appear young, but I'm more than capable."

"You're what? A teenager?"

"Close enough," he replies with a shrug. "But I've been training since before you were born. Don't let the baby-face trip you up."

"Baby-face?" I mutter under my breath, still trying to wrap my head around him.

Calythra leans closer, his big blue eyes unblinking, and I fight the urge to step back. "You don't trust me yet. That's okay. But I'm telling you now, Jack, Jamie's going to be just fine with me. And Tahrionne? He's a ghost when he wants to be. We'll get your kid and keep him safe. Promise."

There's an odd sincerity in his tone that catches me off-guard. Despite his playful demeanour, there's a sharpness to him, a confidence that feels earned rather than forced. And his English? I have no idea how he speaks it so well, but it's impressive.

"Why are you so sure you can handle this?" I ask, my voice quieter, more serious.

Calythra tilts his head, considering the question. "Because this isn't my first rodeo." I blink that he even knows the term *rodeo*. "And because I care. More than you'd think. Kids like Jamie? They deserve to grow up, to have a shot at life without worrying about the likes of the royal guard breathing down their necks. I'm not just doing this because Harith told me to. I'm doing this because it's the right thing to do."

I'm struck silent, the tension in my chest easing just slightly.

Calythra claps his hands together suddenly, breaking the moment. "Right, then. Let's get this show on the road. Got a kid to save, yeah?"

Harith nods, his expression calm but approving. "You're ready."

"Born ready," Calythra replies, his grin flashing one last time before he turns to leave the room.

As the door closes behind him, I glance at Solan, my chest tightening with a mix of hope and fear. "You really think they can do it?"

"Yes," Solan says simply, his golden gaze steady. "And so should you."

His hand finds the back of my neck again, his touch grounding me, but my thoughts are still with Jamie—and with the strange, confident monster who just might be his best chance. "You're exhausted," he murmurs.

I let out a shaky laugh. "Adrenaline crash," I admit.

He pulls me gently towards the cot in the corner of the room, his golden gaze soft. "Rest, Jack. We will protect him. I promise."

And somehow, as his warmth surrounds me, I almost believe him. It's not enough to stop the dread from swirling in my gut, but it does something to settle me.

"I don't think I can sleep." My voice sounds brittle, like it might shatter under the weight of my guilt. Jamie's out there, alone, and the idea of me getting a full night's rest feels like the ultimate betrayal.

"Then don't," he says simply, his tone calm but resolute.

He sits down first, the mattress creaking slightly under his weight. It's not plush, not even close to comfortable, but it might as well be a throne with the way Solan carries himself—calm, deliberate, present. He tugs me down beside him, and I follow without resistance, though I'm not entirely sure why. Maybe it's exhaustion, or maybe it's the pull he has over me, that ever-present gravity that keeps me tethered when everything else feels like it's slipping away.

"What can I do to make this easier while we wait?" he asks, his voice low, his gaze steady.

The question hangs in the air between us, heavy and unspoken. My mind betrays me, flashing with images that have no business surfacing right now—his mouth on mine, his strong grip on parts of me I can't even acknowledge without blushing. Desire stirs, hot and unwelcome, but it refuses to be ignored.

I glance at him, and the intensity of his gaze almost undoes me. He's watching me with such focus, such quiet attentiveness, that it's like he can see straight through me. It's too much and not enough all at once.

"Stay," I whisper before I can stop myself.

He stills. The hand that was brushing against mine pauses, and for a moment, I'm afraid I've crossed some invisible line. But then I feel it—a pulse, an energy that radiates from him like heat from a flame, subtle and warm but unmistakably alive. It dances over my skin, leaving a trail of awareness in its wake.

"I will stay," he says, his voice quieter now, more intimate. His fingers find my pulse point at the side of my neck, the touch electric. My vein leaps under his hand, and there's no way he doesn't feel it.

He leans in slightly, his golden gaze locking onto

mine. "And what else do you need from me?" he asks, his voice dropping to a husky murmur. "You can have anything that I have to give."

There's a fierceness in his eyes that makes me swallow hard, a promise that feels too big to comprehend. And suddenly, I can't think. All I can do is feel—his touch, his presence, the sheer intensity of him.

Fuck it. I want him.

Without a word, I move, instinct overriding hesitation. I swing a leg over his lap, straddling him in one fluid motion. His eyes widen, and for a split second, I think I've surprised him. But he doesn't pull away. Instead, his hands hover at my sides, hesitant, almost reverent.

"Touch me," I say, my voice shaking with a mix of nerves and raw need.

He doesn't hesitate this time. His hands settle on my waist, large and warm, and then they move up my back, trailing heat wherever they go. A soft, involuntary moan escapes me, and I press closer, feeling the hard planes of his chest beneath me.

His hair shifts, the strands brushing against my arms like they're alive and responding to me. When they rest against my skin, it's like a circuit is completed, and I inhale sharply, the connection startling in its intimacy. The scent of him fills my lungs—

earthy, warm, uniquely him—and it's like breathing for the first time.

"Do your people...?" I trail off, embarrassment creeping up my neck as I stumble over the words. "Do you use your mouths to...?"

He tilts his head slightly, his expression curious but patient. "To make love?" he finishes for me, his voice soft.

"Yes." I exhale sharply, trying to ground myself. "That. But also this." I press my fingers to his mouth, then mine. "Kiss."

Understanding dawns in his gaze, followed by something almost shy. "Yes," he says, his voice barely above a whisper. "But only with those who belong to our soul."

His words hit me like a punch to the chest. Horror and guilt slam into me, and I start to pull back, ashamed of how recklessly I've been throwing myself at him. But before I can retreat, his hands tighten on me, keeping me in place.

"I've been waiting for you," Solan says softly, his deep voice vibrating through me. His gaze is locked on mine, fierce but vulnerable, and it's like he's offering me every part of himself in that single moment.

My breath hitches, my pulse racing under his

hand. I can't think, can't hesitate. The words tear through my chest, their impact cracking something open inside me. I surge forwards and slam my mouth against his, my fingers gripping his jaw, his neck, desperate to anchor myself to him.

His lips are soft, impossibly warm, and their heat spreads through me like wildfire. The first touch is almost too much—a shock to my system, a jolt that leaves me gasping against him. But he doesn't pull back. His hands tighten on my waist, dragging me closer, and suddenly it's not enough. I press harder, threading my fingers into his hair, the silken strands wrapping around my hands and my forearms as though holding me in place.

His mouth moves against mine, hesitant at first, as though testing uncharted territory. But the hesitation doesn't last. He learns fast—too fast. His lips part, and his forked tongue brushes mine, tentative and careful, and I swear I shatter. A broken sound escapes me, part moan, part whimper, and the way he responds—growling low in his throat as he pulls me impossibly closer—makes my head spin.

The kiss is consuming, every part of him overwhelming my senses. His heat seeps into me, his scent filling my lungs with every breath. It's grounding and dizzying all at once, like standing on the edge of a cliff and feeling both the fear of falling and the thrill of flight.

The connection between us is electric, his energy pulsing over my skin in waves that leave me trembling. It feels like he's everywhere—his hands roaming my back, his hair curling around my arms, his mouth devouring mine with a hunger that mirrors my own. I press my fingers into his shoulders, hard muscle shifting under my touch, and the strength of him only pulls me deeper into the moment.

I've never been kissed like this before—never felt so completely undone by the press of someone's lips. It's not just a kiss; it's an unspoken promise, a claiming, a merging of something far deeper than just physical desire. I feel exposed, laid bare, and yet somehow, I don't care.

Solan pulls back, just enough to let me catch my breath. His forehead rests against mine, his golden eyes searching, his chest heaving as though the kiss left him as wrecked as it left me.

"I don't think I can stop," he admits, his voice low and rough, his gaze flicking to my lips as though already drawn back to them.

"Don't," I whisper, my own voice trembling, my lips brushing his as I speak. "Don't stop."

He doesn't need further encouragement. He crashes his mouth back onto mine, and this time, there's no hesitation. He kisses me like he's starving, like he's been waiting for this moment his whole life, and I lose myself in him, every rational thought drowned out by the sheer intensity of him.

When we finally break apart, I'm breathless, my body trembling, my head spinning. I can't form a coherent thought, let alone a sentence. All I can do is stare at him, still clutching his hair, my chest rising and falling as I try to process what just happened.

His lips are swollen, his hair dishevelled, and his gaze is fixed on me with a single-mindedness that makes my heart stutter.

"I didn't know it could feel like this," I whisper, my voice barely audible.

His smile is small and genuine, and the sight of it sends a fresh wave of heat through me. "Neither did I," he admits.

For a moment, the weight of the world fades, and there's only him—only us. And for the first time in what feels like forever, I feel something close to peace.

"Now you rest."

"Huh?" Rest? Now? After I almost came in my pants from simply kissing? But fuck if there is anything "simple" about what just happened between us.

"Yes, my bonded needs to sleep."

Bonded. The words from his earlier explanation about soul mates slam into me. And just a few moments ago, he mentioned his soul. I freeze on top of him, eyes widening at the absurdity, at the fucking rightness of his words and everything happening between us.

How is this even possible?

"How can you be mine?" The question spills out with a softness that belies the rush of emotions I'm struggling to contain. My brows shoot high as another thought hits me. "What if the merge had never happened? What if I'd never come here?"

Jesus. My heart aches when I say it aloud. The suddenness of everything doesn't make sense to my human brain, but I feel everything. Feel the rightness, the certainty, the truth.

"There would never be a life where we wouldn't have found our way to each other." Solan cups my cheek, reverence in his tone and the gentleness of his touch. "We have a lot to discuss, to learn."

No fucking shit. I nod rather than spout off.

"But for now, you really must rest."

I don't fight the roll of my eyes even as I remain

on his lap, idly wondering what, if anything, he has under his leather kilt. "I don't think I have to do anything." Amusement colours my words—that and a clear tone letting him know that it's been a long damn time since someone told me to go to bed.

He searches my gaze, his strong hands settling on my back. "*I* need to rest." There's no doubt each word is deliberate. Crafty fucker. "I ran far today."

I narrow my gaze. Not only is he crafty, but he's a manipulative arsehole too. I hold back my lip twitch, liking this side of his character.

"Tomorrow, we should have Jamie. He's going to need the two of us, and then we work out what to do next."

"Fucking hell," I murmur with a shake of my head. "You don't play fair."

"I will do anything within my power to make sure you and Jamie are safe. For now, that means resting." He angles towards me but hesitates.

"What?" I ask, already breathless from our closeness and the thought of his mouth on mine again.

"We will sleep, and I want to hold you."

"O-kay?" I say slowly, not seeing the problem here.

"The... urge for more is hard to ignore."

The hardness prodding at my arse makes it clear

he's not exaggerating. My own cock is so rigid, I'm not sure if the imprint in my jeans will ever fade.

"There is more to our bonding, but it will take time."

My brain misfires. "What do you mean, take time?" Bloody hell. "Is there some sort of blood-exchange voodoo shit we have to do?" Not going to lie, I'll totally do it, but still, I'd prefer a satisfying ride of his cock.

Solan's nose scrunches. "I do not know voodoo shit."

A huff of laughter escapes me, drawing a wide, beautiful smile over Solan's lips. "And the blood exchange?" An edge of cockiness grasps on to our discussion. Though snuggling with Solan in bed is not going to be a hardship.

"No blood exchange, but...." His hesitation rears up again.

"You know, every time you trail off like that, you send my mind whirling and my imagination running wild."

"I am sorry." Genuine worry seeps into his words.

"It's okay, but...?" I prompt, the question clear in my tone.

"I make a promise to talk everything through with you. Once we have Jamie and you are safe."

I arch a brow. Is that seriously all he's giving me? Well, that's annoying as fuck.

A yawn rips through me so wide, my jaw cracks. Damn it. I really do need to sleep. That doesn't mean I'm not frustrated. I stare at him with sleepy eyes.

"Will you trust me?"

Defeat wraps around me. My shoulders sag even as I cup his cheek. "I do trust you. I still can't quite fathom what the hell is going on or how damn accepting of everything I'm being, but yeah, I trust you."

Pieces of his hair shift, undulating as they reach for me. As before, the moment they settle on my skin, a fresh wave of rightness embraces me. What I wouldn't do to have each silky strand permanently attached to me. It sounds weird as fuck, but there's no point lying to myself.

"Rest," he says gruffly, and this time, I nod.

It would be foolish of me not to heed his words. Rest now so we can protect Jamie when he's back at my side. It's with that thought that we settle on the mattress, fully clothed and plastered against each other.

"Your English," I murmur, snuggling up closer to him, "it's better. You seem to be struggling less."

At the press of his lips to my head, I barely repress the sigh of contentment wanting to spill.

"I learn fast. The growing bond helps."

Huh. I wonder if that means I can learn his language. My piss-poor attempt at languages at school was enough to have my Japanese teacher begging me not to select his course for my options. But learning Pyronoxian... being able to speak to Solan in his native tongue is one hell of an incentive.

Our limbs tangle as I consider just how smart he is—and what other changes could happen with our bond—and my heartbeat seems to slow. It's enough that I notice.

"My heartbeat," I say sleepily, pressing my hand against Solan's warm chest.

"Matches mine."

A smile curves my lips, and I close my eyes, allowing sleep to embrace me.

CHAPTER
EIGHT

I STARTLE AWAKE WITH A BUZZ OF AWARENESS and heat trailing over my skin. The room is full of shadows, unfamiliar, but I know where I am. Where we are.

Solan doesn't stop the gentle back-and-forth stroke of his fingers even though it's obvious I'm awake.

"What time is it?" I ask groggily, relaxing into his touch.

"The sun is only just peeking over the mountains."

I stretch and yawn.

"We do not have time like your watch tells you," he explains.

I scoot back far enough that I can see his face.

Golden eyes latch on to mine, and my smile appears immediately. Goose bumps erupt over my skin, and I'm pretty sure my pulse should be racing, my heart fighting to escape my chest to get to him, but it remains a slow, steady thud.

I press my hand against my chest, the other against his, my smile slipping a little as I try to make sense of what's happening. The words we exchanged last night come back to me. My brows jerk high. "What did you mean that my heartbeat matches yours?" I get the feeling he didn't mean figuratively. He wasn't being poetic.

It's also one hell of a conversation to have when I've been awake for less than a minute.

Solan's hand stills on my side, and for a moment, he just watches me, his gaze intense, golden, and unyielding. When he speaks, his voice is soft but carries a gravity that pulls at me. "I mean it as it sounds. No poetry, no riddles. Your heart beats with mine now."

My lips part, but no sound comes out. My mind trips over itself trying to process his words while wondering if he can read my mind. "That's... not normal."

"Nor am I," he replies simply, his lips curving into the faintest hint of a smile. His hand resumes its motion, a gentle glide down my side, anchoring me while my thoughts spiral.

"How?" The question feels inadequate, almost ridiculous given everything that's happened, but it's all I've got.

His expression softens, reverence replacing the intensity as he shifts, propping himself up on one elbow. "From the moment the merge completed, I felt you. My heart...." He pauses, his brow furrowing as he searches for the right words. "It was as if it knew you before my mind could. It beat so fast, so erratically, I thought it might shatter in my chest. I had never felt anything like it before."

I swallow hard, unable to look away from him. "And you just... knew it was me?"

Solan nods, his hair shimmering faintly in the low light as it moves in tandem with him. "It was not a question. It was certainty. I knew you were not of my world, but my heart did not care. It reached for you, called for you, even when I did not yet understand." He presses his hand to his chest, his fingers splaying over his skin. "Our bond is a gift. It is said that when our souls find their other half, even across stars or worlds, they will reach out until they unite."

The words are beautiful, but they hit like a punch.

I try to laugh, but it comes out shaky. "That's… a lot to take in."

"I know." He moves his hand to cup my cheek, and the warmth of his palm steadies me in ways I can't explain. "Over the past days, our hearts have been aligning. What was once two rhythms struggling to find each other has become one. The closer we are, the stronger it grows. Now they beat as one."

I stare at him, my chest tight, my mind a whirlwind. The logical part of me wants to reject everything he's saying—because it's barmy, right? But my body doesn't lie. I can feel the truth in my pulse, in the slow, steady rhythm that matches his. It's as if my soul recognises the bond he speaks of even if my brain is still trying to catch up.

"That's why I feel…." I trail off, unsure how to put it into words.

"Whole?" he offers gently.

I nod, my throat tight. "Yeah. And also completely out of my depth."

Solan chuckles softly, the sound low and soothing. "You are not alone in this. It is new for me too."

I huff a laugh, rubbing a hand over my face. "You make it sound like it's the best thing that's ever happened to you."

"It is." His answer is immediate, unwavering. "You are everything."

The sincerity in his voice, the sheer weight of those words knock the breath out of me. My chest aches, my heart feels too big for my body, and the logical part of me—the part that should be screaming to slow down—falls silent. Instead, I lean into his touch, letting the moment wash over me.

In the back of my mind, I know this isn't normal. This isn't how humans behave, how relationships work. But the connection between us feels immutable, like it's been etched into my very being. And with the way Solan's fingers trace soothing patterns over my skin and his golden eyes hold mine with such fierce devotion, I don't have it in me to fight it. Not now. Maybe not ever.

He leans in, and my breath catches as his lips brush mine, a whisper of a touch that ignites every nerve in my body. It's soft at first, almost tentative, but then he takes control, his mouth firm and claiming, kissing me senseless. His taste floods my senses, warm and electric, and I can't stop the needy sound that escapes me as I shift against him. My body reacts instinctively, my hips rolling against his thick, solid thigh, desperate for friction.

Solan growls low in his throat, the sound

vibrating against my lips as he grips my waist, holding me in place. His hair moves wildly, strands wrapping around my arms, my back, pulling me closer, as if he can't bear even an inch of distance between us.

The tension builds, every touch, movement pushing me closer to the edge. I'm practically grinding against him, my body trembling with the need for release. I don't even care how desperate I must look, how utterly undone I am beneath his touch.

But then he pulls back, breaking the kiss with a reluctance that mirrors my own. His breathing is ragged, his hair reaching for me even as he cups my face. "It is not time."

"Not time?" I pant, my head spinning. "Are you serious right now?" Frustration and desire war within me, my body aching for him, for more.

His gaze softens, though his hair still moves restlessly, a testament to his struggle. "There is more to our bonding, and we must wait. You are not ready."

I gape at him, confusion and need warring in my chest. "Not ready? I'm practically—"

He cuts me off, brushing his thumb over my lower lip. "Jamie needs us. We need to be prepared."

The mention of Jamie is like a bucket of ice water.

The haze of desire recedes, and guilt crashes over me. He's right. As much as I want this—want him—Jamie comes first. He always has.

I sag against Solan, nodding reluctantly. "You're right."

He kisses my forehead, his touch lingering, and whispers, "We will have our time."

Fuck, I hope so. All this pent-up tension is building to heights I've never experienced before. It's tempting to rub one out, but something is stopping me. Something more than me wanting to come with Solan. On him. In him. It doesn't matter which as long as it's *with* him.

"We need to—" He stills, cutting himself off. I can barely register what happens next as he leaps off the mattress, dagger in hand, cemented in front of me and facing the doorway.

I scramble into action, my eyes locked on the dagger. Where was he hiding *that*? I don't have time to process before I lock my gaze on Solan's strong back muscles bunching when a low, threatening growl tears out of him.

The sound wraps around me, turning me on while also setting my teeth on edge. Self-preservation wins as I glance at the door, tuning into the sound outside. The lilt of two creatures speaking in

Glowranthian penetrates the air. One is deep, gravelly, and sounds seriously pissed off. The other is Harith's. Solan's reaction stops me from relaxing.

The desire to know what's going on thrums through my veins, but I keep quiet. Solan's not relaxed a fraction despite Harith's being one of the voices, and tension vibrates from him, settling on my skin. Thank Christ I'm dressed. At least whatever happens next, my bare dick won't be greeting them.

Talk about a boner killer.

Before I can even wonder if I should be hiding— my skin paint long since washed off in Harith's private spring—the crudely sawn door opens with a rush. Solan's muscles bunch, and I hold my breath.

A body fills the doorway, large and... red. I startle, recognising the species as Pyronox, Solan's species. The fuck? I edge forwards, planning to step to Solan's side to get a better look, but his arm stops me, snapping out and barring my way.

Irritation slams into me even as my brain tries to rationalise his behaviour.

Words tear free from Solan in a tone and language I've not heard before. I can only assume they're his mother tongue. The Pyronox's large eyes, his form clear under his own leather kilt and the muscles of his uncovered chest on proud display, keep darting to me. While his curiosity is evident, disdain pushes to the forefront, practically rolling off him in waves.

The Pyronox throws a hand out in my direction. I stand up straight, this time pushing Solan's arm away and settling at his side. It's tempting to lean into him, absorb his heat and his strength, but something tells me any sign of weakness in front of this Pyronox would be a mistake.

"What's going on?" I stare at the Pyronox, aware Harith still stands silently slightly behind him in the doorway. When no one immediately answers, I peer up at Solan as I say his name.

He reacts immediately, gaze on me, eyes softening in an instant as he drinks me in. A sound from the stranger has me losing Solan's attention, a new sneer pulling at Solan's lips as he glares at the Pyronox.

For fuck's sake. Years of working in an environment with daily dick-measuring contests—which is nowhere near as fun as it sounds—has me reacting almost on instinct.

I take a step forwards, putting myself between Solan and the Pyronox. My movements aren't aggressive, but they're deliberate enough to demand attention. "Okay, big guy, let's cut to the chase," I say, keeping my tone firm but not hostile. "Put your dick away and tell us why you're here."

The Pyronox narrows his eyes at me. His large, muscular form looms, and his bright red skin almost glows in the dim light. "You dare speak to me like that, human?" he growls in my native tongue, his voice a deep rumble that seems to reverberate through the room.

I don't flinch. Instead, I cross my arms and raise an unimpressed eyebrow. "Yeah, I dare. Get over it."

Solan's hand brushes against the small of my back, a silent acknowledgment of my boldness, but he doesn't interrupt. His tension is palpable, though, and I can't miss the guilt that flickers in his golden eyes when the stranger glances his way. Interesting.

The Pyronox's attention snaps back to me, his disdain evident. "I have been here longer than you have existed. Solan and I—"

"Are not mates," Solan interjects sharply in English, his voice cutting through the tension like a blade. "Enough, Durandal." Solan's gaze is fierce as it locks onto the other Pyronox. "You know that would never have been."

Durandal's jaw tightens, and his hands curl into fists at his sides. "You made it sound as if there was hope," he says, his tone bitter.

"I made it clear where I stood," Solan replies, his

voice softer now, but no less firm. "I cannot control fate."

I glance between them, my hackles rising at the implication. Whatever guilt Solan feels, it's clear he's been honest about the bond we share. But that doesn't stop Durandal's frustration from colouring his expression. It also doesn't stop me from stepping in again.

"Look," I say, keeping my voice steady. "I don't know what kind of history you two have, and frankly, I don't care. Solan's mine, and that's not up for debate. If you've got a problem with that, I suggest you deal with it somewhere else. We've got bigger issues to handle right now."

Durandal's lips pull back in a snarl, but he doesn't step forwards. Instead, he glances at Solan, who meets his gaze steadily. After a tense moment, Durandal exhales sharply, his shoulders relaxing slightly.

"You're right," Durandal says grudgingly. "There are more pressing matters."

Finally. Though what the hell is the urgent business that this guy has with Solan or me leaves me clueless.

He steps back slightly, giving us a bit more breathing room, though his frustration still simmers beneath the surface. "Tahrionne sent me," he begins. "There is news of your human."

My heart leaps into my throat, and I straighten instinctively. "Jamie? What about him? Is he safe?"

Durandal nods, though his expression remains grim. "He is not with the royal guard as you feared. He is travelling with Calythra and Tahrionne. They have managed to stay ahead of pursuit, but a rogue group of mercenaries is tracking them. They are dangerous and relentless."

Relief and dread crash over me in equal measure. Jamie isn't alone, but he's far from safe. "Why are these mercenaries after them?" I ask, my voice tight.

Durandal hesitates, then answers, "They're hunting anyone who came through the merge. You and your nephew are not the only ones they seek, but Tahrionne's reputation for finding those not of this world has made him a target."

Solan frowns. "Tahrionne's reputation should deter such hunters. These mercenaries must not be from this district, or there is something more driving them."

Durandal inclines his head. "That is my suspicion as well. Regardless, Tahrionne sent a message: They cannot return here. You must meet them at the

Youlander Pass. He plans to outmanoeuvre the mercenaries there."

My stomach twists at the thought of Jamie in more danger. Before I can even think it through, I look at Solan. "We're going after them."

I expect him to argue, to insist I stay behind, but instead, he nods. "Yes. Without you, I would struggle to succeed."

That catches me off-guard. "Wait, no argument?"

He shakes his head, a faint smile tugging at his lips. "You are capable, and I would be weaker without you near. Jamie is your family. I understand."

Gratitude surges through me that I don't have to argue, and I nod. "Good. Let's get ready."

Solan turns to Durandal. "Thank you for bringing this message. And... I am sorry."

Durandal's expression tightens, but he nods curtly. "I understand the bond. But it does not make this easier." His gaze flicks to me, frustration evident along with something that hurts my gut—longing. But he says nothing more.

We gather supplies quickly, and Solan packs essentials while I saddle Geralt, who'd since been brought into Harith's private outbuildings. I can feel Durandal's eyes on me the entire time, but I ignore him, focussing on the task at hand. When everything is ready, I throw my cloak over my shoulders, hiding my human features from prying eyes.

As we set out through a hidden route that Harith directed us to go, the tension finally starts to ease. I glance at Solan, whose determined expression softens slightly when he catches my eye. "You ready for this?" I ask, trying to lighten the mood.

He smirks. "Always. Let us hunt." Then, with a sly grin, he adds in an exaggerated accent, "Come with me if you want to live."

I burst out laughing, the sound echoing through the trees as we head towards the Youlander Pass. Was it really only a few days ago that he said those words to me after saving my life? Even in the midst of danger, Solan manages to make my heart feel a little lighter.

The chill of the alien dawn swirls around us as we step out onto the cracked, violet-hued landscape. Towering trees with crystalline leaves are scattered across the horizon, their shimmering branches casting fractured rainbows across the jagged terrain. The air hums faintly, charged with an energy that makes the hair on my arms stand on end.

Solan walks a step ahead of me, his stride confident but tense. His silence stretches, the weight of Durandal's visit still pressing against us.

I can't let it go. Not yet. "So, are we going to talk about what happened back there?"

He glances back at me, his expression unreadable. "What do you wish to know?"

I let out a slow breath, shoving my hands into the pockets of my cloak. "Everything, I guess. Starting with Durandal. You were holding back, weren't you?"

Solan slows, his golden eyes scanning the horizon before he turns to face me fully. "Durandal and I... we have history. Before the rift, he sought to bond with me."

The words hit like a punch to the gut even though I'd suspected as much. I'm not sure why it stings so much, but it does. "And you considered it?"

He nods, his expression grave. "It is not the same as what we have. A bonded union not ordained by fate lacks the depth, the permanence. But it is... functional."

"Functional?" I snort, trying to mask the wave of jealousy rolling through me. "Sounds romantic."

Solan's brow furrows, his gaze searching mine. "I did not love him, if that is your concern. But I was... tempted. Without a mate, there are limitations. Restrictions."

I don't like the sound of that. "What kind of restrictions?"

"No lasting connection. No real unity," he says, his tone steady but tinged with something bitter. "I could never share my full strength, my full self. Loneliness lingers, no matter how many temporary bonds one forges. It is not... the same."

His words twist something in my chest. A forced bonding might have squashed the edges of that loneliness, but it would never fill the void. I hate everything he's saying, but then again, I'm a man who's fucked his way through life, rarely feeling lonely—though that's not technically true. More like I've been able to lose myself in a man, in dating. It's a bitter thought, one that makes me glance away for a moment.

"Are you two the only ones of your kind in Terrafeara?" I ask, changing the subject.

He hesitates, his steps slowing. "No. I have heard of others. Met some along the way. We are scattered, some in hiding."

That revelation sinks in as we continue walking, the path beneath us uneven and sharp. After several moments, I bring us back to the pressing matter. "Youlander Pass. That's where we'll find Jamie, right?"

"That is where we are to meet, yes," Solan replies.

I'm watching his face as I ask the next question.

"What about the mercenaries? Do you intend to find them first? Stop them?"

His jaw tightens, and for the first time, I see genuine conflict in his expression. He exhales slowly, his breath misting in the air. It's far from cold, but with Solan's temperature burning so hot, it's not a surprise. "My protective instincts demand it. For you. For Jamie. Ending their lives would ensure safety. But more than that...." His gaze locks with mine, unflinching. "I want you safe. Whatever it takes."

The fierceness in his voice is unlike anything I've encountered before. His golden eyes, which I'm used to being calm and measured, burn with an intensity that makes me take a step back. I've seen him kill before, witnessed the precision of his bow and arrow as he struck down a monster without hesitation. But this... this is different. His resolve is terrifying, but not because it feels alien. It's the kind of raw, unrelenting protectiveness that shakes something loose in me.

"You mean that," I say, more a statement than a question.

"With every part of me," he replies, his voice low and edged with steel. "If they harm you or Jamie, I will destroy them."

The sincerity in his voice, in his eyes, makes it hard to breathe. "So, you'll wait and see?"

He nods. "For now."

The conversation lulls as the landscape stretches ahead, surreal and beautiful in its strangeness. The cracked terrain glitters faintly in the pale light, and the trees seem to hum in response, their crystalline leaves swaying as if alive. The air grows heavier, the faint tang of minerals coating my tongue with each breath. The beauty is undeniable, but there's a tension to it, as though the world itself is holding its breath.

Solan breaks the silence after a long while, his voice soft but infused with a faint trace of amusement. "Have I ever told you about Thraxus?"

I glance at him, raising a brow. "Your sister's bonded, right?"

"Yes. The Glowranth who taught me about this world and his language."

I can't help but think how fortunate it was to at least have some understanding of a world you were unceremoniously dumped into. "How did that even happen? Them finding each other?"

Solan smirks, his golden eyes lighting with humour. "Oh, it was chaos. My community had seen other species over the years, thanks to the rifts, but never a Glowranth. They're... not exactly subtle, as you can imagine."

I blink, picturing the Glowranths I'd seen since being in Terrafeara. The faint bioluminescent glow, the sinewy, and sometimes hulking, humanoid figure—definitely not something anyone would mistake for anything ordinary. "I'd imagine not."

"Thraxus didn't just arrive—he *exploded* into our world," Solan continues. "He came roaring like a storm, glowing with so much raw energy, he lit up the sky and scared the life out of everyone."

I can't help but laugh. "And your sister just... knew he was her mate?"

"Instantly," Solan says, shaking his head. "Ignis marched straight up to him, completely ignoring the fact that he looked like some eldritch horror straight out of a nightmare, and declared, 'You're mine.'"

"No hesitation?" I ask, grinning at the image of this fearless female Pyronox. And *eldritch*... really? How the heck does he know such a fancy word? I can't imagine Arnie ever having used it.

"None. Meanwhile, the rest of us were scrambling for weapons, thinking we were under attack. Thraxus... well, he was confused. We both know what it's like being ripped from our worlds and dropped into a new one. But add in being confronted by a fiery woman claiming you belong to her."

My grin forms easily despite how well I can relate. I also wonder if his experience with Thraxus and his sister is the reason why Solan didn't immediately declare me as his. "What did he do?"

Solan's smirk widens, and his tone turns conspiratorial. "He tried to run."

"Didn't work, did it?"

"Not even a little," he replies, chuckling. "Ignis didn't give him the chance. She tackled him to the ground—right there in front of all of us—and wouldn't let go. She just kept shouting at him to stop being a *bumbry* and accept his fate."

I can't hold back my laughter, the mental image vivid and absurd. "That's insane." I can just imagine being a *bumbry* isn't meant as a compliment.

Solan continues, his amusement infectious, "By the time he stopped struggling, Thraxus was completely smitten. Though, if you ask him, he'll say he was ambushed."

"That sounds like something out of a storybook," I say, grinning ear to ear.

"It was... memorable," Solan admits, his smile lingering as his gaze grows distant. "They're happy...

and have a daughter. Thraxus has calmed down a lot, but he still claims Ignis cheated fate."

The levity of the story lingers between us, a much-needed reprieve from the weight of our mission. But before I can ask more, a faint sound breaks through the stillness. A rustling, deliberate and sharp—too deliberate to be the wind.

Both of us freeze, instincts flaring as we strain to pinpoint the source.

The movement grows louder, closer. My heart pounds as I grip the hilt of my blade that Solan insisted I strap to me. Solan's posture shifts, predatory and protective, every muscle coiled and ready.

"We're not alone," he murmurs, and fuck it all to hell. I am so over this shit.

CHAPTER
NINE

"Uncle Jack!"

I'm on the ground in an instant, legs moving, chest constricting, and relief racing through me so fast, my head spins. It's really him. He's flesh and sweetness and trembling as I tug him into my arms, holding him so close, I'm sure he's struggling to breathe. But shit, Jamie... here, as I live and breathe.

"Holy shit, kid." I pull away, holding him by the arms as I peer into his face. Dirt smudges litter his skin, but he's unharmed and bright-eyed. "Bloody hell." I tug him close once again, pressing my lips to the top of his head and hugging him hard. "You're okay." Another kiss and I ease him back. "You're okay, right?" I search for signs of injury. Search his gaze for distress.

He nods, his little bobblehead bouncing up and down as he grins at me. My gaze darts behind him, falling on Calythra. He's speaking to Solan in Glowranthian (maybe), and his hands fly wildly in the air as he points to his right, signalling somewhere far off in the distance.

I follow where he points and don't see anything but trees—a given, since not long after exiting a valley, we entered a forest.

"Cal said we'd find you." Wide-eyed, Jamie glances at Calythra, something close to adoration on his smudged face. "He managed to get us away from the monsters chasing us."

I feel the blood drain from my face while Jamie's cheeks flush, his eyes sparking with wild, almost-frenzied excitement that I have little doubt is laced with fear. *Fuck*. I swallow the lump in my throat and pull him to me a third time while glancing in Calythra's direction. His startling blue eyes are pointed in our direction, and while he's smiling, it's absolutely clear he's on high alert—standing vigil, almost.

"Thank you," I mouth, more than aware the words aren't deep enough to reflect just how in his debt I am.

He dips his head, gaze unwavering, his almost-translucent skin shimmering in the sunlight.

"We must leave." Solan's deep voice grabs all my focus. My eyes travel to him, and just like every time since we shared our first kiss, the sight of him captures the air in my lungs. He's so ridiculously beautiful. And mine.

The tilt of his head is minuscule, but I swear he knows what I'm thinking as I give myself the moment to enjoy him. Jamie's back and safe at my side. Solan's looking like he wants to devour me while taking a knee to worship me. The combination is heady. And for the first time since being in this world, surrounded by monsters and uncertainty over whether each breath I take might be my last, I inhale a breath that fills my lungs, my very being. Air and relief are a peace-giving mixture—who the fuck knew?

Before I can ask what the new plan is, I whip my head around. "Where's Tahrionne?" It's likely I've butchered his name, but still, where the hell is he?

Jamie squirms in my grip, trying to turn and point. "Tahrionne led them away. He said it was the only way to throw them off. He went north."

My heart sinks. "He's alone?"

"He's clever," Calythra interjects, his tone light

but edged with purpose. "He had no choice. They were gaining on us, and he was the best decoy. It worked. We're here, aren't we?"

I glance at Calythra, my chest tight with worry. His casual demeanour might be an act, but his confidence is steadying. "And now?"

"We're on the outskirts of Youlander Pass," Solan says, his voice measured but tight. "It's where we were supposed to regroup. We can't stay here long."

"No kidding," Calythra mutters, scanning the forest with his sharp, ethereal eyes. "We spotted *klaustras* nearby."

The mention of those monsters sends a shiver down my spine. I don't need the reminder of what the car-sized, three-horned creatures can do. "Fantastic," I mutter. "Last thing we need is to tangle with them again."

Calythra gives me a toothy grin that's somehow both reassuring and infuriating. "Don't worry. They don't usually go for seconds. Unless you smell like dinner."

Jamie wrinkles his nose. "Do I smell like dinner?"

Calythra crouches dramatically, sniffing the air near Jamie. "Hmm. Maybe a snack. You're too small for a full meal."

Jamie giggles, and I shake my head, thankful for the levity even if my nerves are still frayed.

But Solan isn't laughing. He's scanning the tree line, his golden eyes sharp with worry. "We need a plan," he mutters. "Without declaring ourselves to the realm, we'll always be on the run. But I can't...." His jaw tightens, and his gaze darts to Jamie, then me. "I can't risk you."

I step closer to him, my voice firm when I ask, "And what happens if we do declare ourselves? They'll split us up. Reassign us like we're inventory, right?"

Calythra's expression flickers, his usual bravado dimming for a moment. He looks twitchy, almost uncertain—a stark contrast to his usual confidence.

"What?" I press, narrowing my eyes at him. "What aren't you saying?"

He hesitates, his fingers flexing at his sides, the faint bioluminescence along his arms pulsing erratically. Finally, he sighs, glancing at Solan before addressing me. "There's an option. It's dangerous, but it might be our best shot. The Riftborn."

Jamie perks up, his curiosity blazing. "What's that?"

Calythra gestures vaguely, his movements sharp with emotion. "Think rebellion. A faction made up of those who've been wronged by the realm. Locals who don't fit their rigid mould, sure—but mostly people like you, me, us." He glances around the small group that contains three different species. "Those of us who weren't born to this world. When the merges started and worlds collided, anyone who came through—whether human or something else—was treated as property. Tools. Soldiers. Experiments. It didn't matter what you wanted; the realm decided your fate."

He pauses, his steady tone turning brittle. "That's what sparked the Riftborn Rebels. They've made it their mission to fight against the realm's oppression, to demand rights for everyone—whether they were born here or dragged here. They believe no one should be forced to serve under the guise of survival. They believe in freedom. Democracy. Equality. The kind of things most of us thought were long lost."

Jamie's eyes widen, and I feel a knot forming in my chest. Calythra's words burn with a truth I can't ignore. It's not just about us, or Solan, or even Calythra himself. It's about everyone who's been crushed under the weight of a system that sees us as little more than pawns.

Solan stiffens, his entire frame going taut. "Absolutely not."

"Why not?" I ask, my gaze darting between them.

Solan's golden eyes, wide with fear, lock onto mine. "They're radicals. The realm considers them enemies, traitors. If we're caught with them, there's no coming back."

"They also don't give a damn about the realm's rules," Calythra counters, his tone firm. "You think the realm will honour your bond?"

The fuck? He knows about our bond? Do I have neon lights above my head? Hell, perhaps my scent has changed or something. I try to give myself a subtle sniff but catch Jamie's attention. He's looking at me like I've gone and lost the plot. I clear my throat, focussing on Calythra.

"Not between beings from different worlds. You'd be fighting every day just to stay together."

The truth in his words lands like a blow, and I see the hesitation in Solan's expression. For all his strength, his defiance, he looks scared. But when his gaze meets mine, something shifts.

He nods slowly as if coming to a decision. "We don't have any other choice."

Jamie raises his hand like he's in school. "So... first we get my horse, right? You did stash it somewhere, didn't you?"

Calythra barks a laugh, his grin returning. "Priorities. Yes, kid, we stashed your horse. He's safe."

Jamie beams, and I find myself smiling despite the tension. "Good. Let's start there. I'll come up with the next step."

Solan turns to me, his golden eyes softening. "You?"

"Yes, me." I meet his gaze, refusing to back down. "I'm capable of making decisions, and I'm not going to sit here waiting for someone else to dictate my life."

He doesn't argue. Instead, he steps closer, his fingers brushing mine. The contact is grounding, sending a quiet thrill through me. He needs this, I realise—this touch, this reassurance. And maybe I do too.

"Uncle Jack, are you and Solan boyfriends now?"

Bloody hell. My fingers twitch, but rather than releasing Solan's hand, I hold tight. "Uhm." I peer down at my nephew, my breath whooshing out of me when he stares back with curiosity and maybe a little amusement.

This kid's met one of my old boyfriends, but it's been a while. Who am I kidding? He was probably too young to remember. But boyfriend? Seriously? How am I meant to explain that Solan is so much more than that even though I don't think we're even officially fully bonded, which the arsehole still hasn't explained properly.

Sure, we keep being interrupted, and there've been nonstop life-and-death situations going on, caused by monsters and plants who are determined to eat us and a realm that wants to enslave us.

Talk about one clusterfuck after another.

"Yes...?" I drag the word out.

"Huh. He's so much bigger than you."

And isn't that a kick to the balls?

Calythra snorts out a laugh while Solan vibrates at my side. Arseholes, the both of them.

"He's not *that* much bigger than me," I say a little defensively. We all know I'm full of shit. Solan is wide and tall, and given half the chance, I'm sure he'd carry me around. Honestly, in the bedroom, I'm more than happy for him to do just that. And being engulfed in his strong arms is like being wrapped in a blanket more than big enough to swamp me.

But still, calling it out like that....

Jamie dips his brows, assessing the two of us together. "If you say so," he settles on, ever the diplomat.

I roll my eyes, mainly at myself. I also nudge Solan with my elbow, since the dick is thoroughly entertained. Stopping short, I slam my hand to my chest. The fuck is that? I turn abruptly, staring at Solan, realising that I felt every ounce of his amusement deep in my chest.

Understanding fills his gaze. And yes, I bloody know that, too, despite no outward change. We communicate silently. No words push into my head, and thank fuck I haven't developed the ability to mind read, but I sense warmth, reassurance, a plea to not panic. Each emotion is a pulse surrounded by affection that's impossible not to react to.

I tug my hat off and press my forehead to Solan's chest. This is not the time or place, and I swear to all that is holy that if those purple monsters burst out and attack, I'm going to go all John Rambo on their arses, but I need a moment to process. To feel. To not freak out. I sense Solan's emotions. There's little doubt he's experiencing mine too.

There's a shuffle at my side, and I tune in, but I'm not quite able to pull away just yet. Calythra has led Jamie a few steps away, talking quietly to him. Strong, warm arms wrap around me, cocooning me. I swallow back the bubble of hysteria that Jamie is right about how big Solan is. I love it and wouldn't want it any other way.

"I'm okay," I finally say, clearing my throat.

Vulnerability is a curse back home—for a man, a farmer, and even a property owner. Fuck, even for an Aussie bloke. I take a breath before trying to bottle that shit up, but Solan knows. He'll always know, right? What I'm feeling? The depth of my emotions? Is that what's happening here? I'm not sure if that's terrifying or liberating. Both, I suspect.

"I'm okay," I repeat, this time receiving a gentle kiss on the top of my head before he releases me. My smile is quick to form and real when I peer up at him. He nods once before I step out of his hold and glance over at Jamie and Calythra.

As though sensing my attention, Calythra stops speaking and turns my way, Jamie following suit.

"So, the Riftborn...." Calythra's words trail off, heavy in the air.

Solan's jaw tightens, his large eyes darting between us. He still looks like he wants to argue, to shoot the idea down entirely, but something stops him. Maybe it's the weight of everything Calythra just said before my realisation, or maybe it's the way my hand instinctively finds his again, grounding him.

I squeeze gently, offering silent reassurance. "How do we even find them?" I ask, keeping my voice steady. "And how do we know they'll trust us?" Or how can we trust them, for that matter?

Calythra lets out a soft huff, crossing his arms over his chest. "That's the tricky part. They don't exactly advertise their base. But I've got... connections. People who owe me favours. I can get us there if we're willing to take the risk."

Solan's lips part, but he hesitates, his gaze flickering to me. "This isn't a decision we can take lightly," he murmurs, his voice low and deliberate. "The Riftborn may oppose the realm, but their methods are... controversial. If we align ourselves with them, there's no going back."

Jamie shifts in my peripheral vision, frowning. "Isn't that better than being on the run forever?" His voice is small but determined, and it makes my heart clench. "They sound like the good guys."

Calythra chuckles dryly. "Kid's got a point. But trust me, Jamie—they're not all heroes. They're desperate, and desperation makes people dangerous. You've gotta decide if that danger's worth it."

I take a breath, letting the weight of the moment settle over me. "We need a plan. Solan, I know you're worried, but we can't keep running blindly. If we're going to survive this—and not just survive but actually live—we need allies. If the Riftborn are fighting for the same things we want, then it's a risk worth taking."

Solan studies me for a long moment, his face etched with uncertainty. But there's something else there, too—trust. He nods slowly, his thumb brushing over my knuckles. "If you believe this is the right path, I'll follow."

Jamie grins, a flicker of youthful optimism breaking through the tension. "Looks like it's settled, then."

Calythra's sharp teeth flash in a crooked smile. "Good. But first things first—we're not going anywhere without that horse of yours. What did you call it again? The Mountain?"

Jamie laughs, his voice light despite the gravity of the moment. "No, it's Ridge. But Mountain works too."

"Right," Calythra says with a playful smirk. "Let's grab Ridge and get the hell out of here before we run into those *klaustras*. Again."

The levity is brief but welcome as we start moving, weaving through the trees towards where Calythra stashed the horse. Calythra keeps up a steady stream of commentary, half for humour, half to mask his own tension. "You know, this 'Ridge' better not be as temperamental as the last horse I dealt with. That thing tried to eat my satchel. And by 'thing,' I mean it was basically a furry demon with hooves."

Jamie snickers, and I can't help but crack a small smile. It makes sense other horses have found their way into this world. I'm sure there're some of my cattle roaming around somewhere. Even Solan's lips twitch, though his shoulders remain taut with vigilance.

When we reach Ridge, the sleek black horse is exactly where Jamie said he would be. The animal tosses his head, snorting softly as Jamie approaches with a grin. "See? Told you he's the best."

Calythra raises a brow, eyeing the horse as though he might suddenly grow a second head. "I'll reserve judgement."

As we prepare to move out, Solan steps closer to me, his hand brushing against mine. I glance up at him, and his expression is softer now, his golden eyes warm and searching. The contact steadies him, doing the exact same to me.

Jamie notices, of course, because he's twelve and impossible to evade. He tilts his head, grinning slyly. "You two are weird."

"Thanks for the observation, kid," I shoot back, my tone dry.

He shrugs, his grin widening. "I mean, it's cute, though. Like... gross cute."

Calythra laughs, a low, rumbling sound that echoes through the trees. "Ah, young love. Makes me glad I'm not involved."

I roll my eyes, but there's a smile tugging at my lips. For the first time in what feels like forever, there's a glimmer of hope threading through the chaos. It's faint, but it's there. And for now, that's enough.

CHAPTER
TEN

For two days, we've travelled—me on Geralt's back, Jamie and Calythra on Ridge, while Solan has stayed on foot. The sun hasn't been as intense as the rays that beat down on me the day before my life changed irrevocably, a relief considering the number of craggy rocks that we've had to sweet talk the horses to trek over.

We've stopped for a few breaks, sometimes pushing on despite knowing Jamie was struggling. Other times, I insisted we stop when I saw him slumping forwards on the saddle, Calythra preventing him from slipping off with a careful grip. And last night we slept under the stars that I'm convinced are identical to the constellations in my world.

My dad would have known. For all his grumpy ways and his inability to stop and rest, the night sky had always shown me a different side to him. He'd regularly sat under the floating patterns of glistening stars, staring up and describing what he saw, the mythology and the mystery. The names had never sunk in, something I now regretted, but that thought doesn't stop me settling down with a smile for my second night under the stars.

"What is it about the stars that causes this?" Solan strokes his fingertips gently over my cheek, finishing with a slow stroke of my lips.

With his arm as my pillow, I feel safe and surprisingly comfortable. It's the first time I've been able to relax all day, too wary of our surrounds, too concerned for Jamie. Only now, with his soft, sleepy breaths floating in the air a few metres away, am I able to truly catch my breath. "They remind me of home, my dad." I keep peering at the inky-black sky.

"They make you feel close to him," he states, and I nod despite him not having asked me a question.

"They do. Beyond the Southern Cross and the Great Bear, I could never remember the constellations. But I recall him pointing them out to me, telling me their stories. He used to say they were a map for the soul."

Solan hums softly, still tracing idle patterns against my skin. "A map for the soul," he repeats, the words heavy with thought. "It's a beautiful idea. Perhaps these stars are guiding us too."

"Maybe." I tilt my head to meet his gaze. His golden eyes glow faintly in the dim starlight, full of warmth and intensity. "Do they mean anything to you? In your world?"

His expression softens as he considers my question. "In my world, the stars were considered... warnings, signs of what might come. But here, they feel different. They don't hold the same weight of fate." His fingers still on my lips for a moment, then slide down to rest lightly against my throat. "Here, they feel like a reminder that there's more. That no matter what happens, there's something vast and unchanging beyond all this chaos."

I smile at the sentiment, feeling a flicker of comfort. "That's a nice thought."

"It's you," he murmurs, leaning closer. "You remind me there's more. That there's still a future worth fighting for."

Solan's fingers return to my face and trace along my jawline, slow and deliberate, the warmth of his touch grounding me. The gentle pressure steadies the current of emotions surging between us even as his gaze searches mine with an intensity that makes my breath hitch.

And no bullshit, I'm close to damn swooning. Have you ever heard prettier words? 'Cause I absolutely have not.

"You're my tether," he murmurs, his voice low and rough like gravel smoothed by time. "No matter what happens, no matter where this road takes us—you're my anchor. My reason."

I don't know what to say to that. His words are heavy with meaning, a weight I'm not sure I can carry but also can't imagine letting go of. Instead, I lean in, letting my lips find his in a kiss that starts as soft as a whisper.

It deepens quickly. Solan's hand moves to cradle the back of my head, tilting me closer. His lips part against mine, and the taste of him sends a shiver down my spine. It's not frantic or hurried; it's deliberate and consuming, the kind of kiss that demands everything and gives me everything in return. His other hand slips around my waist, pulling me flush against him, and I can feel the steady thrum of his heartbeat matching my own.

I lose myself in the feel of him—the heat of his mouth, the roughness of his palm against my lower back, the quiet, desperate sound he makes when I sigh into the kiss. It's overwhelming and perfect, and it's everything I didn't know I needed until now.

But reality crashes back too quickly. A branch creaks somewhere in the distance—likely Calythra shifting his weight in the tree—and I pull back, reluctantly breaking the connection. My forehead rests against Solan's as we both catch our breath, the night air cool against my flushed skin.

"We can't," I whisper even though my body protests the words. "Not here."

His golden eyes flicker with frustration, but he nods, pressing one last featherlight kiss to my lips before pulling back. "You're right," he concedes, his voice tinged with regret. "But don't think I won't find a better time."

I laugh softly, brushing my fingers over the soft skin of his jaw. "I'll hold you to that."

Solan grumbles, a low sound of frustration that makes me laugh. "It's unfair," he mutters, his hand sliding down to rest on my hip. "You make me forget everything else."

"I know," I admit, still smiling. "But we have bigger things to worry about right now."

He sighs even as his gaze softens. "The rebellion,"

he says, and it's clear the shift in focus is as much to ground himself as it is to inform me. "What else do you want to know?"

"Everything," I admit, settling against him, his arm once again my makeshift pillow. "But start with what you think is most important. You know a hell of a lot more about this world than I do."

Solan's brow furrows slightly as he considers my question. "The Riftborn... they're not a united front. Not entirely, I don't think. They're made up of different groups—some of them fiercely independent, others willing to work together for a greater cause. The problem is, their goals aren't always aligned. Some want to overthrow the realm completely, dismantle its structure, and start over. Others just want equal rights for those not born here."

"Like you. And me."

He nods, his jaw tightening. "Like us. But even within the rebellion, there's disagreement. Some believe those not born of this world, like the two of us, shouldn't be part of it. They think the merging of worlds is a curse and that outsiders don't belong here."

"That's... comforting," I mutter, though the sarcasm in my voice does little to mask my unease. "And yet Calythra wants to take us to them?" Confusion prickles through me, tightening my chest. "Even the name *Riftborn* implies they're fighting *for* people like us—those who came through the merges, no matter the species, so why would any of them be against humans or anyone else not born here? Doesn't that go against everything they're supposed to stand for?"

Solan's expression darkens, his golden eyes glinting with the weight of unspoken knowledge. "You'd think so," he says, voice low and measured. "But the rebellion isn't a single mind moving in perfect harmony. It's a fractured body with too many voices. Some fight for the freedom of everyone not born here—humans, Pyronox, and any other species pulled into this world. Others... they see certain groups as a threat. A danger to their fragile cause."

"That's ridiculous," I snap, frustration bubbling over. "We're all in the same boat. All thrown here without a choice."

"It is," he agrees softly, brushing his fingers over mine to calm me. "But fear makes people do ridiculous things. When survival is on the line, some believe unity is strength. Others...." He hesitates, his jaw tightening. "They think isolation and exclusion will protect what they've managed to build."

I shake my head, the explanation doing little to

settle my confusion—or my anger. "And we're supposed to trust them?"

"We're supposed to survive," Solan answers, his voice firm but tinged with something vulnerable. "That's the choice we're left with."

"Do you trust Calythra?" I ask close to his ear, and the weight of the question hangs between us.

Solan hesitates, searching the stars for a long moment. "I don't know. But I trust that he wants us to survive. For now, that's enough."

I let out a slow breath, toying with the fabric of his shirt. "What about you?" I ask softly. "Do *you* think we can survive this?"

His eyes snap back to mine, and the intensity in his gaze makes my heart skip a beat. "With you? I'll survive anything."

It's a bold statement, one that makes my throat tighten, but I don't argue. Instead, I press a kiss to his chest, right above where his heart beats steadily beneath my palm. "Then I guess we better rest and make it our mission to find them tomorrow."

He smirks faintly, brushing his hand over my hair. "You're already thinking ahead. I knew I chose well."

I roll my eyes, but the teasing glint in his gaze is infectious. "You didn't choose me," I say with a small laugh. "Fate did."

Solan's expression softens, and his fingers trail down my arm. "Maybe. But if I could choose a thousand times over, I'd still choose you."

The tenderness in his voice is too much, and I yawn suddenly, the exhaustion of the day finally catching up to me. He chuckles, shifting to pull me closer as my eyes flutter shut.

"Sleep," he murmurs, his lips brushing against my temple. "I'll keep watch with Calythra."

And as I drift off in his arms, I believe him. With Solan by my side, there's nothing I can't face—even a rebellion.

By the time the sun comes up, we're all awake and finalising packing up our small camp. I slept surprisingly well, but I suspect being pressed up against Solan is the reason. Even my blue balls didn't keep me awake.

Jamie's all but bouncing around the camp this morning, getting distracted when he should be packing up. The whole time, he's been "Caly's" shadow, because that's what Jamie's now calling the warrior in training. Sure, I'm a little concerned by the hero worship that's going on—still not completely certain what to make of Calythra's help—but honestly, I'll take Jamie's fixation on Calythra rather than him having a meltdown.

At some point, it's going to happen. All I can do is make sure I'm ready to catch him when all of this stops being an adventure and the reality of Jamie's situation—along with being without his parents and facing the very real likelihood of never seeing them again—hits home.

Selfishly, I just hope it happens once we're safe.

Solan picking up a pack of supplies draws my attention. "I'll scout ahead," he says. "Never more than a call away," he tacks on.

I don't like it, at all, but we discussed this yesterday.

The further into this unknown territory we venture, the more on edge we become. While Calythra offered to venture ahead, Solan insisted he be the one to take on that role. And I get it—albeit reluctantly. Calythra is young and inexperienced. Solan, however, can track. He even gave a big spiel comparing himself to Arnie playing Dutch in *Predator* and being a formidable hunter.

I only smirked a little when he did so, but the thing is, I don't doubt his skills. Neither does Calythra, who told me in no uncertain terms, "Solan's reputation is the kind of thing that gets whispered about in taverns and on training grounds. You know, like: *'Don't wander too far from the campfire, or Solan might track you just to prove he can.'"*

Jamie, overhearing, had burst into laughter. "What, like some kind of scary bedtime story?"

Calythra had shrugged with mock seriousness. "Not a story, Jamie. A cautionary tale. Do you know how many people swear he once tracked a fleeing thief through a sandstorm? A *sandstorm.* Apparently, the guy thought he'd lost Solan, only to wake up with him standing over the campfire like, *'Nice try.'"*

I'd chuckled at that, though inwardly I had no trouble believing it. Solan's sharp eyes, his ability to read the smallest disturbances in the ground, even his predatory stillness when studying his surroundings— it was like he was born for it. He didn't just notice things; he *owned* them. The ground under his feet? His map. The air around him? His compass.

Jamie, however, hadn't been done. "So basically, Solan's the kind of guy who could lose *you* just by standing still?"

"Exactly." Calythra grinned, gesturing grandly, all while Solan had rolled his eyes as he prepared our meal last night. "And when he moves? Forget it. One moment, he's there. Blink, and he's already got your trail memorised, your weaknesses catalogued, and your supply stash raided. He probably knows what you're going to do *before* you decide to do it."

"Well, that's not terrifying," I'd muttered dryly. But even as the banter circled around Solan's almost-mythical skills, I couldn't help the small swell of pride that warmed my chest. If anyone could keep us alive in this strange and dangerous world, it was him.

Bringing me back into the present, Solan adjusts the strap of his pack and leans down to press a kiss to my lips. It's firm, lingering just enough to make my pulse flutter before he pulls away, his golden eyes locking onto mine. "I'll be back before you miss me."

I smirk despite the twinge of unease in my chest. "Too late for that."

His hand brushes my cheek, softness passing over his features. I watch as he disappears into the trees, his movements so fluid and silent, it's like he was never there to begin with. I glance at Calythra, who's watching Solan's retreat with a crooked grin.

"Damn," he mutters, his voice full of admiration. "I've heard all the stories about Solan's skills, but seeing him move? That's some next-level badassery."

Jamie perks up, his curiosity piqued. "What kind of stories?"

Apparently, last night's tales weren't enough for him.

Calythra swings up onto Ridge's back with a dramatic shrug. "Oh, you know, the usual hero stuff. Tracking beasts across impossible terrain, taking down predators twice his size, stealing hearts without even trying."

I snort, rolling my eyes as I guide Geralt forwards. "The last one's news to me."

Jamie laughs, his grin wide as he mimics Solan's quiet footsteps, pretending to scout ahead himself. "If he's that good, maybe we should just follow him instead of worrying so much."

"That's the plan," I say, though my voice is quieter now. We're not sure how close the rebels are, and even though Solan's promised to keep us safe, my instincts tell me to stay on high alert. I look around quickly. Shit, where's he gone? "Barely two minutes, and I can't even see him anymore."

"Don't worry," Calythra says with a teasing lilt, reaching out his hand for Jamie, who eagerly takes it and swings up onto the saddle. "He's not lost. And if he is, I'm sure he'll just charm the trees into telling him where we are."

Jamie snickers, but I give Calythra a dry look. "You're surprisingly chatty for someone who's supposed to be stealthy."

He smirks, though his expression softens a

moment later. "I guess I'm just happy to have company again. Before this, it was just me and my mentor, and that got... quiet. Too quiet." He glances at Jamie, his tone shifting to something wistful. "You know, I almost got adopted once, when I first arrived in this world. By a Glowranth elder. He wanted to train me as a healer, thought I had potential. But the queen decided it wasn't... appropriate."

"Why?" Jamie asks, his brows furrowing.

Calythra's grin turns bitter. "Because I'm not a Glowranth. Apparently, being not of this world makes me 'unsuitable.'" He shrugs it off, but the weight of the memory clearly lingers. "Anyway, here I am, tracking with you instead. Life's funny like that."

Before I can respond, Calythra stiffens, his head tilting as his ears twitch. "Wait," he murmurs, holding up a hand.

I don't hear anything, but I trust him enough to tighten my grip on the reins, stopping Geralt. "What is it?" I whisper, reaching for my rifle.

He doesn't answer immediately, scanning the trees ahead. Then, with barely a moment's warning, the forest erupts into chaos.

They come from all sides—five figures emerging from the dense underbrush, their movements swift and deliberate. Two of them I recognise as

Glowranth, their tall, sinewy humanoid forms shimmering faintly with the eerie bioluminescent ridges that mark their kind. Their glowing skin and smooth, monstrous features stand in stark contrast to the snarling aggression in their expressions. Despite their humanoid shape, the predatory grace of their movements reminds me that intelligent doesn't mean harmlessness.

The other three are something else entirely—alien in a way that defies classification. Their forms are a haphazard blend of limbs and features that seem ripped from different nightmares. One creature stalks forwards on mismatched legs, its jagged carapace reflecting the faint light. Another's elongated arms end in hooked claws that drag through the dirt as it lumbers forwards, its twisted face fixed in a grimace that might once have resembled a smile. The last moves with serpentine fluidity, its body coiling unnervingly as its many eyes glint with malicious intent.

These aren't wild animals acting on instinct; they're intelligent beings—monsters, yes, but with a purpose. There's no mistaking it. Their coordinated movements and the silent, deliberate way they spread out around us scream of a well-executed ambush.

"Hold on!" Calythra shouts, already sliding off Ridge and drawing his blade.

Jamie screams as Ridge rears, and I barely manage to keep Geralt steady as the monsters close in.

I fight back, swinging wildly with the knife Solan insisted I carry, too afraid to use my rifle in such close proximity, but it's not enough. One of the creatures knocks me off my horse with a swipe of its clawed paw, and I hit the ground hard, the air rushing from my lungs.

"Jamie!" I gasp, my vision spinning as I scramble to my feet. I see Calythra holding his own against two of the monsters, his movements quick and precise, but Jamie is cornered, his small frame dwarfed by the beasts.

Panic surges through me. I manage to break free from one of the monsters by swinging my fist at its face with all my strength. It recoils, but before I can shout for Solan, a sharp blow to my side sends me sprawling.

I don't even get the chance to scream.

Then, just as suddenly as the attack began, a commanding voice cuts through the chaos.

"Enough!"

The monsters freeze, their snarls silencing as a

figure steps into the clearing. She's human—or at least, she looks human—her dark brown skin glowing faintly in the filtered sunlight. She's tall and muscular, her braided hair pulled back, and she wears a hooded cloak that she lowers as she approaches. Her accent, unmistakably American and Southern, catches me off-guard.

"You're safe," she says, her voice firm but not unkind. "For now."

I glare at her, blood trickling down my cheek. "Safe? Are you kidding me?"

She doesn't flinch at my anger, her gaze steady. "We didn't know who you were. You're lucky we stopped when we did."

Jamie looks at her with wide eyes, his fear giving way to awe. "Who are you?"

"Shanae," she says simply, scanning each of us in turn. Her gaze lingers on Calythra, then on me. "Now, who the hell are you, and what are you doing here?"

Before I can answer, a distant roar echoes through the trees. My heart leaps into my throat. It's Solan.

He's coming.

And if he sees the blood on my face, I know he won't stop to ask questions. He'll tear through these monsters, this woman, like a storm, and nothing—not reason, not logic—will hold him back.

"Call him off," Shanae says sharply, her composure faltering for the first time. "Whatever you think we've done, we're not your enemies."

Calythra's voice is tight. "You have no idea who's coming, do you? That's Solan."

At the name, Shanae blanches. "Solan?" Her voice wavers, and the others around her exchange uneasy glances.

"Yes," Calythra says, his tone almost smug. "And that's his bonded." He gestures to me. "So, yeah. You've really stepped in it."

The tension in the clearing thickens, the weight of Solan's reputation settling over us like a storm cloud. I can't help the flicker of pride that rises in my chest—ridiculous, stupidly sexy pride. But now is definitely not the time to admit that.

"Stand down," Shanae orders her group, her voice sharp as a blade. "All of you. Now."

The roar grows louder, and I step forwards, ignoring the pain in my side. I have to stop this before it's too late. Before Solan reaches us.

"You need to all back the fuck off and let me handle him," I say, my voice steady despite the chaos swirling around me. I have little doubt this mismatched band of monsters is part of the rebellion. I can't afford for them to be slaughtered, and I absolutely don't want Jamie to be caught in the thick of it either.

The air grows heavy, charged with an almost-electric anticipation. A faint rustle through the trees warns me moments before Solan breaches the clearing.

He's magnificent.

It's not just the feral intensity in his eyes or the powerful way he strides into the open—it's also the flames. Flickering tendrils of fire snake over his skin, glowing orange and gold against the rich red of his.... Fuck me. Are those scales? His movements are fluid and controlled, but it's the fire—raw, living energy—that draws every ounce of my attention. His eyes lock on me, searing and unyielding.

But I know. Oh, how I know. He doesn't see the rebels shrinking back or Jamie's wide, terrified gaze. All he sees is the blood trickling down my cheek, a stark red contrast against my pale skin.

"Solan!" I shout, desperate to pierce through the haze of rage I feel radiating from him. His steps don't falter. He's not charging, not yet, but the deliberate, measured way he moves is infinitely more terrifying.

The rebels must think so too. Their leader—

Shanae—shouts something in a language I don't recognise, and the group scrambles back, positioning themselves behind me like I'm their new shield. Most of them do, anyway. One of the rebel monsters hesitates, its form too slow or too stubborn to retreat as fast as the others.

Solan's hand rises, and with it, the fire around him swirls, coalescing into a burning orb.

"No!" I holler, my voice raw and cracking as I lunge forwards, arms outstretched. "Solan, stop!"

The fireball shoots from his hand, streaking across the clearing with terrifying precision. My heart seizes in my chest as I anticipate the strike—already imagining the blood, the destruction, the smell of charred flesh.

Instinct takes over before I can think it through. I hurl myself forwards, my body colliding with the startled rebel just as Solan's fireball roars through the clearing. The force of it knocks the air from my lungs, but not before Jamie's scream pierces my chest like a dagger.

I feel the fire hit me square in the chest, and for a split second, I think it's over.

This is it.

I picture Jamie's tear-streaked face. Solan's eyes, full of love and desperation. My heart shatters into a thousand pieces, the thought of leaving them behind unbearable. But then...

I gasp. My lungs burn, but not from the fire.

Holy shit, I'm alive.

Flames lick across my skin, but they don't consume me. They dance—bright and mesmerising, curling over my arms and chest like living things, almost playful in their movements. Panic claws at me as I swat them, but they refuse to extinguish.

"What the—" My voice catches, my brain unable to process what's happening.

"Uncle Jack!" Jamie's scream cuts through the chaos, his small frame hurtling towards me.

"No!" Solan is there in an instant, intercepting Jamie mid-run and pulling him back before he can get too close. "Stay back!" His voice is sharp, desperate.

"But he's—" Jamie's words come in frantic gasps as he tries to break free.

"Listen to me," Solan growls, his tone brooking no argument. "He's not hurt, but the flames will burn you. Stay with Calythra."

Jamie hesitates, tears streaming down his cheeks, before Solan shoves him gently but firmly towards Calythra. The young Veilvox steps in without question, his expression unusually serious as he wraps an arm around Jamie, holding him in place despite my nephew's protests.

And then Solan is on me.

His hands are firm but careful as he guides me, his voice a steady anchor amidst my rising panic. "Focus on me," he says, his golden eyes locking onto mine. "You're not hurt. The flames—just breathe."

"I don't know how to stop it!" I rasp, my voice shaking. "What's happening to me?"

"I'll explain," he promises, brushing his hands over my arms, coaxing the fire into submission. "Just focus. Calm your breathing. Feel it."

I do as he says, though my heart is hammering against my ribs. Slowly, impossibly, the flames begin to dim, their wild flickers settling into a soft glow before fading entirely. My skin is unmarked, though it feels warm, tingling with energy that wasn't there before.

"What the hell just happened?" I whisper, staring down at my hands as if they belong to someone else. "I should be dead. That fire—"

"You're not," Solan says firmly, scanning me for injuries even though there's no sign of a burn. Relief wars with something darker in his expression—something that sends a chill down my spine. "My fire will *never* hurt you."

His eyes flick to the blood on my face, and his jaw tightens.

"Solan," I start, but he's already turning, his entire body tensing like a predator scenting its prey.

The rebels.

They're clustered together a few feet away, wide-eyed and wary, but Solan's murderous gaze zeros in on them like a nocked arrow.

"You," he growls, his voice low and lethal. Flames ripple across his arms, and for a moment, he looks every bit the monstrous warrior of stories that are whispered about him—unstoppable, terrifying, and breathtakingly beautiful. From the rebels' reactions, it's clear Calythra wasn't exaggerating.

The American who'd introduced herself as Shanae edges forwards, her hands raised in a placating gesture. "Wait—please. We didn't mean for this to happen."

"You hurt him," Solan snaps, his voice like thunder. "I should burn you all where you stand."

"Solan, stop!" I step forwards, catching his arm. He flinches at the contact, his eyes darting to me as if to ensure I'm still there. "I'm fine. They didn't know."

His gaze softens when it meets mine, but the tension in his body doesn't ease. "They drew blood."

"And we need their help," I remind him, my voice

firm despite the trembling in my hands. "If you kill them, we lose any chance of finding safety."

Shanae takes a cautious step. "You're right. You do," she says, addressing me directly. Her voice is steady, but I catch the way her eyes flicker nervously to Solan's blazing arms. "We didn't know who you were. That's why we acted the way we did. We're trying to survive, same as you."

"Survive?" Solan's voice drips with scorn. "By attacking innocents?"

Shanae holds his gaze, her expression hardening. "You're not innocent. None of us are. But I'd rather fight alongside you than against you. If you'll let me."

The tension in the air is suffocating. Solan's flames flare brighter, but I squeeze his arm right over the flames, grounding him, though I'm still not quite sure how I'm able to do so. Hell, if I'd had this ability when I was a firefighter, my job would have been a whole lot safer and easier. "We need them," I say softly, pleading with my eyes.

For a long moment, he doesn't move. Then, slowly, the fire ebbs, retreating beneath his skin.

"Fine," he says, his voice low and dangerous. "But if any of you so much as breathe wrong, I won't hold back next time."

Shanae nods, relief flickering across her face. "Fair enough."

Jamie breaks free from Calythra's hold and rushes to my side to throw his arms around my waist. "Don't do that again," he mumbles into my shirt, his voice thick with tears.

"I won't," I promise, ruffling his hair. But as I glance at Solan, his golden eyes still burning with barely restrained fury, I can't help but wonder if I'll have a choice.

CHAPTER
ELEVEN

I'VE NO IDEA HOW LONG WE'VE BEEN PLODDING along this track. All I'm sure of is that I stink—the joy of travelling with limited supplies and no washing facilities. Okay, that and we're still no closer to safety or answers.

Shanae's been tight-lipped. The only thing she's asked and—after a shared glance with Solan—I've confirmed is that, yes, Jamie and I arrived in the latest merge just a few days ago. She did reveal that she's been here for close to eighteen years.

I'm still processing.

On the one hand, she's survived this long, and I assume has a life here. It's a relief. But fuck, eighteen years with no chance of returning.

"So, if you happened to be in a rift..." I ponder

how to describe the section of land exchanged in a merge. "... *cell* here, you could technically find yourself back home?" I ask.

Solan tenses beside me, and guilt that my words make him nervous pulses under my skin.

"Technically, yes. Our world or another. Solan's... or Yetaria's." She points at the large, noseless monster a few steps in front of us. "Who's to say where the rift would take any of us?"

Shit, I didn't even consider that. A tendril of unease unfurls in my gut.

What if another happens and takes Jamie away from me... and to somewhere even more dangerous than here? I feel the blood drain from my face. What if I'm taken away from Solan or him from me? A slice of fear threatens to buckle my knees.

I don't have time to spiral—not with Solan's firm, comforting grip on my thigh. I soak in his warmth, the silent reassurance he's giving despite not knowing what I'm freaking the fuck out about. The fact that he does so without an exchange of words is enough.

I'm not sure how to respond. Do I want to think about this further and get myself worked up about something I have exactly zero control over? Fuck no.

Thankfully, Solan angles his head towards Shanae and says, "Where *exactly* are we heading?" Solan's voice is steady, but there's an undercurrent of tension that makes me glance at him. His golden eyes flick briefly to mine before focussing back on Shanae.

She adjusts the strap of her pack, her pace steady as we trudge along the overgrown trail. The air is thick and humid, the jungle closing in around us like a living, breathing thing. Vines hang low, brushing our heads, and the occasional cry of some unseen creature sends shivers down my spine.

"To our headquarters," Shanae replies, her tone clipped but not unkind. "Not the main camp."

"What's the difference?" I ask, keeping a firm grip on the reins of my horse. The animal snorts softly, uneasy in the dense jungle.

"The camp's where most of the rebels are," Shanae explains. "It's a lot bigger, more like a proper settlement. Think of a town rather than a city of tents. The headquarters, on the other hand, is more of a... central node. Fewer people, more secure."

"A town?" Jamie perks up beside me, his eyes wide with curiosity. "What kind of town? Like... one from Earth?"

"Not exactly." Shanae's lips quirk into a small smile. "It was merged here about twenty years ago. We call it Dathanor. Used to be from a world called Fenorith."

"Fenorith?" I echo, the name foreign and intriguing.

"Yeah," Shanae says. "Whole place was apparently covered in bioluminescent veins and floating rivers. Dathanor was one of their smaller settlements, but it's… changed since then."

"Changed how?" Jamie's practically bouncing with excitement now, and I can't help but smile at his enthusiasm. Hell, it's better than him being terrified.

Shanae glances at him, her expression softening. "Well, for one thing, it doesn't have floating rivers anymore. But it's still got its quirks. You'll see when we get there."

At least that's reassuring, the implication that we'll get to see the settlement and make it out of the headquarters alive.

The trail narrows, forcing us into a single-file line. Solan drops back to walk behind me. I glance over my shoulder, catching how his gaze sweeps the surroundings with practiced ease.

"And the shields?" he asks, his tone casual but probing. "How have you managed to protect a place like that?"

Shanae snorts softly. "This world is like one of those crazy movies or video games back home," she directs at me. "You'd be amazed at the kind of skills some species bring to the table."

"Like what?" Jamie asks, eyes wide. He's in front of me, his head angled up, glancing at everything he can.

Shanae flicks a look his way and grins, her teeth white against her dark skin. "There's a species called the Entherians. They're humanoid but have these crystalline structures in their bodies that let them manipulate energy fields. They can embed those fields into objects, creating shields that are damn near impenetrable."

"That's... awesome," Jamie breathes, his eyes wide with awe. "Can they make anything else?"

Shanae chuckles. "Oh, plenty. But shielding's their specialty. Without them, we'd have been discovered years ago."

The pathway opens up again, and Solan rejoins me. The invisible pull between us is strong and makes it all but impossible not to peer at him.

His expression is unreadable. "And what about your defences? Beyond the shields."

Before Shanae can answer, one of her companions—a hulking, tusked creature named Raskar—growls low in his throat. "Why do you care, Pyronox?

Planning to burn us down if you don't like the answers?"

The hostility in his voice is like a slap, and my hackles rise. "Hey," I snap, stepping between Raskar and Solan. "He's asking because we're on your side. Or have you forgotten that already?"

Raskar narrows his beady eyes at me, his lips curling back to reveal sharp teeth. "Trust isn't given freely, human. Not here."

"Then maybe you should stop treating us like enemies," I shoot back, my voice sharp. "We're here because we don't have a choice, not because we want to be."

"Enough," Shanae cuts in, her voice firm. "Raskar, stand down. Solan's questions are valid. And if you can't keep your temper in check, I'll leave you behind."

Raskar grumbles something under his breath but falls silent, his tusked head bowing slightly in submission.

"Sorry about that," Shanae says, her tone softer as she glances at me. "Tensions are high these days. Can't blame anyone for being on edge."

I nod, though my shoulders remain tense. Solan's hand brushes briefly against mine, a silent reassurance that helps ease some of the tightness in my chest.

The jungle grows denser as we continue, the air damp and heavy with the scent of earth and vegetation. Every now and then, I catch glimpses of old structures—crumbling walls overtaken by vines, rusted metal frameworks that hint at a civilization long gone. It's eerie but also fascinating.

"Where are these from?" I ask, gesturing to a half-collapsed tower we pass.

"Hard to say," Shanae replies. "Rifts bring all sorts of things through. Could've been part of a city from another world or even this one."

The conversation slows as we press on, the sounds of the jungle filling the silence. Birds call from the treetops, and the occasional rustle of leaves makes my skin prickle with unease.

Then Shanae holds up a hand, signalling us to stop. "We're coming up on a dangerous stretch," she says, her voice low. "There's a predator that hunts this area."

"What kind of predator?" I ask, my grip tightening on the reins of my horse.

"Something native to this world," Shanae replies. "Big, fanged thing. Likes to ambush its prey. You'll know it if you see it. Just stay alert and quiet."

The group moves cautiously now, every step deliberate. My heart pounds in my chest, the tension in the air palpable. Even Jamie is quiet, his earlier excitement replaced by a wary nervousness.

The jungle seems to hold its breath as we navigate the final stretch. Every shadow feels like a threat, each rustle of leaves a potential attack. But as we step into a small clearing, the tension eases slightly.

"Looks like we're clear," Shanae says, her voice barely above a whisper.

I let out a breath, but the relief is short-lived. A low growl rumbles through the air, followed by the sound of snapping branches.

"What was that?" I whisper.

Solan looks intently at me, a tight-lipped smile aimed my way. "If it bleeds, we can kill it." His hand goes to the hilt of his blade.

The growl is joined by others, and then they're upon us—a swarm of waist-high creatures with wiry bodies, sharp claws, and teeth that glint like polished knives. This is definitely not the large monster Shanae warned us about. Their eyes glow with a feral intensity, and they move with terrifying speed, their snarls filling the air.

"Jamie, stay back!" I shout, drawing my rifle as my horse rears in panic.

Solan is already in motion, his blade flashing as he cuts down one of the creatures. Shanae and her team form a defensive line, their weapons raised as the mini monsters close in. Fuck, they're ugly and terrifying.

I'm off Geralt in a beat, my gun coming up instinctively, the weight familiar and comforting in my hands. I fire twice, each shot precise. The first freaky gremlin drops with a shriek, clawing at the bloody hole where its eye used to be. The second stumbles as my bullet catches it in the shoulder, but it doesn't fall.

Behind me, Jamie cries out as one of the monsters lunges towards him. I pivot, sighting down the barrel in an instant. The report of the shot is deafening, and the creature collapses at Jamie's feet. He stares at me, wide-eyed, but I don't have time to reassure him.

"Stay close to Caly!" I bark, already turning back to the fray.

Solan is a whirlwind of flame and steel, his movements as fluid as they are deadly. The air around him shimmers with heat, the flickering flames on his skin casting eerie shadows across his sharp features. He moves with terrifying precision, each swing of his blade cutting down another creature.

One lunges at him from the side, and he doesn't

even flinch. A column of fire erupts from his hand, engulfing the attacker in midair. It screeches, the sound high-pitched and awful, before collapsing into a smoking heap.

I can't help but stare for a moment, caught between awe and something far more dangerous—a primal, breathless appreciation of his sheer power. He's magnificent, a force of nature, and the sight of him is enough to make my pulse race.

But there's no time to dwell on it. Another creature charges at me, its jaws wide and slavering. I side-step, driving the butt of my gun into its skull with all my strength. It yelps, momentarily stunned, and I take the opportunity to fire point-blank into its chest. "You're one ugly motherfucker." The words spill out even as a slightly hysterical grin forms.

Then Solan is in my space, his own grin wide, his eyes heavy with lust. "Did you just...?"

I roll my eyes, my smirk still in place, my adrenaline flying so high, I don't even give a shit that I'm sharing an Arnie moment with him in the middle of a bloody battle. I lose his smile when he spins—a dagger soaring from his hand to land in the centre of the mini monster's forehead.

"Behind you!" Shanae shouts.

I whirl just in time to see another ugly fucker

leaping for me, its claws outstretched. There's no time to aim—I raise my arm instinctively, bracing for impact.

Before it can reach me, a fiery whip lashes out, catching the creature and yanking it to the ground. Solan strides forwards, his eyes blazing as he finishes it off with a clean slice of his blade.

"Are you all right?" he asks, his voice tight with concern.

"I'm fine," I snap, adrenaline coursing through me and all humour long gone. "Focus on those fucking monsters!"

He hesitates for the briefest of moments, his gaze flicking over me to ensure I'm unharmed before turning back to the fight.

The monsters are relentless, their snarls and screeches filling the air as they press their attack. Shanae and her team hold their ground, their weapons a mix of advanced tech and brutal simplicity. Jamie clings to Calythra's side, his face pale but determined.

"You dirty fucking Fraggles!" Shanae shouts, her voice sharp.

I glance over in time to see two creatures circling towards her. Without thinking, I aim my rifle and fire, dropping one. The second leaps for her, but she meets it head-on, driving a wickedly curved blade into its chest.

I take stock, the sounds of screams and grunts lessening. For all their ferocity, the weird-arse monsters are no match for our steel and determination. What the hell am I talking about? No match for Solan. Sure, my rifle came in handy, and the others protected and took down a few, but it's Solan who's unstoppable, his flames cutting through the growing darkness like a beacon. Every movement is purposeful, each strike devastating.

As the last creature falls, semiquiet descends over the clearing. The only sounds are our ragged breaths and the distant calls of jungle birds.

The clearing is a mess of scorched earth and fallen bodies, the air heavy with the acrid scent of smoke and charred flesh. Jesus, there are so many. What I'd thought of as a small group of maybe ten is so not right. There must be twenty, maybe more, scattered monsters at our feet.

Solan's flames have burned out, leaving him standing amidst the wreckage like some mythic warrior, his blade dripping with dark ichor. He breathes heavily, his chest rising and falling, the faint glow of embers still flickering across his skin.

The rebels are staring at him, their expressions a

mixture of awe and thinly veiled horror. Shanae, previously so composed, looks like she's not sure whether to thank him or step cautiously away. Yetaria mutters something low in a language I don't understand but with a tone that doesn't need translating—disbelief, reverence, and a touch of fear.

"That was…," Shanae begins, trailing off as her gaze sweeps over the carnage. "Impressive doesn't quite cover it."

"Terrifying fits better," Yetaria says bluntly, his eyes fixed on Solan as though he might burst into flames again at any moment.

"I can't believe I'm saying this," Shanae mutters, rubbing her temples, "but I think I'd rather face another pack of those things than him in a fight."

I glance at Solan, and my pulse skips. The rebels might be horrified, but I'm a far cry from that. Watching him fight was like watching raw power unleashed, each movement precise, every flame-tipped strike beautiful and deadly.

And maybe that's part of the problem—how much I felt it, the sheer pull towards him. Even now, blood smeared across his cheek, his shirt torn, he's standing there like he's walked out of a dream designed to ruin me.

I swallow hard, trying to keep my voice steady as I step closer to him. "Are you okay?"

He doesn't answer right away, his molten-gold eyes scanning my face for any sign of injury. Finally, he nods, his voice low and quiet. "You?"

"I'm fine," I manage, though the look in his eyes makes it hard to breathe.

"You didn't have to protect me like that," he says, his fingers brushing the back of my hand briefly. "Didn't have to fight."

"You were protecting me too," I point out, though my voice wavers just slightly. "It's what we do. I know you're the warrior here, but I can handle myself."

The corners of his mouth lift ever so slightly in a hint of a smile that makes my heart stumble.

Fuck, I want to kiss him. Lose myself in him so completely that all the carnage around us disappears.

I don't know who moves first. Our lips connect, mouths part, tongues stroke and tangle. I hold him close, clinging to his shoulders as I groan against him, kissing him with everything I have. One firm hand on my spine holds me steady while the other cradles the back of my head. Another lick into his mouth and Solan shudders. Fuck, I love this. How he loses control, is close to unravelling completely.

The clearing of a throat, or maybe more than one,

cuts through the lust connecting me to Solan. I pull back, wide-eyed and gasping for breath. Solan peers down at me, his chest rising and falling in a rapid beat. He's beautiful. It doesn't matter that he has black splats of blood on him or even that—

"Are they... are they gone?"

Fuck. Jamie. I turn quickly towards him, relief flooding through me when I see him pale but unscathed.

"For now," Shanae replies, wiping her blade on the grass. "But we need to move. There could be more nearby."

I swallow hard as I look around, reaching out for my nephew to hold him close. "That wasn't the monster you were worried about, was it?" I confirm even though I already know.

Her gaze shifts to me, and she shakes her head. "No."

Fuck it all to hell.

Solan steps into my line of sight, his golden eyes scanning me for the second time. "You're hurt," he says, his voice low and intense.

"It's just a scratch," I say, brushing at the blood on my sleeve. "Nothing serious."

His jaw tightens, but he nods, brushing his fingers against mine for a brief moment.

But before I can say more—or worse, do something like throw myself at him and kiss him senseless again—Shanae interrupts.

"We need to get moving," she says, her tone brisk. "That fight might've drawn more predators. We can't linger."

Solan steps back, his hand falling away, and I curse the timing. With a nod at Shanae, I gather my things, giving Jamie another quick once-over to ensure he's still in one piece. He's pale and shaky, but he meets my gaze with wide, determined eyes.

"You okay, kiddo?" I ask, crouching down to his level.

He nods quickly, his voice small but steady. "Yeah. You were amazing."

"So were you," I say, ruffling his hair. "You kept your head. I'm proud of you."

Calythra shoots me a look that I think might be approval, and the group begins to move again.

The jungle opens up as we press on, the air hot and humid. Despite the tension and how battle-weary we are, Jamie seems to have found his second wind and peppers Shanae with questions, his curiosity undiminished.

"So, you're not taking us to the main camp right away?" he asks.

"No," Shanae replies, glancing over her shoulder. "We're going to the headquarters. It's smaller, more secure."

"What's the main camp like?" I ask, curious despite myself. She gave the basics earlier, but I need to have a better understanding of where I'm leading my nephew. I click at Geralt to keep up, his reins in my hand as he walks at my side.

Shanae pushes a low-hanging branch out of the way. "It came through in one of the early merges—a whole chunk of another world, including buildings, streets, and people. We've built onto it over the years, but the original structures are still there."

Jesus. The whole thing boggles my mind, but damn if the excited curiosity isn't bubbling in my gut too. I peer up at Solan, whose gaze immediately lowers to meet mine. "Have you seen lots of evidence of rifts since you've been here?"

He bobs his head. "Yes, a few larger settlements and areas, but more like your home."

"As in my house, my property?" I clarify, checking he's not simply talking about my world.

"Yes. We can return one day, gather your things."

That would be incredible, but what would be even better would be staying there. If not for my own sense of self-preservation, then definitely for Jamie. It's something I'll ask Solan, but not right now when surrounded by rebels who may or may not want to welcome us in. Hell, from some of the initial sneers and what we've already discovered, them trying to kill us might still be on the cards.

Though I suspect after Solan's earlier display, they're even warier than they were.

"Thanks," I offer, squeezing his large palm.

Shanae pauses as we break free from the dense jungle, her eyes narrowing towards something in the distance. I follow her gaze, blinking rapidly as the sight before me registers.

At first, I think it's a mirage, some trick of the heat and exhaustion. But no. It's there. It's real. And it's... a bowling alley.

Not just any bowling alley, mind you. The alley is bright pink, its gaudy neon lights still somehow flickering faintly despite what must be years of wear and tear, with a massive sign on top that reads *"Strike It Rich Lanes!"* The smiling caricature of a bowling pin holding a sack of cash winks down at us, though one of its eyes is cracked and darkened.

Jamie is the first to react. He stops dead in his tracks, jaw dropping. "What... the... heck?"

I bark out a laugh, the sound sharp and unhinged.

"Bloody hell. It's a bowling alley. In the middle of a jungle."

Shanae sighs, running a hand over her face. "It came through in one of the merges. No one knows why or how. We use it now, but… yeah. It's a bowling alley."

I can't stop laughing. The absurdity of it all hits me square in the chest. After everything we've been through—fireballs, monsters, jungle predators—this is what finally breaks me. Tears sting my eyes as I double over, clutching my stomach.

Solan steps closer, his expression one of deep confusion. "I don't understand. Is this structure… important to your people?"

"Not in the slightest," I wheeze, wiping at my face. "It's for a game. You roll a heavy ball at pins and try to knock them down. That's it. That's all it's for."

Solan's brow furrows, his golden eyes darting between me and the garish building. "And this… entertains you?"

Shanae groans. "Welcome to Earth culture."

Jamie chimes in, "It's fun, though. And they have burgers and hot chips and arcade games!"

"Burgers?" Solan repeats, his expression even more bewildered. I suspect he's filtering through his memories of every Arnie movie he's ever watched, trying to recall if he's ever heard of a burger being mentioned.

I lose it again, laughing so hard, I can barely stand. The bubbling hysteria feels cathartic, a release of everything I've been holding in since this nightmare began.

Even Shanae cracks a small smile, though her amusement is short-lived. She steps forwards, her tone turning serious. "All right, laugh it up now, but keep it together when we go inside. The rebel leader is... intense."

I blink, sobering slightly. "Intense how?"

"You'll see," Shanae says cryptically. "Just... don't provoke him."

The laughter peters out completely as her words sink in. A ripple of unease moves through our group, the rebels exchanging wary glances.

As we approach the building, I notice more details—reinforced steel plating bolted to the walls, makeshift barricades around the perimeter, and several sentries perched on what used to be the roof. They watch us closely, their weapons trained but not raised, their expressions unreadable.

Shanae leads us through the entrance, the glass doors now replaced with heavy metal ones that creak ominously as they swing open. Inside, the transformation is even more jarring.

The bowling lanes have been repurposed into a training area, the polished wood now scuffed and scratched from years of use. Tables and chairs from what must have been the snack bar are arranged in clusters, covered with maps, blueprints, and weapons. The air is thick with the hum of activity—people of various species moving with purpose, their voices a low murmur beneath the steady clatter of... is that someone actually bowling in the distance?

Shanae leads us towards the back, where an over-sized table has been constructed from salvaged materials. Seated at its head is someone who I assume to be the rebel leader.

He's humanoid, but only just. His skin is a deep, iridescent purple that shimmers like oil under light, and his eyes are a piercing silver that glow faintly in the dim room. Horns curve elegantly from his temples, framing a face that is both striking and unnerving. His build is massive, his presence commanding.

He watches us approach, his gaze sharp and assessing. When he speaks, his voice is deep and resonant with an almost-musical quality. "Shanae. You've returned."

"Yes, and with new arrivals," Shanae says, gesturing to our group. "This is—"

"I know who they are," the leader interrupts, his eyes locking onto me with unsettling intensity. "The ones from the latest rift."

I straighten instinctively under his scrutiny, my heart pounding. Solan moves closer to my side, his protective presence both comforting and grounding.

The leader's gaze shifts to Solan, and for a long, tense moment, the two of them simply stare at each other, as though sizing each other up.

Finally, the leader's lips curve into a faint enigmatic smile. "Interesting," he says, his tone unreadable.

Great. Just what we need—more cryptic commentary. But at least we haven't been eaten on the spot. Plus, he's still smiling, and not in an "I wonder if you'll taste like chicken or beef" kind of way.

"Welcome to the Riftborn," the leader says, his deep voice cutting through the room's low hum of activity. He rises from his seat with deliberate grace, the faint glow of his silver eyes never wavering from me. His towering frame seems to fill the room, the curved horns on his temples lending him an almost-regal menace.

Shanae steps forwards, offering a tight nod. "This

is Solan, Calythra, Jack, and Jamie. The humans arrived during the latest merge."

"I know," he replies smoothly, his lips curving into that faint enigmatic smile. "Their arrival was… notable." His gaze locks onto mine, and for a moment, it feels as if he's looking through me, peeling back layers I didn't even know I had.

Solan shifts beside me, his imposing frame stiff with tension. I suspect he's not used to being measured up like this, especially by someone who radiates confidence and control.

The leader's smile deepens just enough to make it clear he's noticed. He turns his attention to Solan, the weight of his piercing gaze palpable even from where I'm standing. "Pyronox," he says, the single word rolling off his tongue like an old secret. "It's been a long time since I've seen one of your kind."

Solan's eyes narrow. "And you are?"

"Commander Varek Zathrian," the leader replies, inclining his head slightly, a gesture that feels halfway between respect and amusement. "I lead the Riftborn."

Jamie tugs at my sleeve, his wide eyes fixed on Varek. "He's huge," he whispers, earning a faint chuckle from Shanae.

Varek's sharp hearing doesn't miss it. His silver

gaze flicks to Jamie, softening just a fraction. "You have courage, little one," he says, his tone almost... kind. "But courage without understanding can be a dangerous thing."

Jamie shrinks back slightly, and I instinctively place a hand on his shoulder, stepping forwards to shield him.

"Why don't you tell us what you mean by 'notable'?" I ask, keeping my voice steady despite the tension coiling in my chest.

He studies me a beat before his attention shifts to Jamie, then back to me.

"I know why you're here." He takes a step closer, his towering frame somehow even more intimidating up close. His smile sharpens, a predator's grin, as he says his next words. "You're running from the crown. You're searching for allies. What you don't yet realise is that the Riftborn aren't just your best chance of survival. We're your only chance."

My breath catches in my throat. There's no way he could know that. None. Plus, talk about not answering my damn question.

Varek's gaze shifts to Jamie, who instinctively moves closer to me. "The boy too," he adds, his tone darkening, though it's hard to tell if it's concern or something else entirely. "You brought him here... but do you even understand why?"

"What do you mean?" I ask, my voice sharp. And brought him *here*? As in, to the rebels, or to this other world? Because fuck him if that's the case. I had zero control over anything that happened.

Varek chuckles, a low rumble that sends a shiver down my spine. He turns his back on us and strides towards the window overlooking an incongruous building looming in the distance.

He says over his shoulder, "I'll give you one piece of advice—keep a close eye on your little shadow."

Jamie flinches at the word, and I pull him closer.

Varek turns back to us. "It's interesting, don't you think?"

Fuck it all to hell with his cryptic bullshit and his nonanswers.

"What is?" Solan asks, his stance protective, his voice brooking no shit.

"Almost every human who's been dragged into this world has found themselves bound to someone— or something—not of their kind," Varek finishes, his piercing silver eyes scanning me, Jamie, and Solan with unsettling precision.

"What the hell are you talking about?" I demand, holding Jamie tighter.

Varek tilts his head, his oil-slick skin catching the dim light of the room. "You know exactly what I mean. What do you humans call us? 'Monsters'? You may as well call us your destined mates."

The words slam into me, a weight I wasn't prepared for. I open my mouth to protest, but nothing comes out. It's not like I haven't already accepted that Solan and I are connected, bound by something more than choice or circumstance. But hearing it so bluntly, so universally applied to every human who's come through a merge, makes my stomach churn.

Solan stiffens beside me, his flame-kissed hand brushing mine in silent reassurance. "You're saying this happens to all humans?" His voice is taut, like a bowstring pulled too tight.

"Almost humans we've encountered," Varek clarifies, his tone calm, almost academic. "There's just been one exception."

"That's ridiculous," I blurt, my voice trembling with disbelief. "How is that even possible?"

Varek's enigmatic smile deepens. "A theory—one I've spent years piecing together. This world isn't just a random dumping ground for rift fragments. It's the centre, the nexus. A hive pulling threads from countless worlds into one chaotic web."

He paces slowly like a predator sizing up prey.

"And humans? You're the common denominator. Since the first one arrived and bonded with someone from this world, the balance shifted. The merges became more frequent. The worlds blended more chaotically. But one thing remains constant: Humans have the unique ability to forge these bonds—mates, fated partners, whatever term you prefer."

"It's not unique," Solan interrupts. "We have bonded in my world."

Varek doesn't appear deterred. Instead, he nods. "That may be the case, but here in Terrafeara, my world, and several other worlds, including Earth, the very possibility of having a fated mate ceased to exist hundreds and, in some cases, thousands of years ago."

The room seems to tilt around me. "No," I whisper, shaking my head. "That can't be right."

"Oh, it is," Varek says with grim certainty. "And it makes you—humans—a hot commodity."

A cold dread creeps up my spine, and I instinctively look at Jamie. "You're saying monsters... creatures... would hunt us for this?"

Varek shrugs as if it's the most obvious thing in the world. "Some would kill to sever a bond, to prevent the power it brings. Others would do worse to claim it for themselves. Particularly those still unbonded."

I can barely breathe. "What the fuck?"

"I didn't know," Solan says suddenly, his voice breaking through the fog of my thoughts. He turns to me, his gaze fierce and unwavering. "I swear I didn't know."

"I...." My throat is dry, my thoughts scattered. "I know."

"It's just a theory," Solan presses, looking back at Varek. "How certain are you?"

Varek's lips curve into a wry smile. "Certain enough to have survived this long by taking it seriously. Shanae?"

She steps forwards, her expression sombre. "He's right. I met my fated within the first week of being here. It's real. And it's not just humans who feel it—this world seems to draw us together, across species, across worlds. It's like gravity."

Shanae's words hit me like a punch to the gut. This isn't just about me. It's about Jamie too.

"You mean...." My voice falters. "Jamie...."

Shanae nods. "Once he's old enough to bond, yes. He'll be highly sought after."

Jamie looks up at me, wide-eyed and scared. "What does that mean, Uncle Jack?"

"It means I have to protect you," I say firmly, gripping his shoulders. My voice turns to steel. "It means you're safe with me."

"With us," Solan adds, his tone leaving no room for argument.

Varek watches the exchange with an air of detached amusement. "You're starting to understand. This world isn't just dangerous because of the monsters roaming its jungles, its plains. Or even because of the realm and the crown that wants to control all species. It's dangerous because of what you represent. Power. Connection. Change."

Power. It's the second time he's used that word.

A niggling thought at the edge of my brain demands my attention. Something Solan said... or didn't say, more like.

"There is more to our bonding, but it will take time."

I think of our heartbeats falling into sync. Then there's the whole me going all "flame on!" like the hot guy in *Fantastic Four.*

That could be it, right? The extent of the power Varek's referring to.

"Varek." Solan's deep voice takes me by surprise. "You know who I am, correct?"

If he had eyebrows, I'm sure Varek would be

arching one at Solan right now. Instead, he nods. "I've made sure everyone in the Riftborn knows your name and your capabilities."

Well, damn… talk about his reputation preceding him. I've no idea why Solan doesn't have an ego the size of a great white.

"I need to speak to Jack in private."

My gaze snaps to his. No way am I leaving Jamie. Not after—

Solan grips my shoulder, his focus still on Varek. "I need your oath that Jamie is kept safe and does not leave this room. Him or Calythra."

"Jamie will always be safe with me," Calythra is quick to say, a terseness in his tone that makes it obvious he's offended. But still, he's a kid in training surrounded by a bunch of rebels armed to their eyeballs in steel… and even a few guns (some I don't recognise as being Earth-made).

Solan turns to Calythra. "And I know you will continue to protect him. But I also need Varek's oath."

"You have it," Varek says after a beat. "They are safe and under my protection while you seek the privacy you have requested."

I narrow my eyes at his wording. "How can you trust his… oath?" I ask, trying not to choke on the word. It feels ancient, like something out of a myth. But the way Solan's expression tightens, I know it carries far more weight here.

"Oaths are binding here," Solan replies, his voice low but firm. "More than words. They hold power. To break one...." He hesitates, his jaw tightening. "It's not something anyone survives intact. Physically or otherwise."

Varek smiles faintly, the expression both amused and grim. "To betray an oath is to unravel yourself. Painfully. Permanently. Not a risk I'm inclined to take, especially when I've given my word to protect."

Jamie steps closer to me, and I squeeze his shoulder, not entirely reassured but unwilling to push further.

"So, what now?" I ask, glancing at Solan, then Varek.

"You go with him," Varek says, his tone a blend of command and nonchalance. "I'll ensure the boy is comfortable. That way...." He gestures towards a hallway leading deeper into the converted bowling alley.

I don't move immediately. "And it's safe down there?"

"Just a private room. Space for conversation,"

Varek replies smoothly, his silver eyes gleaming. "Nothing more."

The unease prickling my spine intensifies, but Solan touches my elbow lightly, drawing my focus.

"It's necessary," he says, his voice quiet but insistent.

"Fine." My voice comes out sharper than intended, my nerves fraying at the edges. "But this better not be one of those 'I'll tell you the bare minimum' conversations, because I've about had it with those."

Solan's lips twitch, a hint of dry amusement, but he doesn't respond. Instead, he turns to follow Varek's directions, and I reluctantly trail after him.

The hallway is dimly lit, the air cooler than in the main area. My boots thud softly against the polished wood floor, and with every step, my stomach tightens. Whatever Solan needs to tell me, it's big. And the dread pooling in my chest tells me I might not be ready for it.

CHAPTER
TWELVE

It turns out being in an enclosed space with Solan is possibly the worst or best thing in the world. It depends on how I look at it, because fuck, all I see and smell and bloody well feel is him.

How the hell am I meant to concentrate on anything beyond the two metres between us that are too damn wide?

"Jack." The word is one long rumble. It's a deep caress. A gentle sweep of heat and longing and so much need— "Jack," Solan repeats, the flash of hunger in his gaze nearly enough to have me whipping out my dick and falling to my knees.

Or onto my back.

Hell, on my hands and knees.

I'm pretty sure I'd do a damn headstand if that turns out to be his kink.

Words that I don't understand pour out of him— the additional clue that he's struggling to be in such close proximity to me.

We came here to talk. For Solan to explain whatever it is that I'm sure is going to get a reaction that isn't simply me wanting to see his dick and hoping like hell he has a peen that's going to send me spiralling and exploding.

The sheer size of my handsome, brutish monster —and don't get me started that I'm wading into Mills & Boon territory here, since this is what Solan does to me (and yes, I may not be a big reader and my mum's soft porn was man-on-woman, but when I was fifteen and restricted from internet use, I took my thrills however I could)—must mean he's packing, right?

All it will take is me stepping into his space and running my palms up his strong red thighs. I'm still not convinced he's wearing undies—or hell, a loincloth or something—under t—

"Jack." This time my name's garbled, a desperate plea that I'm pretty sure means he wants me to stop and get to business that doesn't involve his monster peen in my arse.

I should be taking it easy on him. There's little doubt that whatever he needs to tell me is as serious as a giant dick in my butt, but since my mind is apparently solely on his junk, there's only a slim chance that I'm going to make it easy and stop eye fucking him. Wanting him. Needing him.

"I need you to try to stop blasting your intentions to me for one second and clear your mind," he says through gritted teeth, as though each word is painful.

His words are enough to have me considering what he means, though my hard cock isn't at all fazed. "Blasting my intentions?" Somewhere in the recesses of my brain, I know my reaction to Solan, to finally being alone with him, is excessive... desperate, even. The awareness doesn't help in the slightest.

Especially when the strands of his hair are undulating, reaching for me. A shiver racks me, wanting their touch... Solan's touch more than is logical, let alone healthy.

Hell, we're both still splattered with dried monster blood. I have zero fucks to give, though, apparently.

"Please, Jack."

It's the tremble in Solan's voice that has me swallowing hard and trying to clear my head from the desire that's doubling down and taking over every cell of my body.

"Okay." I nod a little stiltedly. "Intention? What do you mean?"

Solan exhales heavily, his chest rising and falling in a deliberate rhythm, like he's trying to ground himself. His molten gaze flickers to me, his expression taut with restraint.

"You're broadcasting," he says, his voice a low, trembling growl. "Your emotions, your desires... everything. I can *feel* it, Jack. It's like a firestorm, impossible to ignore, impossible to—" He cuts himself off, his jaw tightening.

Broadcasting? The hell? I stare at him, trying to piece together what he means, but my focus keeps slipping back to the way his hair moves—those tendrils of living flame undulating with his every breath once again stretching towards me like they have a mind of their own.

"I don't—" I start even as I recall our earlier moment when I was sure I could feel his emotions, but he raises a hand to stop me, his red fingers gleaming faintly in the dim light.

"You don't realise you're doing it," he says, his tone softening. "It's not your fault. The bond... it's incomplete, but it's already strong. Stronger than I expected. And after everything we've just discovered...." He trails off, something like desperate urgency in his eyes that begs me to understand the significance of what's happening between us.

My heart skips a beat. "The bond," I echo, the words thick on my tongue.

"Yes," he murmurs, his gaze holding mine. "The connection between us. It began when we exchanged blood—the cut on your hand—that was the first step." I look at my hand, then his, a frown dipping my brows low. "I cut it not on purpose," he says quickly, and I nod, sending him a soft smile, knowing that instinctively. "The connection," he continues, getting back on track, "It's only a fragment of what it will become."

I swallow hard, my mouth suddenly dry. "And the rest?"

This is absolutely something we both know we should have spent time talking about, but in fairness, we've been busy trying to stay alive. That kinda took precedence.

Solan hesitates, his tendrils curling and uncurling with a kind of restless energy. "The bond completes through the exchange of body, mind, and soul. Only then will our connection be whole. It's... irreversible, Jack. Eternal. When one of us dies, the other will follow immediately. But until that time, we would share everything—strength, power, life itself. Even the fire I've already shared with you, the one you barely understand, will become something more."

My mind reels, the weight of his words pressing down on me like gravity cranked to eleven. Eternal. Irreversible. Life itself.

I stare at him, the weight of his confession settling like a stone in my chest. Despite everything—the danger, the confusion, the sheer absurdity of this situation—there's one thing I can't deny: The thought of being without him is unbearable.

"Solan...," I begin, but my voice falters as his hair brushes against my arm, the tendrils, warm and alive, sending a shiver down my spine. Apparently we're no longer a couple of metres apart, our bodies working like the moon and the tide.

"I need you to understand," he says, his tone urgent. "The bond isn't just about us—it's about what we can become together. My strength, my fire... it will become yours. And your fire will grow, become something neither of us can predict. But the connection goes both ways. Your emotions, your desires...." He trails off, his eyes darkening. "They already affect me more than you know."

My breath catches, heat pooling low in my gut.

"So... when you say exchange of body, mind, and soul...."

"It means what you think it means," he says, his voice dipping into a growl. "And it means more than that."

He steps closer, his presence overwhelming, the heat of him wrapping around me like a living thing. "The exchange of body... it's the final step, the catalyst for the merging of our minds and souls. When that happens, we'll be bound completely. Nothing will separate us—not distance, not death. We'll share everything, Jack. Every thought, every feeling, every breath."

I should be terrified. Hell, maybe I am. But all I can think about is the way his voice wraps around me like a promise, how his hair reaches for me like it's as desperate for this as I am.

"And your hair," I say, my voice rough. "It reacts to me because of the bond?"

He nods, his expression softening. "As you know, it's part of me. A sensory extension. It responds to you because I respond to you. Because you're mine."

The possessiveness in his voice sends a thrill through me, and I know I'm in deep. Too deep. But there's no going back now—not that I'd want to.

"Solan," I whisper, my throat tight. "If we do this... if we complete the bond...."

"There's no 'if,'" he says, his voice like a vow. "Only 'when.'"

The finality in his tone sends a shiver down my spine, but I nod, my resolve hardening. Whatever this is, whatever it means... I'm all in.

The air between us is charged, heavy with unspoken words and the kind of tension that has a life of its own. Solan's eyes burn into mine, heated and alive, as if the fire in him could consume the space between us. His hair, those strange tendrils of living flame, flickers towards me, and I can feel the heat of them even before they touch.

Then he moves.

It's not a tentative kiss, not the kind you ease into, testing the waters. It's desperate and claiming, the kind of kiss that demands surrender. He cups my face, his hair ghosting just shy of my skin as his mouth crashes against mine.

The world tilts, my thoughts scattering like leaves in a storm. His lips are hot and insistent, his sharp teeth brushing my lower lip, sending a jolt of something electric through me. A promise, a declaration, a *claim*... every single one of those things is pressed against my lips, stroking my tongue, consuming me.

I'm lost in him, his taste, the way his body presses against mine like he's trying to carve himself into my very being. I clutch at his sides, the heat of his skin burning in the most incredible way as he licks into my mouth with his forked tongue.

Bang, bang, bang.

The sound echoes through the room like a gunshot, shattering the moment.

I pull back, gasping, my heart pounding against my ribs like it's trying to break free. Solan's eyes are wild, his chest heaving, his hair sparking and curling in agitation.

"Whoever that is," I growl, my voice rough, "is about to die."

Solan's lips quirk into something like a smirk, but the moment doesn't last. The knock is a sharp reminder of everything waiting for us on the other side of the door—the rebels, the mission, and Jamie. My chest tightens at the thought of him, his wide, uncertain eyes, and the way he clings to me like I'm the only thing keeping him tethered.

I let out a shaky breath, stepping back reluctantly. "We'll finish this later."

Solan nods, his gaze lingering on me, his hair still reaching like it doesn't want to let me go. "Later," he agrees, though the word is thick with reluctance.

Before we move towards the door, there's something I have to know. "Wait," I say, my voice softer now. "I need to ask you something."

His expression shifts, wary but open. "What is it?"

"You said... we'd share thoughts and feelings," I begin, struggling to keep my voice steady. "Is there a way to... block that? To stop it?"

The question seems to hurt him, the flicker of pain in his eyes a knife to my chest. His lips press into a thin line before he answers. "Sort of," he says after a moment, emotion making his English momentarily halt again. "We can... shield. Like dimming a light. Can block thoughts with practice."

"And emotions?" I press.

His gaze meets mine, intense and unyielding. "Emotions... always there. A shadow. Faint, but... always."

I nod, though the answer makes my stomach churn. The idea of someone else, anyone else, having that kind of access to my inner world is... unnerving. But with Solan, the thought isn't terrifying. It feels... right, somehow.

"There's one more thing," I say, my mind turning back to the rebel leader's words. "About the power— what we learned from Varek. You said you weren't sure of the true impact it would have on us."

Solan's jaw tightens, his gaze darkening. "I still don't know," he admits. "But Varek is right. Others could try to use it. Our bond... it's a strength but also a weakness. If someone took you, if they controlled you...." He trails off, the thought clearly unbearable.

I swallow hard, my horror mirrored in his expression. "Or you," I whisper, the enormity of it settling over me like a weight.

"It's why we must be careful," he says, his voice low and fierce. "Together, we are strong. Stronger than anyone other than other bonded pairs. But apart...."

The silence between us speaks volumes, the implications sinking in.

"It explains why Varek was so eager to welcome us," I say, my thoughts racing. "We could be a game-changer for them, couldn't we? Turn the tide of their rebellion."

Solan nods grimly. "Yes. And others will see it too. Not just the rebels. The realm... others.... They will all want what we have."

My mind flashes to Jamie, his small frame, and the weight of his trust in me. A pang of guilt cuts through me, sharp and relentless. What kind of life has he been dragged into?

"Jamie," I say, the name a plea. "What does this mean for him? He's just a kid."

Solan's gaze softens, but his expression remains serious. "It means he must be protected. Always."

"Should I...." I hesitate, the thought forming even as I speak. "Should I try to find a way to send him home? Isn't that the only way to keep him safe?"

Solan's brows knit together, his hair flickering with unease. "Home... if it's possible... it may be safer. But also...." He hesitates, his voice dropping. "It may not. There is no way to know if it is even... possibility."

I don't correct him, just wait for him to continue while recalling our much earlier conversation about the likelihood of returning home.

"No one person has made the rifts happen. It is all... fate," he lands on.

The ambiguity of his answer does little to ease my growing dread. "That you know of. Right?"

He tilts his head. "That I know of." He pauses. "You think it may not just be fate... the gods?"

I have no fucking clue. "Who knows?" I shrug my tense shoulders. "You didn't know about all humans being bonded, so you... *we* can't be absolutely certain someone or something isn't behind the merges." A tendril of excitement... of hope unfurls in my chest. "A single entity or more than one could be orchestrating this whole thing. Shaking up the whole damn universe and its dimensions... for this very reason."

"To pull together bonded pairs?" Solan asks slowly.

I shrug again. "I don't know, but it's a possibility, isn't it?" At his nod, I say, "And if that's the case, it means we can help Jamie. Protect him. Send him home."

Holy shit. This could totally work. If I'm right, all we need to do is figure out the arsehole pulling the strings and get him to create a new rift wherever Jamie is. My half-formed smile cuts off abruptly when my gaze catches Solan's. He looks.... Fuck. He's devastated.

His red skin has lost its warm glow, looking almost ashen. Solan's silence stretches between us, heavy and suffocating. His usually bright, fiery gaze is dim, the tendrils of his hair curling inwards as if in retreat. The sight of him—a creature so full of power and life—reduced to this haunted, vulnerable version of himself sends a pang of guilt straight through me.

"Solan...," I start, but he cuts me off, his voice low and strained.

"You wish to leave." The words aren't a question

but a quiet, gut-wrenching conclusion. "You do not want this bond."

"What?" I blink, startled. "That's not what I—"

"Why would you?" he interrupts, stepping back from me. His movements are slow, deliberate, like he's fighting to keep himself together. The inches feel monumental. Too far. The distance is jagged and gaping, slicing pain into my gut. "I am a monster. You have called me that. Perhaps you meant it as... jest or mistake. But it is truth, isn't it?" He gestures to himself, his four-fingered hands and towering red frame. "This form. This fire. I am not... human. And you...." His voice wavers. "You would not want this for Jamie. You want him free, with a choice."

My heart hammers in my chest knowing I've caused him so much harm, so much pain. I know better. Should have done better. What the fuck had I been thinking being so damn careless... so insensitive? I open my mouth to protest, to apologise, to try to fix this, but he barrels on, his voice thick with emotion. "The bond is not a cage, Jack. It is completion. It is life. It is finding the one being made for you. Jamie... he would *want* this when the time comes. To find his fated. To feel whole."

His pain is palpable, cutting through me like a blade. I don't miss the way his gaze flickers over me, cataloguing every difference, every reason he thinks I might reject him. The fingers, the flames, the tendrils of his hair that I've been mesmerised by. Things I've called monstrous, even in passing.

Fuck, what have I done?

The term *monster* burns in my mind now, the casual way I've used it feeling like a slap to both of us.

"Solan," I say, stepping towards him, but he retreats further, shaking his head. My heart cracks open, shame seeping through the break as emotion crawls up my throat.

"You wish for Jamie to have a choice," he says, his voice cracking. "And you resent that you did not. That this bond was... forced upon you."

His words hang in the air, heavy and damning. Do I resent it? I should, shouldn't I? But the truth is more complicated than that. My feelings are a tangled mess of logic and instinct, doubt and undeniable connection.

"I don't know what I feel," I admit, my voice raw. Tears sting my eyes. "It's too soon. Too much. I'm trying to figure it out."

Solan flinches, and the sight of it twists something deep in my chest.

He retreats further, the space feeling like an expanse impossible to cross over.

No. No fucking way.

"But," I race to add, willing to bare my soul, expose my damn throat if necessary, drop to my knees and beg for him to believe me as I take another step forwards and say, "I know one thing for certain."

He doesn't meet my gaze, his shoulders tense and braced for the worst.

"I don't want to leave you." My voice is firm despite the emotion I reveal, the tears clogging my throat. I exhale, and the truth of my words settles over me like a calming wave. "You're mine, Solan." Steel slithers into my tone, pushing away the swell of tears. "Whether it's fate or whatever the hell brought us together, I'm not walking away."

His eyes snap to mine, wide with something I can't quite place—maybe relief, disbelief, hope all tangled together. His hair flares slightly, a flicker of life returning to it.

"Mine," I repeat, softer this time. "I don't have all the answers. But I'm not going anywhere."

Solan exhales sharply as if he's been holding his breath, but the tension in his frame doesn't fully ease. "You say this now," he murmurs, his voice still tinged with doubt. I want to smack myself in the nuts for causing this doubt. "But you still question. Still hesitate," he adds.

"Of course I do," I say, my honesty cutting through the crackling air between us. "This is big, Solan. Huge. But it doesn't change how I feel about you. I don't want to leave you. I want to figure this out, seal the deal, as it were. I'm all in."

His expression softens, the fire in his wide gaze flickering back to life. "All in," he echoes as if testing the words. He steps closer, and I drag in air, my relief immediate. His towering frame fills my vision, a comforting presence, overwhelming in the best way possible. "You are certain?"

"I'm certain," I say, the steel in my voice returning. I reach for him and press a steady hand on his chest. "But I also want answers. About the merges, the rifts... everything. I can't argue with fate, but if fate has a hand in this, it has to work both ways. If Jamie's meant to stay, then fine. If he's meant to go home, then we need to find a way to make it happen."

Solan's lips press into a thoughtful line, but there's a flicker of understanding in his gaze. "You would trust fate?"

"Do I have a choice?" I shrug, a small wry smile tugging at my lips. "If this whole bond thing is fate, then yeah. I'm not about to argue with it. But it doesn't mean we can't try to figure things out along the way."

He studies me for a long moment, then nods slowly. "You are... unpredictable," he says, his voice lighter now, almost teasing. "I think I like that."

"You'd better," I shoot back, the tension easing between us.

His hair reaches towards me again, tentative but hopeful. I let out a shaky breath, feeling a small surge of warmth in my chest. I don't have all the answers—not about Jamie, not regarding this bond, not for what the hell comes next. But standing here, with Solan's fire brushing against my skin and his eyes locked on mine, I feel like maybe—just maybe—I'm exactly where I'm meant to be.

I ask, my voice quiet, "What age can someone become... bonded?"

"In my world," Solan says, his tone cautious, "it is... adulthood. For humans... I do not know. It is something you must... learn."

I nod, my mind already churning with the implications. Jamie is young, but since bonding is a possibility for humans, it's a danger I can't ignore. It also means we have time. It doesn't have to be worked out today, tomorrow, or even a year from now.

The knock comes again, sharp and impatient. Solan steps towards the door, his hair still flickering with residual agitation.

"Come," he says, his voice tense but steady. "We must go."

I follow him reluctantly, the weight of everything we've discussed pressing down on me. There's no denying it anymore—this bond, this power, this *world* —it's more than I ever bargained for. And somehow, I have to find a way to navigate it without losing myself —or the people I care about—in the process.

CHAPTER
THIRTEEN

The building they've given us isn't human-made, that much is obvious. The walls have a seamless, almost-organic quality to them, curving in places where sharp angles should have been. The ceiling arches slightly, faintly glowing veins running through the material like bioluminescent threads that cast a warm golden hue over the rooms. There are two small sleeping quarters and a main living space where Calythra has unrolled a mat, clearly intending to sleep there.

The structure is nestled among other similar ones only a short distance from the bowling alley the rebel leader's claimed as headquarters. Solan and I agreed—tentatively—to support the cause, or at least to take the refuge they've offered for the time being. Varek's made it clear there will be terms, but tomorrow, we'll talk shit out and figure out what exactly those are going to be.

For now, the focus is on rest. Or at least, that's been the idea.

Jamie has finally started to slow down, though it has taken some effort. Calythra's knack for engaging him, distracting him while making him feel seen, is impressive. My trust in him is growing even if I still don't understand what his intention is. But he's kept my nephew alive and safe, and now he's practically a second shadow, promising to keep an eye on everything as he settles into the living space.

I catch Jamie faltering. A quick swallow, a sudden glassiness in his eyes, and then he physically shakes it off, diving back into a game with Calythra. He's trying so damn hard to hold it together, and I hate it. I hate that he feels like he has to.

But as his yawns grow more frequent, I'm selfishly relieved. Tonight won't be the night reality hits him. If it does, I'll be here—with hugs, with quiet reassurances, with whatever he needs. But for now, I just need to get him to bed.

"Come on, mate," I say, nudging him towards the sleeping quarters. "You're about two yawns away from falling over."

"I'm not tired," he argues, but the words are punctuated by yet another yawn.

"Right," I say, grinning. "And I'm not your uncle."

Jamie rolls his eyes. "Fine. But if I have nightmares, I'm waking you up."

"That's what I'm here for," I say, guiding him into the small room. It's cosy, with a low, rounded bed that seems to mould itself to his shape when he sits on it.

As he settles under the strange silken covers, I kneel beside him, brushing his hair back from his face. His dark eyes meet mine, a seriousness in them that never fails to catch me off-guard.

"You okay?" I ask softly.

"Are you?"

I hesitate, then smile. "I'm supposed to be the one checking on you."

"Yeah, well," he says, shrugging. "You've got a lot of horse crap on your plate. I can tell."

My throat tightens, but I force a grin. "Stop being so bloody perceptive. It's annoying."

Jamie smirks, but the expression quickly fades. "I miss Mum and Dad." His voice is small, barely more than a whisper.

His words hit like a punch in the gut. "I know, mate." My voice is thick. "I miss them too."

He reaches out, his hand small but firm as it grips

mine. "We'll figure it out," he says, echoing words I've said to him countless times before. "Right?"

"Right." I squeeze his hand. "We'll figure it out."

For a moment, we just sit together, the silence heavy but not unwelcome. Finally, Jamie's eyes droop, and I lean down to press a kiss to his forehead. "Goodnight, kiddo."

"'Night," he mumbles, already half-asleep.

I stand and slip out of the room, closing the door quietly behind me.

In the shared space between where Jamie's snoring softly and where I plan to ruin Solan, I find my mate deep in conversation with Calythra. Their tones are serious but not heated, and I catch the occasional flicker of Solan's hair flaring before settling again. When he sees me, his expression softens, though he doesn't immediately break away from the conversation.

I wait until they finish, exchanging a brief nod with Calythra as he settles onto his mat. Then Solan and I make our way to our sleeping quarters, the tension from earlier still lingering between us like a taut wire.

The moment the door closes behind us, it snaps. The energy between us is palpable, an electric current humming through the air, charged with every unspoken word, each promise we've exchanged but haven't yet fulfilled. My pulse quickens, the space between us shrinking with every ragged breath I take.

Solan's hair reacts first, the tendrils flaring to life, wild and unrestrained, flickering like fire caught in a storm. It reaches towards me, seeking, just as his golden eyes lock onto mine with an intensity that steals my breath. That heated gaze burns through every barrier I thought I had left, leaving me raw and exposed.

"Jack," he starts, his voice a low, gravelly rumble that sends a tremor through me. There's a question in the way he says my name, a hesitance that tugs at something deep in my chest.

But I'm not about to let him second-guess us. "No more waiting," I murmur, stepping closer, my voice rough with the weight of everything I feel. The words are a promise, a declaration, and I see the way they land—his breath hitching, his stance faltering as if I've knocked him off balance.

I move my hands with deliberate slowness, finding the straps of his weapons first. I unclasp them one by one, the metal buckles releasing with quiet clicks that echo in the charged silence between us. Solan's chest rises and falls, each breath heavy, his eyes tracking my every move as if he's unsure whether to stop me or surrender entirely.

"Are you certain?" he asks. His voice is barely above a whisper, but it trembles with emotion, his hair tangling around my wrists, seeming desperate to pull me closer. The sensation of it—silken yet alive—sends a jolt through me, heat coiling low in my stomach.

"Absolutely," I say, my voice steady despite the storm raging inside me. I step even closer, so close that his warmth radiates into me, the faint scent of him—earthy and wild—filling my senses. "You're mine, Solan," I tell him, my tone firm, my conviction absolute. "And I'm done waiting to prove it."

His lips part, a soft exhale escaping him, but whatever he's about to say is lost when I find the fastener of his leather kilt at his waist. My fingers brush against his skin, the contact igniting something primal between us. His hair flares around us, a fiery halo that bathes the room in golden light, as though the bond between us is alive, pulsing, demanding to be acknowledged.

I feel completely certain—of him, of us, of the bond tethering us together. Every instinct screams that this is right, that he is mine and I am his. There's no more room for hesitation, no more room for fear.

And I am done holding back as I finally unclasp his kilt and let it fall to the floor.

I part my lips, my brows jumping high, my eyes widening.

"Holy fucking goodness and hail to monster dick." I can't look away. I try. Sort of. Okay, I barely try to meet his gaze to check that his huff is one of amusement at the way I'm eye fucking his cock like it's a trophy.

"I—" I've got nothing. No words. All I can do is stare. I'm pretty sure I'm drooling too. Definitely salivating. "Nnngh..." is the garbled mess of a word I finally land on.

"Jack."

The concern in his tone has me reluctantly pulling away. When I do, I wince at the uncertainty in his golden eyes and am quick to reassure. "You've...." I huff out a breath and clear my throat. "You've been freeballing all this time." Heat stings my cheeks. "Not that you appear to have balls, but fuck, anyone could have seen your cock." A flash of.... Fuck a duck.... Yeah, that's jealousy that swims in my vision.

Solan reaches for his kilt. Sod it all to hell. I'm doing a piss-poor job of letting him know what the sight of his dick is doing to me.

"No," I all but yell, making us both startle.

Another flash of heat touches my cheeks, this time in pure embarrassment. "You're fucking beautiful. Incredible." I manage to keep my eyes firmly on his rather than following the tempting trail down his tight abs to his mesmerising dick. It's a siren calling to me.

But I will not look away from his face. I can't. I need him to know I speak the truth.

The tightness around his eyes softens a fraction.

"You are... honestly, you're everything. Not a single inch of what I see doesn't do it for me."

"You're not... worried about our differences?"

My gaze widens before I narrow it, a sly smirk forming. "How exactly do you know we're so differ-ent? I'm pretty sure there are no movies with a full frontal of Arnie." Though I think there was an impressive one of his tight buns.

Holy shit. I stare hard, laughter trying to make its way out of my chest when somehow Solan turns an even deeper shade of red. "What exactly have you been looking at?"

When he glances away, I tug off my now-clean shirt, so relieved we were able to make use of the hot springs and herb-scented soap a short walk from the base. My movements immediately pull his gaze back to me.

"I'm teasing. I don't really want to embarrass you," I reassure him, softening my smile and reaching out for his large hand. Somehow, I still keep my attention away from his tempting dick. As soon as I catch a glance, I'm going to be done for. Mouth, arse, hand—whatever part of my body I can get on his cock, I'm good with.

"I—" His forked tongue peeks out, his eyes flashing, his tendrils going haywire as he rakes his gaze over my bare chest.

Do I preen a little? Fuck yes, I do. My muscles used to be gym created when I worked as a firefighter. These days, I'm farm strong... and hard. That Solan's clearly besotted with the fact that I have hair is a fuck of a turn-on.

"You?" I push, making quick work of my belt, jeans, and socks, revealing myself fully to him.

Words I don't understand fly out of his mouth. The heat in his gaze rises to inferno levels as every muscle of his locks up tight, as though he's restraining himself from pouncing on me.

Fuck that.

Before I can pounce right back, he says, "I found picture books in an Earth house."

I arch my brow, a salacious grin appearing. "You did, huh? What exactly was in these picture books?"

Solan's swallow is loud. "Humans, free of material."

When I stay quiet, he steps closer, his muscles losing some of their tension. Since every cell in my body is screaming, "Fuck me, Solan," he's undoubtedly more than certain that I'm on board with everything he's saying and absolutely everything I want us to do together while naked.

"The one male had his hand on his"—he dips his gaze down to my dick—"cock. Another picture was of two men. Both on their middle legs."

Middle legs? Their dicks?

"Here." He leans forwards slightly, pressing his hand to my knee.

"The men were on their knees? Fucking?" A breathy moan punctuates my question. Just saying "fucking" aloud makes the pull almost impossible to ignore.

"Fucking?" Solan repeats, his head tilting further, a crease forming between his brows. The flickering tendrils of his hair freeze midair as though his brain has hit a processing error. "That is... the loud word humans shout? The angry one? Like Arnold Schwarzenegger?" He deepens his voice in an uncanny imitation of the actor. "*What the fucking hell are you doing?*"

I freeze. For half a second, I just stare at him, torn between laughing so hard, I can't breathe and sinking into the floor to die of second-hand embarrassment. "Bloody hell," I manage, pinching the bridge of my nose as my shoulders start to shake. "You've been learning English from *Schwarzenegger* movies." It's a reminder to myself more than anything.

Solan frowns, confused by my reaction, his hair beginning to flicker again. "He is... human leader, yes? Very respected?"

That does it. The chuckle bursts out of me, loud and uncontrollable, and I struggle to get words out while inwardly preening that his English has devolved because he has sex on the brain. "He's not—he's not a leader!" I gasp, tears pricking my eyes. "He's a movie star, Solan. An actor." I don't want to get into the whole "leadership" position he had in the US. Plus, I should perhaps have had this whole conversation with him when I first discovered the DVDs. I can't help but wonder why he didn't realise that movies are fictional. Christ knows what he really thinks about Earth and what a human's purpose is.

His frown deepens, his glowing golden eyes narrowing. "But he commands. He says the fuck word with great authority."

"That's... not what it means in this situation." I

swipe my face, trying to rein in my laughter, though my body is still shaking with aftershocks.

Solan looks utterly bewildered, which only makes it harder.

"Okay, okay, listen." I hold up a hand, attempting to restore some semblance of seriousness. "Yes, *fucking* can be a cuss word, but it also means... uh...."

He leans closer, his tendrils practically vibrating with curiosity. "Means what?"

"It's...." I clear my throat, suddenly feeling a little warm under his intense gaze. "It's also what we're about to do. When people have sex, Solan. Making love. Complete the bond with our bodies. That kind of *fucking*."

Understanding dawns in his eyes like a sunrise, warm and bright—and then it turns into something far more dangerous. His lips curl into a slow, wicked smile, and his hair whips the air like a wildfire catching a gust of wind. "Ah. *This* is fucking." He steps closer, his towering frame blocking out everything else, his voice dropping to a seductive rumble. "You will teach me the human way."

I swallow hard, the laugh in my throat replaced by a rush of heat. "Oh, I'll teach you," I murmur, meeting his gaze, my chest rising and falling as the tension between us spirals higher. "But I promise you'll pick it up pretty quick."

Does my brain stutter, wondering what sex means to his species? A little. And I definitely want to know more, but considering he's absolutely down for exploring human sex, the knowledge takes over every other thought or possibility.

He leans in, his hand brushing my hip, the barest contact making me shiver. "Then fuck me, Jack," he growls, clearly testing out the phrase. His attempt at confidence wavers for half a second before his lips twitch into a grin. "Did I say it correctly?"

I groan, my head tipping back as I release a strangled laugh, the sound mingling with the heat building between us. "You're a bloody menace," I tell him, reaching for him, my hands tangling in the tendrils of his hair, which causes a shiver to rack his body as I pull him close. "But, uh... yeah, you got it right. But I'm kinda hoping you want to fuck me."

And it's no use; I can't hold back anymore: I finally look down at his cock.

Fuck. Me. Dead.

Or sideways.

Or anyway he wants.

I sink to my knees, wide-eyed and fixated, desperate to get a closer look. Tingling buzzes through my fingers, which are eager to touch and explore, and yeah, I'm definitely salivating.

His dick is a good nine inches. Big enough to make me know I'll feel the sting, the burn, and every delectable inch, but not enough to horrify me.

Without a doubt, I can take him.

I swallow hard. He definitely doesn't have balls.

The deep red of Solan's skin is darker on his dick, a shade that reminds me of glowing embers, rich and mesmerising. It's impossible not to stare, to trace the fascinating details with my eyes. His cock is smooth and thick at the base, tapering into a blunt point that's narrower at the tip. There's no foreskin, no opening, just unbroken, gleaming skin that looks both alien and breathtakingly enticing.

I reach out, my fingers trembling slightly, unable to resist touching him. The ridges circling the end draw my gaze first—three rings, subtle but prominent enough to promise sensations I've never even dreamed of. My cock twitches, and I clench reflexively, imagining what those ridges will feel like inside me.

But it's the barbs that truly capture my attention. Small, no more than five millimetres, they line the underside of his cock, each one perfectly symmetrical and somehow... beautiful. They don't look sharp, though they make my heart race in anticipation. When I run a tentative finger along one, it pulses under my touch—a soft, rhythmic movement that has my breath hitching.

"Holy shit," I whisper, my voice shaky. "What... how does that even—?"

Solan groans low in his throat, his head tipping back as his tendrils whip through the air, glowing faintly in the dim light. "Jack," he rasps, his voice rough and strained. "You are... killing me."

I force myself to tear my gaze away and look up at him. His face is a picture of intensity, golden eyes molten, his teeth gritted as if he's barely holding himself together. But it's his hair that leaves me speechless. The tendrils have grown longer, the strands thinning and shimmering, almost translucent. They're slick, wet with something that glistens faintly. I realise, with a jolt, they're creating lube.

"You're kidding me," I breathe, unable to stop the awed laugh that escapes. "Your hair is making lube? That's a thing?"

"They are to prepare you," Solan says, his words tight, like he's forcing them out through sheer will. "They will help... stretch, make you ready. If you allow it."

I blink, overwhelmed but achingly curious. "And

the barbs?" I return my hand to his cock, ghosting my fingers over the ridges before brushing the underside. I can feel the faint heat they're emitting, small pulses that resonate with his energy.

"They will not hurt you," Solan promises, his gaze locking with mine, fierce and protective. "They secrete heat, small pulses. Their purpose is... pleasure. To make you fall apart, to ensure your release. To make you mine."

Bloody hell. My head spins, and my body feels like it's on fire just from hearing him describe it. "You're really stacked for this, huh?" I murmur, a teasing grin tugging at my lips. "Designed to ruin me."

Solan's lips twitch, and he huffs a shaky laugh. "Ruin you?" He leans closer, his voice dropping to a growl. "No, Jack. Bond with you. Cherish you. This is what I am for."

His words, raw and sincere, hit me like a double kick from a roo, leaving me momentarily speechless. But I'm not done exploring. Not by a long shot. Leaning in, I press my lips to the ridged head of his cock, tasting him for the first time. The heat is intoxicating, and the slight saltiness of his skin leaves me hungry for more. I swirl my tongue over the ridges, savouring the texture, before trailing down to the barbs. When I flick my tongue against one, Solan groans so deeply, it vibrates through my chest.

"You taste incredible," I tell him, glancing up to see his reaction. "Are you always hard like this?"

He shakes his head. "No. But since meeting you, all it takes is a thought."

Fark.... He's a walking, talking, perfect mate, always ready to go. Hell if that knowledge does make my dick swell.

His tendrils are practically writhing now, some curling down to brush against my shoulders, slick and warm.

"Jack," he chokes out, his voice trembling. "If you do not stop, I will...."

"Fall apart?" I grin, emboldened by his reaction, before taking him deeper into my mouth. The barbs pulse against my tongue, sending a rush of heat through me, and I moan, my own cock throbbing painfully.

It's almost too much for both of us. Solan's hands come down to my shoulders, his strength evident as he tries to pull me back. But I'm not ready to stop. Not until he's gasping my name. I hollow my cheeks and take him deeper, letting the ridges and barbs tease my lips and tongue.

Suddenly, with a growl, Solan grips me more

firmly, lifting me effortlessly from my knees. His lips crash into mine, swallowing my startled gasp. His hair wraps around us both, slick tendrils pressing against my skin in ways that leave me trembling. They trail down my back, exploring, teasing, and then —holy shit—they find my entrance.

I break the kiss, gasping as the first tendril presses gently, stretching me in ways that make my head spin. "Solan," I breathe, clutching at his shoulders. "What—?"

"They will prepare you," he repeats, his voice a husky whisper. "If you wish."

"Oh, I wish," I pant, arching into him as a second tendril joins the first. They're warm, slippery, and impossibly gentle, probing and stretching until I'm trembling and moaning against him. Each touch is a promise, every movement laced with care and reverence.

And hot—so fucking hot and sexy.

The growing bond between us pulses, a living thing, heightening every sensation, every emotion. I can almost feel his need, his desire, his love, and it's close to being overwhelming. "I need you," I whisper, my voice shaking. "Now, Solan. Please."

He doesn't make me wait. His tendrils withdraw, leaving me gasping at the loss, but then he lowers me to the bed and positions himself, his cock pressing against my slick hole. His hands cradle my hips, strong and steady, his gaze searching mine.

"You are mine, Jack," he says, his voice rough but tender. "And I am yours."

I nod, unable to speak, and then he pushes forwards, slowly, carefully, until he's fully seated inside me. The stretch is intense, the ridges and barbs igniting nerves I didn't know I had, and I cry out, my head falling back as pleasure overtakes me.

Solan stills, his tendrils wrapping around me, holding me close. "Are you all right?" he asks, his voice filled with concern.

"Better than all right," I manage, my words coming out in a breathless rush. "You feel... amazing. Don't stop."

And then he moves, and I swear I see stars.

The heat of Solan inside me is consuming, all-encompassing. It burns and stretches me in ways I didn't know were possible, and I welcome it, every inch of him. His cock moves with deliberate intensity, and the ridges at the tip drag against my walls, sending shivers through me with each stroke. But it's the barbs that undo me, pulsing lightly as they press into me. Every pulse feels like a small explosion of pleasure, radiating outwards and igniting my nerves.

His thrusts pick up speed until they are hard and fast, punishing, and I feel every drag, push, and pull of him inside me. The sound of our bodies meeting—skin against skin, the wet slap of flesh—fills the room. It's raw and animalistic, but beneath it is something deeper, more intimate. Our whimpers intermingle, his low groans syncing with my desperate gasps, and the quick, frantic beat of our hearts is a rhythm I can't escape.

It's everything. It's too much. And yet I want more.

His tendrils don't stop their exploration. Two of them are already wrapped around my cock, slick and warm, stroking me in perfect time with his thrusts. My head falls back, a guttural moan spilling from my lips as I lose myself to the sensations. The tendrils move with a precision that feels designed to drive me insane, their grip firm yet gentle, coaxing me higher with each movement.

A third tendril joins the others, and I can barely distinguish the sensations anymore. I'm so far gone in the haze of pleasure that I don't even realise I'm gasping his name until I hear him respond.

"Jack," he growls, his voice low and primal. The sound is like a physical touch, curling through me and making me clench around him.

"Solan," I manage, gripping his shoulders, my nails digging into his skin. My body is on fire, every nerve ending alight with sensation. The heat is unbearable, but I embrace it, letting it consume me. "I... I don't know how much longer I can...."

Before I can finish, two more tendrils press against my entrance. My eyes widen as they slide in alongside his cock, the stretch almost too much. Almost. The burn is exquisite, a perfect counterpoint to the pleasure, and I cry out, my voice breaking.

"Fuck!" The word is half curse, half plea.

His mouth crashes against mine, swallowing the sounds I make. His fangs graze my lower lip, drawing a sting of pain that only heightens the pleasure. His forked tongue slides against mine, teasing and tasting, and I melt into the kiss. It's possessive, claiming, and I let him take everything he wants because I want it too.

"Jack," he murmurs against my lips, his voice thick with emotion. His golden eyes blaze with an intensity that leaves me breathless. "You're mine. Always."

"Always," I echo, my voice trembling. I mean it with every fibre of my being.

The tendrils inside me begin to move, pulsing and stretching me further. The sensation is indescribable, a mix of pleasure and pressure that has me trembling. I can feel his cock still thrusting, the ridges dragging against my walls in a way that makes my eyes roll into the back of my head. The barbs pulse with heat, tiny bursts of warmth that send me spiralling closer to the edge.

"Solan," I gasp, my voice breaking as my release builds. "I'm... I'm gonna—"

"Let go," he says, his voice rough but tender. "I've got you."

The tendrils around my cock tighten, stroking me faster, and I can't hold back anymore. My orgasm hits me like a tidal wave, my body locking up as I spill between us. The intensity of it is overwhelming, my vision blurring as pleasure courses through me.

As I come, I feel a new sensation—a heat spilling inside me. It's not from his cock but from the tendrils, which pulse as they release, just the ones deep inside me. The warmth spreads through me, filling me in a way that feels impossibly intimate.

And then it happens.

The bond snaps into place, a surge of energy and emotion so powerful that I cry out again, my body racked with another orgasm. A fresh rope of cum spills from me, my oversensitive cock twitching in his tendrils' grip.

"Jack." Solan's voice fills my mind, not out loud but felt. It's a prayer, a plea, filled with love and reverence. The connection is everywhere, wrapping around my soul and binding us together. His emotions flood me—his love, his devotion, his awe—and I can't hold back the tears that spring to my eyes.

"Solan," I whisper aloud, my voice trembling. "You're... you're in my head."

"And you in mine," he replies, his mental voice soft and reverent. *"It is... everything. You are everything."*

I am?

I have no idea how, but though the connection is strange and overwhelming, it feels right. It feels like coming home.

As the tendrils inside me begin to retreat, I shudder at the sensation. My body is hyperalert, every nerve ending tingling as they leave me one by one. When the last one withdraws, I feel an ache—a sense of loss—but it's quickly replaced by the warmth of Solan's arms around me. His cock is still inside me, pulsing gently, and I hold onto him, not ready to let go.

"You were made for me," I whisper, my voice thick with emotion. "And me for you."

And fuck if I don't feel like a sappy shit, but this is

what he does to me. Turns me inside out and makes me feel complete in ways I don't fully understand.

He kisses me then, soft and slow, his forked tongue sliding against mine. It's a dance, a promise, and I lose myself in it, letting him claim me all over again. His tendrils, no longer inside me, stroke my skin instead, gentle and soothing. Even as my cock softens, they continue to pet me, coaxing every last tremor of pleasure from my body until I'm completely spent.

Finally, Solan pulls out, slow and careful, his sated golden gaze locked onto mine. I wince slightly at the emptiness, but his hands on my hips and his tendrils wrapping around me make me feel grounded.

"Rest," he murmurs, his voice soft but commanding.

I nod, too exhausted to argue, and let him guide me under the soft covers. His arms wrap around me, his tendrils cocooning us in warmth. The steady beat of his heart against my back lulls me into a blissful haze, and as sleep takes me, my last coherent thought is that I've never felt more whole.

CHAPTER
FOURTEEN

"DID YOU HEAR THAT TIME?"

A huff of amusement is Solan's initial answer. "No, Jack." He nuzzles my neck.

For the past hour since we woke—still too early for Jamie to be racing around—I've been testing the whole "read my thoughts" thing that Solan previously mentioned.

Something clearly got mixed up in translation, which, honestly, thank fuck for that.

Solan *can't* simply read my thoughts, and I can't his. And if I could, he'd be thinking in Pyronoxian anyway, right? Unless being bonded transcends the need for thought translations. And if not, it would mean I wouldn't understand a bloody thing. But I've been "thinking" everything from the lyrics to "Down

Under" to memories on the farm to my days as a trainee firefighter. Each time, what Solan's received are impressions of emotions—the key feeling linked to whatever I'm thinking.

"Talking" directly to him, however, mind to mind is a whole new ball game.

It took exactly two seconds for me to open up the pathway to speak to him in my mind. The words, the first time and every time since, have reached him in a flash. I don't know how exactly I do it, or even what the difference is between random thoughts and speaking to him—intention maybe—but it works, which is bloody awesome.

It's also a lot less intimidating or worrying than I'd thought just yesterday when he told me more about our bond.

"Okay, try again," I say, half grinning as I shift closer to him.

"Jack," Solan groans, a mix of amusement and exasperation in his low, gravelly tone. "You are relentless."

"You love it."

"Perhaps."

He's toying with me now. I can feel his affection mingling with his amusement through the bond, and it makes me grin. I close my eyes, focussing on sending him a clear message: *"I'm starving. Breakfast soon?"*

His answering laugh is a rich rumble that vibrates against my chest. "You could just say that aloud, you know."

"But where's the fun in that?" I tease, rolling onto my back. The movement makes me more aware of that strange thrumming sensation in my skin. It's been there since last night, when the bond snapped into place, and I haven't quite figured it out yet.

I frown, focussing on the energy. It feels warm, like it wants to move outwards, and I... push at it?

The bed bursts into flames.

"Shit!" I yelp, scrambling to my knees as the fire licks at the sheets.

Solan is already moving, laughing so hard, he's practically wheezing. He grabs the jug of water from the table to the side of the room and douses the flames in one swift motion.

The fire goes out, leaving the sheets scorched and steaming. The mattress, miraculously, seems salvageable.

"I'm so sorry," I blurt, horrified. "I didn't even know I could do that!"

Solan sets the jug down, still laughing, his golden

eyes sparkling with amusement. "You truly are a marvel, Jack."

"Marvel? I just set the bloody bed on fire!" I gesture at the ruined sheets.

"Yes," he says, still chuckling. "But you did it with such enthusiasm."

I groan, rubbing my face with my palm. "This is not how I imagined testing my new abilities."

Solan sits beside me, draping an arm around my shoulders. His tendrils, still slightly damp from the water splash, wrap around me soothingly. "When I was young, my flames first emerged while I was hunting with my father," he says, his voice warm with nostalgia.

"Yeah?"

He grins, his sharp fangs catching the morning light. "I got... excited and set an entire field of *halyse* ablaze."

"Oh shit," I say, horrified but unable to suppress a laugh. It doesn't matter that I don't know what *halyse* is. I can read between the lines.

"My father was not pleased," he continues, his expression turning sheepish. "He said I was lucky the elders didn't banish us from the village."

"Well, at least you didn't burn your own bed," I mutter, glaring at the ruined sheets.

Solan's laughter booms again, and I form a smirk.

"I think we might need flameproof everything if this keeps up," I say. "Do you reckon the rebels are desperate enough for our help to give us fireproof accommodation?"

Solan raises an eyebrow, his expression sly. "We'll have to see. In the meantime…." His gaze dips to my bare chest, and the bond hums with a wave of heat and affection.

"Don't even think about it," I warn, though I can't keep the smile off my face. "We've got to get dressed before Jamie rocks up."

As if on cue, the faint sound of movement echoes from the other side of the building.

"See?" I say, scrambling for my jeans. Fuck, hearing that means there's little doubt Calythra heard us last night.

Solan moves with far more grace, pulling on his leather kilt and strapping it in place.

I pause, my mouth going dry as I realise he's going commando. Again.

"Do you have to?" I ask, gesturing vaguely at his kilt.

His golden eyes gleam with mischief. "Do I have to what?"

"Never mind," I mutter, yanking on my jeans and

shirt. It's a little torn from yesterday's scuffle, but it's clean, so it'll do.

When Solan straps on his leather chest harness and weapons, I feel a twinge of possessiveness. The way he looks is... distracting. And if anyone else notices, I might actually lose my mind.

"Jack," Solan says, his voice low, pulling me from my thoughts. "You're staring."

"Am not," I mumble, turning away to find my boots.

He chuckles, and I feel his amusement through the bond.

By the time we make it to the main room, Jamie is sitting at the table, looking far too awake for this early in the morning. Calythra is standing nearby, a plate of food in hand.

"Morning," Jamie chirps, his smile wide.

I breathe a sigh of relief. He looks good—better than he has in days. "Morning, kid."

Calythra passes me a plate, a smile aimed our way. "We need to move soon. The leader is expecting us so he can take us to the camp."

I nod, glancing at Solan. "What do you think?"

He settles into a chair beside me, his tendrils brushing lightly against my arm. "I think we'll need to be cautious. The rebels may need our help, but their priorities might not align with ours."

I nod, taking a bite of the surprisingly decent food. "Our priority is keeping Jamie safe."

"Agreed," Solan says, his golden eyes serious. *"And you,"* he tags on in my mind.

Jamie looks between us, his expression a mix of curiosity and determination. "You think they'll really trust us and want us here?"

Calythra snorts. "Trust is a luxury we can't afford right now. Prove ourselves useful, and they'll keep us around."

"Awesome," I mutter, earning a smirk from Calythra. I then glance at Solan and say to him through our link, *"I think Jamie being human and our bond is enough to make them keep us around."*

He answers with a grunt in my mind, one of clear agreement but a whole lot pissed off. Solan glances at me and says aloud, "We need to find out more about their plans. A rebellion has a score, right?"

"Score?" It takes a beat. "Goal?" At his nod, I say, "Yes. They don't seem to simply want to live out their days peacefully outside of the sovereign's rule. You know, like a separate state or something"

"Agreed." Calythra bobs his head. "From the maps

and parchment I saw yesterday, they have a plan to take down the monarchy."

"Shit, really?" Panic claws at my chest. I don't want any of us to be in the thick of that.

"From what I can tell. I only saw a few sheets, but it doesn't seem like they're only looking for separation, nor is it just about saving those who came through the merges over the years."

"They couldn't possibly take down a whole monarchy, right?" I look at Calythra, then Solan. To do such a thing would be all-out war. Human history has taught me that. "Based on the headquarters alone, it doesn't seem like they'd have the capacity or numbers to do that."

Solan answers, "Remember, we only saw what they wanted us to see. We don't know their true strength or numbers."

"Maybe we should just leave."

I startle at Jamie's words, a pang of emotion smacking me in the chest that he's listening and involved in such discussions. But he's also not wrong.

"This is a big world, right?" I ask Solan. Hell, are there other continents or at least different land masses? Are there oceans? I could kick myself for not paying better attention to the maps littered around the rebel HQ yesterday. "We could go somewhere

else, find a place to live, to be safe, away from...
everything?"

Solan's expression darkens, but it's Calythra who
speaks first. "Where, exactly, would you go?"

I frown, the question hitting me harder than I'd
expected. "Somewhere safe. Somewhere far from all
of this."

"And how would you get there?" Calythra's tone
is matter-of-fact, cutting through my flimsy hopes like
a blade. "You don't know this world. You don't know
its dangers."

I bristle, but Solan's hand on my arm stops me
from snapping back. His voice, calm and steady, cuts
through the tension. "Jack, this world isn't like yours.
The dangers aren't just in the people. They're in the
land, the waters, the very air you breathe in some
places."

Jamie shifts uneasily in his seat. "But we have
tons of deadly creatures in Australia. Right, Uncle
Jack?"

Solan exhales, his golden eyes locking onto Jamie
with a seriousness that makes my heart ache. "It's a
little different here. There are three main land
masses in this world. This one—" He gestures
vaguely. "—is the only habitable one. The Green
Waters separate the condiments, but they're filled

with creatures so large, they could swallow a water vessel whole."

Continents. Shit, and only one can be lived on.

"Wait, what? Like, something big enough to take down a giant ship?" Jamie's voice rises slightly, his face paling.

"Think of them like the monsters in your big waters," Solan continues, his tone grim. "But worse. Much worse."

I think back to the *klaustras* on the first day in Terrafeara and struggle to hold back a shudder.

Jamie's jaw tightens, and for a moment, he resembles his mother so much, it hurts to look at him. "And the other countries?"

I exhale a heavy breath, feeling a knot tighten in my gut. "Solan's right. Leaving isn't an option. Not if we're talking about crossing the ocean." I glance at Solan, then Calythra. "What about the land?" I ask, backing Jamie's request for more information about what he called "countries." I have a feeling things work very differently here and that everything is governed by a single monarchy. "You said there are three land masses. What about the others?"

Calythra answers this time, his voice low and grim. "One's a wasteland. Too wild and dangerous for anything to survive for long. The other is plagued by earth fire and shakes."

Jamie blinks, clearly confused. "Earth fire?"

It takes me a beat to figure out what Calythra means. "Volcanoes," I say, my voice quiet. "And shakes are earthquakes." Or at least I think so.

The realisation dawns on him, and his face falls. "So... this is really the only place we can stay?"

Calythra smiles, the expression kind. "I'm afraid so, kid."

I slump back in my seat, the weight of our reality pressing down on me like a physical thing. My chest feels tight, my mind racing with all the possibilities— none of them good. "Brilliant," I mumble, deadpan. "So, what? We're stuck here, dodging a tyrant queen and hoping not to piss off the wrong people?"

"Basically," Calythra says with a shrug.

"Encouraging," I grumble, earning another sharp-toothed grin from him.

Jamie's voice, quieter this time, pulls me from my spiralling thoughts. "Someone has to stop her, right? If she took people and is making them do bad things for her. She's using them as slaves, right, Uncle Jack? We did a whole project at school, and Mr Johns said...." He pauses, his brow furrowing as he searches for the exact words. "He said slavery isn't just about chains and whips. It's when people get treated like they're not people. Like they don't matter. It's the worst thing you can do to someone. And if no one stops her, it's like saying it's okay, right?"

His words hang in the air, heavy and sharp, cutting through my haze of worry. I glance at Solan, whose golden eyes are focussed on Jamie with an intensity I can't quite place. Calythra, too, has stilled, his usual smirk replaced by something unreadable.

I swallow the lump forming in my throat and force myself to respond even as my chest tightens at the weight of Jamie's understanding. "You're right, mate. It's not okay. It's never okay."

Jamie's gaze meets mine, steady and unflinching. "So... someone has to stop her," he says again, the quiet determination in his voice making it clear that he's not asking this time. He's telling me.

His words hang in the air, heavy with the kind of idealism that only comes from youth. I want to tell him he's wrong, that it's not our fight, but the truth is, I don't know if I believe that myself.

I place a hand on his shoulder, giving him a reassuring squeeze. "Let's focus on staying alive first, yeah?"

He nods reluctantly, but I can tell the fire in him hasn't dimmed.

The conversation shifts to plans and next steps as we finish our meal. Solan and I exchange glances, the unspoken understanding between us clear—we need to tread carefully with Varek. I'm about to suggest we start preparing when a thought hits me, sharp and unwelcome.

"Wait," I say, pausing mid-motion. "If we're going to talk to Varek about staying and helping... what's their plan for us all?" Yesterday, Varek didn't disguise the hard-on he had that he was welcoming a fated pair or a young human. But I refuse to be used as a pawn or for our growing power.

"We'll make it clear that our priority is Jamie's safety," Solan says. *"And yours, always,"* Solan adds in my mind, his tone firm.

It takes all my willpower not to roll my eyes. *"Yeah, yeah, mine too. But that means us and no one trying to abuse our bonded power."* It takes everything in me not to add air quotes to "power" as I think the word. That wouldn't earn me any strange looks. *Not.* Sure, I can set a bed on fire, but the rest is hard to grasp and come to terms with.

Solan's lips twitch, but he doesn't argue. Instead, he stands, his broad frame casting a shadow over the small table. "Let's go."

THE WALK TO VAREK'S QUARTERS FEELS longer than it should, tension thick in the air. Calythra's presence is a steadying one. Jamie stays close, his yabbering about everything he sees and everything else on his mind a contrast to the heavy mood.

And Solan.... Hell, I couldn't do any of this without him or his gentle waves of reassurance travelling through our bond.

When we arrive, the same monster—I hold back a wince... *guard*—I noticed before is stationed outside. Its eyes—too many and too sharp—follow us as we approach. I swallow hard, forcing myself to focus on Solan's steady presence at my side.

The guard steps aside without a word, allowing us entry into the bowling alley. Varek stands near a wall covered with writing I can't even begin to decipher. His massive frame appears even more imposing today. Beside him is Shanae, her piercing eyes appraising us as we enter, despite her small smile.

"Welcome," Varek says, his voice low and resonant. "I trust you've had time to consider your position here."

As far as greetings go, I suppose that one makes it clear what his priorities are.

Solan steps forwards. "We have concerns," he starts, his tone measured but firm. "We're willing to support the Riftborn, but our agenda isn't to take down the monarchy."

Shanae's gaze sharpens, but Varek raises a hand, silencing whatever comment she might have made. "Not everyone here seeks the monarchy's destruction," he says slowly. "But you must understand, many do. This isn't just about survival for them—it's about freedom."

I step in, my voice steady despite the nerves twisting in my gut. "We get that. But our priority is keeping Jamie safe. If that means staying here and pulling our weight, we're willing to do that. But we're not soldiers."

Not technically true, I know, considering Solan's job title and that Calythra is in training.

Varek's silver eyes lock onto mine, piercing and sharp, his expression unreadable. He nods once, a slow, deliberate gesture that carries weight, before looking away. "You're a hunter, aren't you?" His gaze is trained on Solan, calculating and curious. "*Kelvarra.*"

Solan tenses slightly, though his expression remains neutral. "I was. Once."

I glance between them, reality setting in. *"Shit,"* I murmur through our bond. *"When you left, you really left. Will there be a warrant out for you or something?"*

"And now you're here, tied to a human and playing rebel," Varek muses, his smirk sharp. "Interesting turn of events."

As he speaks, Solan uses the bond to say, *"I do not know warrant, but the queen's soldiers will be looking for me."* He seems to hesitate.

"What?" I push. Everything about what's happening here needs to be shared. There can be no holding back.

"If they find me, they will take me to the queen's assembly and demand answers. It is unlikely they'll let me leave, at least not without a way to ensure loyalty."

"How?" Before he can respond, he focusses back on Varek.

"I'm here because I choose to be," Solan replies, his voice carrying a quiet authority that silences any further probing.

Despite his calm demeanour, I can feel the undercurrent of tension in him through our bond. His voice is low and measured when he says, "I can offer what little insight I have. I worked outside the queendom, in the market town of Myra's Crossing. It wasn't the same as being within the sovereign state, but I observed enough to understand their methods."

It's a carefully chosen explanation vague enough to satisfy curiosity without revealing too much. What he doesn't say is that his connection to the head merchant of that town—the man who is his sister's father-in-law—is a secret he intends to keep. The rebels might see such a tie as a liability or a threat—though more likely as something to be bargained with—and Solan knows better than to risk it.

Varek offers a smile, though it's not one I wholly trust. "Any insight is valuable," he says simply, though there's an edge to his tone that suggests he'll be keeping a close eye on Solan.

The heavy air between us doesn't dissipate, though his demeanour shifts slightly. He tilts his head, studying us both for a moment before his lips curl into the faintest smirk. "Good. Then we'll take you to Dathanor."

He's about to turn away when his gaze flicks back to me. His smirk deepens, a gleam of amusement flickering in his silver eyes. "Congratulations on completing your bond."

Heat floods my face in an instant. I whip my head around to look at Solan, who seems utterly unbothered, his smug expression making my mortification ten times worse. I resist the urge to groan aloud.

"How does he know?" I ask through our link, my mental voice sharp and indignant.

Solan shrugs and speaks with the mental equivalent of a casual drawl, *"Does it matter?"*

"Yes!" I snap, glaring at him.

He smirks in response, clearly enjoying my discomfort.

Varek doesn't linger on my embarrassment, turning instead to issue orders to his people. As the group begins to move, I take a steadying breath and fall into step beside Solan.

We walk in silence for a while before Solan's voice threads into my mind, softer now. *"Varek's not entirely wrong about bonds. They're... obvious, in a way. To those who know what to look for."*

I glance at him, my curiosity momentarily overriding my irritation. *"And what exactly should I know about what's obvious?"*

Solan's lips twitch into a faint smile, though there's something guarded in his gaze. *"Your scent has changed. Stronger, more entwined with mine. Your energy too. To someone like Varek, who's lived long and seen much, it's unmistakable."*

That doesn't make me feel any better. *"Great. So*

now everyone knows we're bonded because I smell different?"

"Not everyone," he assures me, though the teasing glint in his eyes suggests he finds my indignation amusing. *"Only those who are perceptive."*

I narrow my eyes at him. *"You're enjoying this far too much."*

"Perhaps," he admits, his voice rich with amusement.

Solan's amusement still caresses my mind by the time Varek has finished talking with his crew and gets us to leave. The first thing we do is collect Geralt and Ridge. They've been fed and watered, and I thank Shanae profusely when I realise she's also organised for them to be brushed down. I've been a pretty shitty horse owner since being here.

The journey to the rebel town—Dathanor—stretches out in quiet tension as we make our way. The group moves at a steady pace, Solan and I sticking close together while Jamie shares his horse with Calythra. My stockhorse, Geralt, surprises me with his composure. Even in this strange terrain, with different species and odd contraptions surrounding us, he handles it with the same steady gait I've trusted for years.

Most of the rebels travel on foot, their movements

ranging from fluid and swift, while some are heavy and lumbering over the uneven, rocky ground. It's like they've been shaped by this terrain, their strides effortless where mine feel precarious. Thank fuck I'm on Geralt's back. Solan walks beside me, his steps powerful and deliberate, his eyes ever watchful. He doesn't stray from my side, his hand occasionally brushing Geralt's flank as though anchoring us both.

A few among the group ride peculiar vehicles—contraptions that remind me vaguely of scooters, though sleeker and more "other" in design. Their purr is subtle, almost like the whisper of wind through tall grass. How silent they are is impressive. It's clear they're not powered by anything familiar. No electricity hums in the air, no engines roar. The energy feels... alive. I think of the elemental trick Solan showed me before—the way, with a flick of his hand, he powered the light in his home. Is that what drives these machines?

Jamie's voice drifts to me as he chats with Calythra, his awe at the strange landscape and the company of monsters bubbling over into endless questions. Calythra answers him with surprising patience, his voice a gentle rumble punctuated by Jamie's sharper, more eager tones. For a moment, I'm grateful for the distraction it gives my nephew.

The terrain grows rougher as we progress, jagged rocks jutting up like the bones of the earth. The air takes on a different quality, heavier and tinged with a faint metallic taste that sits on my tongue. I feel it the moment we cross through the wards, an almost-imperceptible ripple that tingles across my skin.

Then, as though the world shifts around us, the rebel town comes into view.

Nestled against a ridge of rocky hills, Dathanor is unlike any place I've ever seen. The settlement seems to rise organically from the landscape, its structures carved directly into the rockface. Glowing veins of bioluminescent green and blue trace patterns along the cavernous walls, casting an otherworldly light over the area. The effect is eerie but mesmerising, like standing inside a living, breathing organism.

The town is layered, with pathways spiralling upwards and downwards, connecting a network of caves and platforms that cling to the cliffs. Wooden bridges, ropes, and ladders stretch precariously between levels, swaying slightly with each breeze. At ground level, makeshift tents and lean-tos are scattered in clusters, their inhabitants bustling with purpose.

"This used to be underground," Shanae says to us as we dismount. "The rift brought it to the surface.

The floating rivers obviously didn't stick. The gravity of Terrafeara makes it impossible."

Varek gestures for us to follow, his silver eyes glinting in the bioluminescent glow. "The wards don't keep anyone out," he explains as we walk. "That's not their purpose. They work as a cloak, concealing the town from view unless you pass through them."

The ingenuity of it impresses me, though it doesn't loosen the knot of unease in my stomach. This place isn't just a refuge. Apparently, it's a war camp, and the purpose behind its creation is evident in every detail.

Armed rebels move with precision, their steps purposeful as they go about their tasks. A group practices with weapons on a platform above, their strikes sharp and deliberate. The clanging of blades echoes faintly through the cavernous space.

"This isn't just a place for people like us to live safely," I mutter to Solan through our bond.

"No," he agrees, his golden eyes scanning the surroundings. *"It's not. There's a lot of activity and weapons."*

I catch sight of Jamie as Calythra helps him dismount. My nephew's wide eyes are glued to the glowing patterns on the walls, his curiosity unbridled. Despite everything, a small smile tugs at my lips. His awe is a comfort, a reminder that even during chaos, there's room for wonder.

Solan steps closer to me, his presence steadying as the weight of our situation settles heavily on my shoulders. *"Stay sharp."* His voice is low and grounding in my head. *"This is no place for carelessness."*

I nod, sweeping my gaze over the town as Varek leads us deeper inside. The activity around us is relentless, the air thick with tension and purpose. This is a community on the brink, not just surviving but preparing for something far greater.

It's fucking terrifying.

Sure, there's a small collection of market-type stalls and cave-shaped domes being used as stores. There are smaller species racing around, and I think they're young... kids rather than small monsters.

"How many live here?" I ask. I can't see the end of the settlement or how many dwellings are here.

Varek stops and glances at me, his gaze assessing. I completely get it if he doesn't te—

"With the four of you, it brings us to 527."

Parting my lips in surprise, I gasp, looking around once more.

"There are also several hatchlings due and eight births imminent."

Fuck.

Shanae steps to Varek's side. "This is what we're trying to protect. Almost every single person is Rift-born, born outside of Terrafeara. Children, parents, grandparents. Some have lost loved ones to the queen. Everyone else is running for their lives, refusing to be used to empower the sovereign state. Used until they're no longer of value." Her words are impassioned, determined, her American accent thick and her deep brown eyes swimming with emotion.

"Shanae lost someone."

Somehow I don't startle at Solan's voice in my head. I study Shanae, my gut hurting at the pain she reveals. And it's not only that, but as a Black Southern woman, it's likely she has some pretty fucking harrowing family history with enslavement, right?

"This is why it's not enough to just hide. We have to make things change."

I open my mouth, but no words come. I don't know what to say. What can I possibly offer in the face of what she's experienced? I've never faced this kind of loss, this kind of fight. Okay, I've been ripped from Earth, but I'm not ready to truly deal with that just yet. And sure, I've seen tragedy. I've pulled people from burning buildings, watched as homes crumbled to ash. But this? This is something else entirely.

Shanae's gaze shifts to me, and it's not accusatory—it's just steady, waiting.

I glance at Solan, my thoughts brushing against his like reaching for a hand in the dark. *"I have no idea how to respond to this. I've never been in her shoes. Not even close."*

"You don't need to have been," he replies, his mental voice calm and reassuring. *"You listen. You acknowledge. That's enough for now."*

I nod slightly, his words a perfect cool breeze on a hot Queensland day. Shanae doesn't press, instead turning back to Varek to ask something about supplies. Jamie, however, is watching her like she's just lit up a classroom.

"What did you do back on Earth, Shanae?" he asks, his voice carrying that innocent curiosity that only kids can pull off. "Before you came here?"

Shanae's lips twitch into a faint smile. "I was a teacher. High school history and government."

"Did you teach about slavery?" Jamie asks, his expression serious.

Her smile fades, replaced by a softer, more reflective look. "I did. We talked about a lot of things—slavery, civil rights, Indigenous rights.

Things that shaped the world and still affect people today."

"What did your students think?" Jamie tilts his head like he's filing away her answers for later.

Shanae sighs. "Some of them understood how big and awful it was… still is in some countries. Others…. Well, some thought it didn't matter anymore. That it was just history, something they didn't have to worry about."

Jamie frowns, clearly not satisfied with that. He shifts on his feet, his mind visibly working through her words.

Solan steps closer to me, his voice low in my mind. *"Jamie's thinking harder about this than most adults."*

I nod, watching my nephew. His voice comes again, quieter this time. "Mr Johns said it's everyone's responsibility to make things better, even if it's hard. 'Cause if you don't, you're just letting it happen."

My chest tightens at his repeated words from earlier. Jamie's always been sharp, but this? He's still making statements, asking probing questions that I'm not sure I have the courage to answer. He's right, though. I know he is.

Solan clears his throat, speaking aloud now. "Wise words, Jamie. It takes courage to face something wrong and do what's needed to stop it. But it's not always clear what the right thing is."

Jamie looks up at him, his expression steady. "So, what's the right thing now?"

Solan hesitates, the weight of the question clear in his golden eyes. "We learn. We understand what's happening here and why. And when the time comes to decide, we stand together."

There's a flicker of approval in Shanae's gaze as she listens. I feel a similar surge of admiration, both for Solan's words and for Jamie's determination.

Still, the questions linger in my mind. I reach out to Solan telepathically. *"I've been thinking more about the rifts. About why they happen. If someone is creating them deliberately, maybe it's the queen—under her order—or someone else entirely. Varek said the crown fears the power bonded pairs have. What if this is about controlling that power?"*

His thoughts sharpen, his attention immediate. *"Go on."*

Before I do, I see that Calythra is speaking to Jamie, while Varek is talking to Shanae, giving us a moment to speak silently. *"If they bring people here and intercept them before they meet their fated mates, then they control the power that comes from the bond. They could harness it for themselves. But if that's the case, why? What's the endgame?"* I wonder if it is her or someone acting on her behalf and if it's about securing the strength of her queendom.

Solan doesn't answer right away. When he does, his voice is cautious. *"It's a possibility. But it's not something we should bring up to Varek yet. Not until we have more answers."*

I agree, but the thought gnaws at me. If we're right, it means this entire situation is more deliberate —and more dangerous—than I'd imagined.

Jamie looks back at me, his gaze steady and far too wise for his age. "Uncle Jack, we can't just do nothing."

His words cut through my swirling thoughts. He's right. Again. As much as I want to shield him, to keep him safe and hidden, and to brush aside his words, I know it's not that simple.

"Yeah, mate," I say quietly, the weight of his conviction settling over me. "You're right. We'll figure it out. Together."

Varek is quick to pounce. "So, you'll join the cause?"

Bloody hell. Is that what I'm agreeing to? "It's not just up to me."

Calythra straightens. "If it's what Jamie wants, then I'm here."

I wince, not wanting this responsibility at all. But wanting and the right thing to do are two different things.

Jamie looks at me with determination. "I'm in, Uncle Jack. We have to stop her."

Fuck it all to hell.

Solan, standing beside him, nods firmly. "Count me in too. We'll do whatever it takes."

I glance at Calythra, then back at Jamie and Solan, my heart sinking. "All right. We'll do this together. But no one gets hurt." *Or taken or gets dead,* I add silently to myself.

Varek's grin is wide and disarming as he takes a step towards us. "Welcome to the rebellion."

CHAPTER
FIFTEEN

I can't look away. Solan's pearlescent horns in my grasp while I fuck his throat is quite possibly the hottest thing I've ever seen, let alone experienced. His large fingers clutch my arse, spreading me open and holding on. But it's the third tendril slipping inside my channel that finally has me looking away from his sexy-as-fuck horns.

"Fuuuckkkkk." I drag the word out, arching my back and looking at the rough-cut ceiling of our cave room, eyes catching on the blue veins pulsing with light. "There." My grunt follows as my hips stutter.

My cock is wedged in his throat. I try to pull away, but he holds tight, swallowing around me while brushing one of his tendrils over my prostate.

"Holy fucking shitting hell... fuuuckkkkk!" I love

everything about his hair, his tendrils: how much control he has over them, when he chooses, how they react almost instinctively to me and my needs. Everything.

He pulls away with a pleased grunt, loosening my cock from the tight squeeze of his throat and then lapping at me.

"Solan." I snap my eyes to his, then down to his forked tongue, which he strokes over my dick. "So fucking good." I shudder, and his eyes move to mine, heat and lust swirling in their depths.

Last night, Solan took great delight in finding my prostate and discovering what exactly it does to me. Right now, what we should be doing is cleaning the group of cave rooms we've been assigned while Calythra entertains Jamie, but it's taken us less than seventy-two hours of completing our bond to work out that once we're alone, it's damn near impossible to keep our hands—or our mouths—off each other.

"You taste like molten fire," Solan murmurs against my skin, his voice low and rough, sending a shiver through me. "Like sunsets over burning fields, all heat and sweetness." He presses a hot kiss to my thigh, then another, trailing up until his mouth closes around my cock again.

I groan, tightening my grip on his horns, the

smooth surface warm under my fingers. There's a faint texture to them, like glass kissed by the sea, polished but alive, radiating his energy. When my thumbs trace the ridges near their base, his entire body jolts, his throat tightening around me.

"Fuck, Solan," I gasp, sliding my hands along the length of his horns, savouring the way his breath hitches. I wonder, wild and half-drunk on lust, if I could actually ride one of them. Am I dexterous enough to pull it off? I almost laugh at the absurdity of the thought, but the idea clings, sparking heat in my veins. Even if I can't, his tongue is plenty long enough to hit my deepest spot—and those damn tendrils—

One snakes deeper, teasing my prostate again, and I lose all coherent thought. My hips jerk forwards, forcing him to take me further into his throat, and he growls, the vibration echoing through my core.

I tighten my fingers instinctively on his horns, and he moans, the sound almost a plea. His arousal spikes, a physical wave that crashes into me through our bond. I feel him grow harder and hotter against my thigh, his need feeding mine in an endless loop.

"Shit—Solan—I'm—" The words barely escape before pleasure explodes, ripping through me like wildfire. His tendrils tighten their hold, his mouth working me through it, and I swear I see a whole sparkling galaxy.

He groans around me, and I feel his release follow, the pulse of his orgasm hitting me as if it were my own. Our bond flares, emotions tangling together—desire, love, satisfaction—until I can't tell where I end and he begins.

He pulls away slowly, pressing one last kiss to my oversensitive cock, then drags himself up to hover over me. His tendrils curl possessively around my thighs, and his lips brush my ear as his voice slips into my mind, molten and sweet. *"You're mine, Jack. Always."*

I shudder, pulling him down into a fierce kiss. We stay tangled together for a moment, catching our breaths, his weight grounding me even as the lust between us still simmers.

But reality isn't far behind. I sigh, breaking the silence. "We should probably get to work before Jamie starts asking too many questions."

Solan grins, a devilish glint in his eyes. "Agreed. But you're not leaving this bed until I've kissed every inch of you."

I laugh, swatting his chest, though I don't entirely disagree. "You've got five minutes. Then we clean."

"Deal." He nips at my neck, his fangs scraping my

skin, before finally pulling away, his expression shifting to something more serious. "After we clean, we have to meet Varek. Strategy talk."

I groan, half hoping he'd forgotten. "Not sure how much help I'll be there. Running a cattle farm and fighting fires isn't exactly rebellion training."

Solan brushes his hand over my cheek, his confidence steadying me. "You bring more than you realise. You've already brought me back to life."

I flush at his words but don't argue, letting him pull me into another kiss before we untangle ourselves to face the tasks ahead.

Once we've organised our new—temporary?—home a little better, we seek out Jamie and Calythra. They're with the horses, and Jamie's apparently been giving a young Glowranth riding lessons.

There are several Glowranth here in the rebellion settlement. From what Shanae has mentioned over the past couple of days, more than thirty Glowranth, some with families and from all walks of life here on Terrafeara, have joined the Riftborn cause. Though, as Calythra mentioned, not all are necessarily here with the freedom of the Riftborn as their reasoning. They're focussed on their freedom too.

Go figure that it's not only humans who struggle to live in a society oppressed by dictatorship.

"How many Glowranth are there in this world?" I ask Solan, my gaze remaining fixed on Jamie and the way he's using a mix of hand gestures, facial expressions, and Calythra's translations to explain to a Glowranth, who I can't even begin to guess the age of, how to hold the reins correctly. He's smiling and encouraging, and fuck if his enthusiasm and kindness don't make my heart ache.

Solan's warm palm presses against my spine, comfort pulsing through our bond. I swallow hard but don't mention how grateful I am for his silent support. I don't need to. Not when he feels everything so acutely.

"The queen likes to keep an accurate record," he says.

"I bet she does," I respond, deadpan. All the better to control if she knows who her citizens are.

He grunts in the affirmative. "Each town and district has a record keeper who works with the *Harethrin*."

I nod, recalling the mention of the *Harethrin* before and it being the mayor of sorts.

"Myra's Crossing is the largest merchant town in Terrafeara outside of the city's merchant quarter. Each district, and there are seven in total outside of the main city where the queen's stone castle is, has a merchant town for exchanging and purchasing goods." He turns his large eyes on me. "They are surrounded by settlements, usually within a few hours' travel, some much closer depending on if the Glowranth have access to transportation."

There's still so much to learn about this world. It's going to take me years to discover and process everything.

"Myra's Crossing has a population of 7,315. That was the last count."

My brows spring high at the number. So much bigger than I expected but still a small town compared to Earth's standards—or at least Australia's. But back home, we have a huge expanse of land and a tiny population. I'm sure it's something like 40 percent of Australia is uninhabitable while 90 percent of Aussies live within fifty kilometres of the coast.

If Terrafeara, this... dimension... is the same size as Earth, that means the population is tiny. But then again, I have no idea how big this land mass is. Do I even need to know? Maybe I'm getting caught up in the wrong details.

"So that means what...?" I fall quiet, trying to figure out the maths, albeit only loosely with no idea of the population of the city. "The whole population of Terrafeara is close to... say, a hundred thousand, max?" That's a super loose guestimate.

"That sounds accurate. Remember, lots of creatures enjoy the taste of Glowranth and any other species that have found themselves here."

I scrunch my nose just thinking of our first encounter with the six-legged monster the size of a Jeep. While Glowranth are the dominant species, there appear to be more than enough dangerous other varieties around to cull the population.

"And procreation for Glowranth is not easy."

Curiosity about why that is threatens to get me off track. There was a reason I was asking about the population in the first place, and that was because of the number of rebels in the Riftborn rebellion. Maybe 527 isn't as terrifyingly low as I first thought. But that absolutely doesn't mean I want to be fighting in a war.

There has to be another way.

The ground shifts violently beneath my feet with a tremor so strong, it feels as though the entire world is threatening to split open. I steady myself, my pulse thundering in my ears as I look up.

A jagged crack slices across the sky, luminous white and impossibly bright, like lightning frozen in place. The air vibrates with an otherworldly hum, a deep resonance that sinks into my bones and makes every hair on my body stand on end. My stomach lurches, my instincts screaming at me that this is wrong—fundamentally wrong.

The sound comes next, a deafening roar like a thousand mirrors shattering at once. It's everywhere, all-consuming. Around me, there's yelling, a scramble for balance, but it's Jamie's voice that cuts through the chaos.

"Uncle Jack, loo—"

My gaze snaps to him just in time to see Ridge, his horse, rear back in panic. Jamie's small form teeters precariously in the saddle, his eyes wide with fear as he struggles to hold on.

Shit. He's going to fall.

My legs move instinctively, but it feels like I'm running underwater, every step heavier than the last. The pressure in the air is oppressive, thick, and suffocating.

"Solan!" I shout, but he's already moving.

Solan's form blurs as he surges forwards with inhuman speed, his golden eyes locked on Jamie. I don't even have time to process what's happening before Solan reaches the horse, his strong arms catching Jamie mid-fall with a precision that makes my chest tighten with relief.

The blinding light in the sky pulses again, brighter this time, and the rumbling intensifies. Ridge bolts, his hooves pounding against the ground as he vanishes into the chaos. I don't blame him.

By the time I reach them, Jamie is clutching Solan tightly, face buried against his shoulder. His small frame trembles, but he's safe, and that's all I care about.

"Got him," Solan says, his voice calm despite the commotion. His emotions, though—relief and worry tangled together—flood through our bond.

"Thanks," I manage to say through our telepathic link, my gratitude almost overwhelming. *"I don't know what I'd do if—"*

"He's fine, Jack. Focus," Solan cuts in, his tone firm but gentle.

He's right. The ground has stopped shaking, but the sky is still wrong, the crack bleeding white light through the green sky that seems to ripple outwards. The air feels charged, almost electric, and there's a low, persistent hum like the world itself is holding its breath.

Around us, the settlement is bedlam. Rebels and residents alike are either frozen—their faces etched with fear and uncertainty—or racing around in panic. Some are shouting orders, others are checking on loved ones, but one thing is clear: Everyone knows what this is.

Another rift.

"What the hell just happened?" I mutter, fixing my eyes on the sky despite being pretty bloody confident I know what this is.

Shanae appears beside me, her expression grim. "Another rift. A big one, by the looks of it."

"It didn't look like this when I came through," I say, the words slipping out before I can stop them. My memory flashes back to that day: the disorienting pull, the blinding light, and then waking up in this strange, terrifying world. This is not the same.

"Each one's different," Shanae says, her voice tight. "Depends on the worlds being torn apart."

A chill runs down my spine. Worlds. Plural. Somewhere, right now, entire pieces of another dimension are being dragged into this one. And something from Terrafeara is gone, replaced in the blink of an eye.

Jamie lifts his head from Solan's shoulder, his face pale but determined. "Is it over?"

"For now," Solan says, rubbing Jamie's back soothingly. But his golden eyes are fixed on the crack in the sky that's slowly fading, his jaw tight.

"Solan, Jack." Varek's voice snaps my attention

back to the here and now. The rebel leader is striding towards us, his silver eyes sharp and his expression unreadable. Behind him, several figures I recognise as part of the rebellion's inner circle are gathering.

"You felt it," Varek says, though it's not a question.

"Hard to miss," I reply, my tone dry despite the tension.

"Then you know what this means." His gaze shifts to Solan. "We need you and Calythra on this. Shanae will lead the team, but you're the best hunter we have, and Calythra is apparently trained."

Solan's emotions flicker through our bond—duty, resolve, and a flash of something I can't quite name. But there's hesitation, too, and I know why.

"We can't be apart," I say quickly, stepping forwards. "Not yet."

Varek's eyes narrow slightly. "You'd be going, too, then?"

"Not without Jamie," I add, my tone firm. "He's coming with me. I'm not leaving him behind."

"You want us bring weakling child into field?" one of the rebels asks in broken English, her tone incredulous.

"He's safer with us than without." Solan's voice is calm but laced with steel. And he doesn't give a shit that he's making it clear that we don't fully trust the Riftborn.

Shanae steps in, her expression unreadable but her voice steady. "They're right. If they can't be apart, it's better they stay together. And the kid's no liability. He's smart and tougher than he looks."

I glance at her, surprised by her support, but she doesn't look at me. Instead, she crosses her arms, her attention fixed on Varek.

After a long moment, Varek nods. "Fine. But if you're going, you follow Shanae's lead."

"You're sure about this?" Solan looks at me, his gaze steady. *"I can refuse. We can all stay here,"* he says just for me.

"Do I have a choice?" I ask, trying for levity but falling short. *"Besides, you're not getting rid of me that easily."*

His lips twitch into the faintest smile, but his worry bleeds through our bond. *"Stay close to me. No risks."*

"Same goes for you," I reply, my hand brushing his.

Jamie shifts in Solan's arms, his eyes wide but unafraid. "Are we going now?"

"Soon, mate," I say, ruffling his hair. "But first, we gear up. We've no idea what we're walking into."

The crack in the sky finally fades. Whatever's been pulled into this world is out there, alone and terrified. Hell, unless it's from a dimension filled with dinosaurs or some shit and gobbles us all up, it's better to convince myself that it's a person or a species who isn't going to try to eat our faces off.

And if they are defenceless—or even worse, human—then the crown will be hunting them before they can even catch their breaths.

We have to find them first.

The next hour is a blur of activity.

Jamie and I prepare our kit for travel while Solan and Calythra join the others to make a plan. The whole time, Solan keeps me in the loop with a constant flow of updates. It means that by the time the group of fourteen is gathered, I'm prepared to leave without any big surprises.

Well, almost no surprises.

One of our companions steps forwards, and I can't help but stare. The creature, called a *Sornath*, looks like it crawled out of a fever dream. It has a sinuous, serpentine body covered in iridescent scales that shimmer between green and gold. Its head is vaguely dragonlike with six gleaming eyes that seem to take in everything at once. When it moves, it doesn't walk so much as glide, its body undulating with an eerie grace.

"That's Nera," Solan says, sensing my curiosity. Yeah, we'll go with "curiosity" rather than the need to check my undies. "They're one of the few species with the ability to track rifts."

"No shit?"

"Exactly," he replies, his tone calm. "Nera can sense the energy left behind and follow it like a trail."

I watch as Nera turns their head towards the horizon, their forked tongue flickering out as though tasting the air. They make a low, guttural sound—completely incomprehensible to me—but one of the other rebels, a humanoid creature with bark-like skin, nods.

"Nera says the trail is faint but clear," the barkman translates, his voice a low rumble.

"Of course they do," I mutter under my breath, earning a glance from Solan.

"What?"

"Nothing," I say, shrugging. "Just trying to figure out how we're the ones who ended up ordinary. Humans, I mean. No super-senses, no dragon eyes, no tongue-tasting-energy tricks."

Solan's lips twitch into a small smile. "You can create fire."

"Yeah, because of you," I counter. "Before that, my greatest skill was being able to quote *Terminator 2* on command. Not exactly world-saving material, mate." I'm talking shit, nowhere near as big of an Arnie fan as Solan.

That gets a chuckle out of him, the sound warm and easy. *"Your skills are more impressive than you give yourself credit for."*

"You're just saying that because you're stuck with me," I reply through the bond, grinning when I feel his amusement ripple in return.

"Ready to move," Shanae says, cutting into our private moment. She's dressed in leather armour that looks well worn but sturdy, her black hair tied back into a loose braid. She catches my eye and smirks. "You coming, or are you too busy making googly eyes at your mate?"

Jamie snickers, and I glare at her. "We're coming."

We set out, the group moving in a loose formation with Nera leading the way. The scenery is unlike anything I've ever seen back on Earth. The ground beneath us is a deep slate grey, cracked and uneven like the surface of an ancient lava flow. Strange spindly trees twist skywards, their branches tipped with glowing orbs of light that pulse faintly, as if in time with the heartbeat of the world.

"Stay close," Solan murmurs, his hand brushing briefly against mine.

I nod, my grip tightening on Jamie's shoulder as he walks beside me. This is not the direction we came from a few days ago.

As we move, I fall into step with Shanae, who seems perfectly at ease despite the tense atmosphere.

She catches me glancing at her and raises an eyebrow. "What?"

"Nothing," I say quickly. Then, unable to resist, I ask, "So... you have a mate?"

She grins, her teeth Colgate white. *Fuck, I really need to figure out what to use to brush my teeth with when my toothpaste runs out.* "I do. Their name's Ril."

"Ril?" Jamie pipes up, clearly curious.

"Yep," Shanae says, her tone fond. "They're a *Gildryn*—a kind of species that looks like a cross between a giant praying mantis and a jellyfish. Beautiful, really, if you're into the whole bioluminescent, translucent vibe."

"Sounds... unique," I say, unsure how else to respond.

"Oh, they are," Shanae says, laughing. "I met them when they saved my ass from a pack of *klaustras*. I was pinned under one of those six-legged bastards, and Ril swooped in like some kind of glowing avenger. Scared the hell out of me at first. I thought they were going to eat me."

"Romantic," I say dryly, which earns me another laugh.

"Hey, it worked," Shanae says, shrugging. "Turns out *Gildryns* are big on loyalty. They've been by my side ever since—well, except for scouting missions. And let me tell you, having a mate who can paralyse enemies with a single touch is a real game-changer."

I glance at Solan, who's walking a few paces ahead. "Paralysing enemies. Sounds useful." And holy shit, that must mean she can do the same, right?

He doesn't turn around, but I feel his amusement through our bond. *"Don't get any ideas."*

The banter helps ease some of the tension, but the farther we travel, the more the unease of the group grows. The landscape becomes more rugged, the terrain littered with jagged rocks and deep crevices that force us to pick our way carefully.

Everything we pass looks part of this land. It doesn't seem like we've stumbled—or are even close to crossing—into a sliver of another world.

Nera suddenly halts, its head snapping to the side. It makes another guttural sound, this one sharper and more urgent.

"What is it?" I ask, my voice low.

The bark-man translates. "Something's ahead. Faint, but... there." He shakes his head. "But not the rift."

Shanae raises a hand, signalling for silence. The group falls still, every sense on high alert.

Then we hear it.

A distant scream, sharp and human, cuts through the air, followed by a deep, guttural roar that makes my blood run cold. The sound is close enough to send a flock of birdlike creatures erupting from a nearby tree in a flurry of iridescent wings.

Jamie presses closer to me, his eyes wide with fear.

"Stay with me," I whisper, my hand tightening on his shoulder.

Before we can react, another sound splits the air —a piercing, otherworldly shriek that vibrates through my skull. The pain is immediate and over-whelming, forcing me to my knees as I clutch at my head.

All around me, the others are dropping to the ground, covering their ears and eyes as the sound intensifies. Even Solan, usually so composed, so fucking strong, is grimacing in pain.

Through the haze of noise and agony, one thought pushes through: *We're too late.*

The scream cuts off as abruptly as it began, leaving a deafening silence in its wake. My ears ring, and I stagger to my feet, my vision swimming. Around me, others are slowly recovering, groaning and shaking their heads as they regain their bearings.

Solan is beside me in an instant, gripping my arm like a lifeline. Through our bond, I feel his fear and fury, a tempest barely held in check.

"I'm fine," I rasp.

"Stay close," he murmurs, his tone sharper than usual. His eyes flicker with golden light, his power stirring beneath the surface.

Ahead, Nera hisses low and urgent, its serpentine body coiling tightly. The bark-skinned rebel translates. "They've found something."

We move cautiously towards the source of Nera's focus, the tension palpable. The group fans out slightly, weapons drawn, every step deliberate. Then we see it.

The body lies sprawled across the cracked ground, unmistakably lifeless. It's not human—its skin is mottled grey, its limbs elongated, and its face bears no nose, just slitted nostrils and a wide, lipless mouth. A creature I've never seen before.

Before anyone can say anything, Jamie calls out, "There's someone else!"

We all turn to see him standing over another figure—a man, human, unconscious, dressed in snow-boots, a thin undershirt, and boxers.

"Jesus," I mutter, rushing to his side. "Snow-boots? Where the hell did he come from?"

The man's skin is pale, his lips chapped, and he's shivering despite the heat of the air around us. I press two fingers to his neck and feel a faint pulse. Relief floods through me.

"He's alive," I say, looking up at the others.

Blood smears across my fingers as I check his head for injuries. "Shit." I wipe my hands on my shirt, removing the stain.

One of the stronger rebels, a hulking creature with leathery skin and thick, hornlike protrusions, steps forwards. "I'll carry him," it rumbles, its voice deep and gravelly.

The man is hoisted onto the creature's back as Shanae instructs the leathery-skinned creature and one other to turn back, return to Dathanor, and let Varek know we're going to press on. We've still yet to find the rift, and we don't even know if the dead crea-ture was killed by the human or something else.

As they head away, my gaze remains on the limp form. The guy looks young, maybe early twenties. He's slim, fit... and those damn snow-boots just leave me scratching my head as I finally look away to follow the big centipede.

The next hour is tense, the group moving cautiously as we search for any other signs of the merge. The heat is oppressive, but there's no sign of snow—just more of Terrafeara's rugged, alien terrain. We stop for a break near a cluster of strange bulbous plants that hum faintly, their tendrils pulsing with colour.

I sit beside Jamie, who looks exhausted but determined. Solan stands nearby, his gaze sweeping the horizon, ever vigilant.

The attack comes without warning.

A hand clamps over my mouth, and I feel the cold press of a blade against my throat.

"Don't move," a voice hisses in my ear, thick with a heavy accent.

My heart races as I'm yanked backwards onto my feet, my captor dragging me away from the group. Out of the corner of my eye, I see another figure emerge—a Glowranth, its bioluminescent markings glowing fiercely. This one is larger, its movements precise and deliberate.

"Jack!" Solan's voice is a roar, and I feel his rage ignite through our bond.

The first Glowranth—the one holding me—steps

slightly to my side so I'm able to take them in. He... definitely male... is different from the others I've encountered, his features more refined, his presence commanding. A distinctive mark glows on his chest, a sigil etched into his skin like a birthmark.

"Prince Aelith," Solan spits, his tone dripping with venom.

The fuck?

This dick is the missing prince?

The Glowranth prince narrows his luminous eyes at Solan. "Hunter," he says in English, his voice cold. "Interesting company you're keeping, and days away from Myra's Crossing."

Solan steps forwards, his fists clenched, literal steam rising from his body as his anger reaches a boiling point. "I don't answer to you," he growls.

He says something sharp that pisses Solan off in Glowranthian. "Enough!" the prince then snaps, his gaze shifting to me. His nostrils flare as he sniffs the air, his expression darkening. "The human. Where are they?"

I manage a strangled, "What?"

The blade at my throat presses against my skin, and I feel a sharp sting as it nicks me.

"The human who arrived with the last rift," Aelith says, his tone icy. "I can smell them. We've been tracking the human for days. Tell me where they are, or—"

"Back off," Solan growls, his voice like thunder. His body is a furnace of heat, and I feel his power building, a storm waiting to be unleashed.

"Solan," I say through our bond, trying to calm him. *"Don't lose control."*

The tension is unbearable, and I see Jamie struggling against the bark-skinned rebel holding him back.

"Let him go!" Jamie shouts, his voice breaking.

"Stay back!" someone orders, but Jamie doesn't listen. He breaks free, charging towards me, and for a terrifying moment, I think the prince's bodyguard—a massive Glowranth in heavy battle armour—is going to strike him down.

Panic surges through me, and I react instinctively. Fire erupts from my hands, wild and untamed, forcing the bodyguard to back off. The flames don't touch anyone, but the heat is intense enough to make everyone hesitate.

I seize the opportunity to shove the prince's blade away and dive for Jamie, pulling him to safety the moment I douse my flames.

The prince's expression darkens, but there's something else there—shock. His gaze locks onto me, and for a moment, the world seems to hold its breath.

"You," he says, his voice low and dangerous. He sniffs again and seems to scent the air. "You're mine."

"Wh-What?" I manage, my chest heaving, the word somewhat strangled.

"I felt it the moment you arrived in this world," he says, his tone laced with grim certainty. "You're my fated mate. My bonded."

The words hit like a thunderclap, leaving me reeling. Solan's fury flares hotter than ever, his body trembling with rage.

Shanae steps forwards, her expression grim. "This just got a hell of a lot more complicated."

CHAPTER
SIXTEEN

THE TENSION IN THE AIR IS A TANGIBLE THING, thick and suffocating. Solan's hands are clenched into fists at his sides, his golden eyes blazing as he glares at the Glowranth prince. His entire body is practically vibrating with suppressed fury. I can feel his emotions through our bond, the raw mix of protectiveness and rage like a wildfire threatening to consume him.

"Solan, calm down," I murmur, though my voice is tight. I don't know who I'm trying to reassure—him or myself.

"Calm?" His voice, low and dangerous, feels like a warning growl. "He thinks you're his fated mate. *You.*"

"Yeah, well, that makes two of us who think it's bullshit," I snap back, but my throat feels dry.

The Glowranth prince, tall and elegant in that unnervingly monstrous way, watches me with narrowed eyes. His skin, that deep, dark blue that gleams faintly in the dim light, practically pulses with a faint bioluminescent glow along the ridges of his arms. The effect is both hypnotic and infuriating.

"It's not bullshit," he says, his voice smooth and cool, conveying just the right amount of condescension to make me want to punch him. "You carry his blood."

I glance down at my shirt, still stained from when we found the human man—the blood that I put there to rub the red stains off my hands. Realisation dawns, and a wave of awkward heat creeps up my neck.

"Wait, you think this blood is mine?" I bark out a laugh, the sound a little more frantic than I'd like. "Oh, mate, you've got it all wrong."

The prince's lips curl into a faint, disdainful smile. "Do I? You wield fire. You're strong. Stronger than any other human I've seen. Only someone worthy of my bloodline could—"

"Whoa, whoa, whoa." I hold up a hand, cutting him off. "First of all, thanks for the compliment, *Your Highness*." Sarcasm drips from my tone. "Second, this isn't my blood. It's from the guy we just found. Y'know, the unconscious, dehydrated bloke in his boxers."

The prince's sharp features tighten into an imperious glare, but before he can snap back, his bodyguard steps forwards.

The bodyguard is a beast of a Glowranth. Where the prince is lean and graceful, this one is towering and broad, his blue skin a shade darker, his glowing markings subtler, almost hidden in the shadow of his massive frame. His voice, when he speaks, is a low rumble in their native language.

I glance at Solan for a translation, but I don't need to ask. His voice slips into my mind, warm and steady.

"He's saying that it's possible you're telling the truth. The prince shouldn't make rash assumptions."

The prince snaps something back in Glowranthian, and for a moment, the two of them argue, their voices a mix of sharp and guttural tones.

"What's he saying now?" I ask, casting a wary glance between them.

"He says it's impossible for the human you found to be his fated," Solan replies aloud, his voice tinged with irritation. "He's basing that on...." Solan pauses, then lets out a scoffing laugh. "On your strength. He thinks you're *too strong* to not be his fated."

I gape at him. "Are you serious? What kind of logic is that?"

The bodyguard cuts through the prince's tirade with a firm, measured response in English. "My prince," he says, his voice deep but calm, "there is merit in his words. If the blood is not his, we must consider that the human he speaks of is the one you seek."

I blink in surprise at the sudden switch to English. Solan arches a brow, clearly as taken aback as I am.

"Wait, you speak English?" I ask, though why I'm surprised, since the prince spoke English better than some Aussies I know, is beyond me.

The bodyguard inclines his head slightly. "I do. My name is Kael."

"Well, Kael," I say, pointing at him with a faint smirk, "you're already my favourite Glowranth in this conversation."

The prince bristles at that, his bioluminescent markings flaring slightly.

Solan, though still fuming, lets out a quiet snort at my attempt at humour. *"Careful,"* he says in my mind, his voice tinged with reluctant amusement. *"You're going to make him jealous."*

Kael steps forwards, his massive frame casting a shadow over the prince. "We must consider what is best for all involved," he says firmly. "If the human you found truly carries your bond, then they are in danger. The queen will stop at nothing to claim them for her own purposes."

The mention of the queen sends a ripple of unease through the group. Even the prince's arrogance falters slightly, his expression tightening.

"Hold on," I say, stepping closer, "didn't you disappear? Everyone thought you'd been sucked into a merge. But you... you ran, didn't you?"

The prince's sharp gaze locks onto mine, and for the first time, there's something other than haughtiness in his expression. There's anger, yes, but also something raw.

"I left," he admits, his voice low, "to find my fated. To find them before my mother did."

The admission hangs heavy in the air, and for a moment, the tension shifts.

Kael nods, his glowing markings pulsing faintly. "We have been tracking them since the last rift," he says. "Not the one from earlier today."

I control my expression, aware that the last merge before today's was the one I came through. It must mean more than one happened at the same time. I wonder if that's happened before.

"We have always been a step behind." His gaze flicks to my bloodstained shirt. "This is the first sign we're close."

Shanae, who's been quiet during the exchange, steps forwards. "So you want your human?" she asks, her tone sharp. "We can't take him to the camp. It's too dangerous." She glances at her team.

"That's not your decision to make," the prince snaps, his arrogance back in full force.

"Actually," Shanae retorts, crossing her arms, "it kind of is. See, I'm the one who's responsible for keeping this group alive. And if you think I'm just going to hand over a Riftborn to you, you've got another think coming, *Your Highness*."

I'm pretty sure she's taking the piss with that emphasis, just like I did.

A faint smile tugs at my lips. Shanae's got guts, I'll give her that.

"What do you want, then? In exchange?" the prince demands, his bioluminescent markings flaring brightly.

The fuck? "What the actual fuck? You think you can bargain your way to get your hands on a human? Mate, you are responsible for a whole lot of bullshit surrounding Riftborn."

He snaps his teeth at me, and Solan steps close, releasing a deep, threatening growl.

Kael intervenes. "What Prince Aelith is most concerned about is his fated's health. Their well-being. He has no desire to use them or exchange them or even barter for them. He wants them safe and well and to have the opportunity to know them."

The prince stiffens at Kael's words, his lips pressing into a thin line, but he doesn't refute them.

Honestly, I'm impressed as hell with Kael. It's not every day you meet someone who can smooth over a Glowranth prince's ego while also diffusing a tense standoff.

"*You think he's telling the truth?*" I ask Solan through our bond, my thoughts dripping with scepticism.

"*Glowranth, especially those of the royal guard, pride themselves on their integrity,*" Solan replies, his mental tone even, but there's a hint of tension beneath the surface.

I scoff aloud before responding through the bond.

"Integrity? Really? Even though they're responsible for kidnapping Riftborn and hand-delivering them to their queen? Doesn't exactly scream 'moral high ground' to me."

Solan's golden gaze flicks to me, his jaw tightening slightly. *"Their role is to serve their queen, their queendom. As such, they believe they are upholding their integrity by following orders. It's deeply ingrained in their culture."*

"So kidnapping innocent people is just another day at the office for them?" My scathing tone filters easily into our bond. *"Great. Love that for us."*

Kael's deep voice pulls me back to the present. "The prince has no intention of harming anyone here," he says, glancing pointedly at Solan before his gaze shifts to me. "And while I cannot speak for the queen's actions, I can assure you that my prince's motivations are his own."

"And what are his motivations?" I ask sharply, my rifle still angled protectively in front of me.

Aelith's gaze locks onto mine, sharp and unyielding. "I will not allow harm to come to them," he says, his voice low but full of conviction. "Not to my fated."

"Right," I say, crossing my arms. "And what if your fated has no interest in you? What if they"—I use the pronoun deliberately, certain the prince doesn't even know the gender of his fated—"don't want to be here? What if—"

"Enough." Kael's voice cuts through my tirade, not loudly but with enough authority to make me pause. He sighs, a sound that's almost human in its exasperation. "Prince Aelith, perhaps now is not the time for declarations. If we are to gain their trust, we must first work together."

The prince bristles but says nothing, his glowing markings dimming slightly as he visibly reins himself in.

Shanae steps forwards, her voice cutting through the tense silence like a blade. "Here's the deal," she says, her tone brisk but unyielding. "We're taking you to our headquarters. You'll wear blindfolds to ensure the location stays secure. Once there, you can speak to our leader directly. We'll also check on the human we found, make sure they're coherent and healthy, and get them up to speed on what's going on, once they're awake and well enough."

Kael inclines his head, the glow along his skin dimming slightly as he considers the proposal. His gaze shifts briefly to Aelith, whose bioluminescence flares in protest.

"You expect me to trust you enough to blindfold me?" Aelith snaps, his voice dripping with disdain.

"Yes," Shanae replies bluntly. "Because if you don't, you'll have to figure out another way to deal with getting to your fated and keeping them away from your mom. Good luck with that."

Aelith's jaw tightens, his teeth slightly bared, but Kael intervenes again, his calm and steady presence a stark contrast to the prince's fiery arrogance.

"My prince," Kael says in Glowranthian, which Solan continues to translate for me, the guard's voice low and firm, "this is a reasonable compromise. We need their cooperation as much as they need ours. For your fated's sake, let's proceed."

Aelith mutters something under his breath that sounds distinctly unflattering, but he finally relents with a sharp nod. "Fine. But if this is a trick—"

"It's not," I cut in, tired of the back-and-forth. "We just want answers, the same as you."

Kael's gaze flickers to me, and there's something almost like respect in his expression. "We'll comply."

"Good," Shanae says briskly, clearly done with the posturing. "Let's move. The route's going to be complicated, so keep up."

THE JOURNEY BACK IS A TENSE ONE. WE'RE ALL aware we've not found the rift's location or anyone who came through it. There's no doubt that we all agree that this new development is more important, though.

Shanae leads us through a deliberately convoluted path, weaving through dense, thorny underbrush and terrain that shifts unpredictably. At one point, we cross a shallow stream, the cool water a brief respite from the oppressive heat of the forest.

Jamie clings to Calythra's side, his small face pinched with fear but resolute. I catch his gaze and try to smile reassuringly, but the ball of dread in my gut only tightens. How much more can he endure? How much longer before this world breaks him—or worse?

Through our bond, Solan's voice cuts through my spiralling thoughts. *"You're worrying again."*

"Of course I'm worrying," I reply, glancing back at Jamie as he stumbles slightly, Calythra steadying him with a gentle hand. *"He's been through hell. I don't know what kind of life he's going to have here—or if we'll ever get him home."*

Solan's golden eyes meet mine briefly, filled with quiet determination. *"He's strong. And he has you. That's more than most in this world."*

The thought warms me slightly, but the ball of dread doesn't entirely dissipate.

Once we reach a particularly dense grove, Shanae orders the prince and Kael to be blindfolded. Kael complies without protest, his calm acceptance once again impressive. Aelith, on the other hand, snarls in irritation but ultimately allows it.

"You're enjoying this far too much," he mutters as the blindfold is tied around his glowing face.

"Not nearly as much as you think," I reply dryly, though I don't bother hiding my smirk, given that the prince can't see it.

Jamie stays close, his small hand brushing mine occasionally as we move. I squeeze his fingers briefly in reassurance, but my mind is spinning. Aelith's arrogance aside, the idea of having the queen's son—even one who's apparently on the run from her—on the same side could change everything for the rebellion.

Through our bond, I reach out to Solan again. *"Do you think this could work? Having him on our side?"*

Solan doesn't respond immediately, his thoughts cautious. *"It's possible. If he's willing to stand against his mother, he could be the leverage we need to end the kidnapping and forced servitude of Riftborns."*

The term "servitude" stings, but it's an undeniable truth. If there's a chance to change that....

"And if he's not willing?" I ask.

Solan's mental voice turns sharp. *"Then we'll find another way. But for now, we focus on getting him—and us—safely to headquarters."*

The sun dips low as we finally approach the hidden rebel base, the dense forest opening into a concealed entrance carved into the side of a cliff. The air is cooler here, the shadows longer.

As we remove the prince's and Kael's blindfolds, Aelith glares at me, his bioluminescence flaring faintly. "Is this where you plan to keep me prisoner?" he sneers.

"Relax," I say with a sigh, not even sure why he's speaking to me since I'm not in charge of this shitshow. "No one's keeping anyone prisoner. We're just trying to figure out what the hell's going on—and make sure your fated is okay."

At the mention of his fated, Aelith's expression tightens, but he doesn't respond.

We enter the converted bowling alley. The air inside is cool and damp, the faint smell of mildew lingering beneath the metallic tang of supplies and machinery. It's an odd mix of comfort and chaos, but it's safer than anything out in the wilds.

The human we found isn't in the main area. I excuse myself from the group, unable to shake the thought of him lying unconscious. If he's awake, he'll need to see another human—someone familiar, or at least not a... well, a monster.

I find him in one of the side rooms, a small infirmary lit by soft, flickering lanterns. He's still unconscious, his pale face slack against the pillow beneath him. My years as a firefighter have taught me enough first aid to do a basic check, and what I find makes my stomach churn. He's malnourished, his skin drawn tight over his cheekbones, and his cracked lips scream dehydration.

"Is he stable?" I ask, my voice low to avoid disturbing the quiet.

A creature is working at his side, attaching a drip with deft movements of clawed hands. The creature is squat and hunched with mottled green skin and a trio of beady black eyes. It looks up at me briefly, emitting a low series of clicks.

To my surprise, Solan's voice echoes in my mind. *"She says the human will recover. The drip contains nutrients and rehydration fluids. Someone called Sonny, another human, has been tasked to look out for him."*

I blink at the new information. There are more

humans here? My heart picks up a little. I nod at the mottled-skin creature who's clearly taking good care of the unconscious man. "Thanks."

She inclines her head slightly, then returns to her work, her focus impeccable.

I leave the infirmary and return to the main area, where Aelith stands, his arms folded, in front of Varek. The leader is leaning casually against the counter of what was once the bowling alley's snack bar, but his sharp eyes are locked onto the prince like those of a predator sizing up its prey.

Aelith refuses to speak, his entire demeanour a fortress of stubborn silence. But as soon as he sees me, his glowing eyes snap to mine, and his rigid posture softens, just slightly.

"They're unconscious," I report, loud enough for everyone to hear, and still holding back the guy's gender (assuming they identify as male, that is). "But they're stable for now. Malnourished and dehydrated, but one of the medics is taking care of them. They'll pull through."

For a moment, Aelith doesn't move. Then his shoulders drop a fraction, and the tension in his jaw eases. His relief is palpable even if he'd probably rather die than admit it outright.

Kael, standing a few steps behind him, catches my eye and gives a small nod of approval.

Varek raises a brow, his expression caught somewhere between curiosity and amusement. "So, royal brat, ready to talk now? Or do I need to get more humans to give you updates?"

Aelith bristles at the nickname, but he doesn't rise to the bait. "I'm here to ensure my fated's safety," he says, his voice clipped. "If that means answering your questions, so be it."

His words surprise me, but even more surprising is the faint flicker of vulnerability beneath the arrogance. Maybe—just maybe—having him on board could actually work.

LATER THAT NIGHT, AFTER THE INITIAL CHAOS has settled, Solan and I sit outside, not too far away from the bowling alley, the quiet hum of the forest surrounding us. Jamie is safely asleep, and for the first time in hours, I feel like I can breathe.

Solan sits close, his presence grounding. His hand brushes mine, and I feel the steady warmth of his emotions through our bond—love, protectiveness, a quiet determination to see this through.

"You're thinking too much again," he says, a teasing edge to his mental voice.

"Can you blame me? This is all...." I gesture vaguely, letting the bond carry my tangled thoughts. *"A lot."* And that includes meeting Sonny, the Aussie who found himself here so long ago that it itches my brain.

Solan chuckles, the sound deep and rich. *"It's a lot. But we'll figure it out. Together."*

I turn to him, the weight of everything we've been through settling heavily on my shoulders. "You really believe that?"

He cups my face gently, his golden eyes locking onto mine. "I do. Because no matter what happens, we have each other. And that's enough for me."

The sincerity in his voice steals my breath, and for a moment, the chaos of the day fades away. His hand on my face feels grounding, anchoring me in the present when everything else seems to be spinning out of control.

"Okay," I say softly, leaning into his touch. "Together."

Solan's lips twitch, his expression softening but still carrying that signature intensity. "If it bleeds, we can kill it." The Arnie quote is delivered with a dramatic edge, his accent adding an unintentionally charming flourish.

I blink, caught completely off-guard. "Seriously? You're quoting *Predator* at me right now?"

He grins, unapologetic. "It felt appropriate. Besides, you like when I reference Earth movies. Admit it."

A laugh bubbles out of me, easing some of the tension coiled in my chest. "I don't know whether to kiss you or smack you."

"Both are acceptable," he replies smoothly, his golden eyes sparking with mischief. His hand trails down my face to brush my jaw, his touch igniting a shiver. "Though I'd prefer the first option."

"You're unbelievable," I mutter, shaking my head, though a small smile pulls at my lips.

"Unbelievably yours," he counters, the playful tone giving way to something deeper, more serious.

And damn it if that doesn't make my chest tighten.

Before I can reply, his expression shifts again, his gaze dipping lower as if cataloguing every inch of me. "An orgasm might help with the tension," he says, his voice low and teasing.

"Bold of you to assume I've got the energy for

that," I shoot back, though the heat creeping up my neck betrays me.

"True," he muses, his mental voice brushing against my mind like a caress. *"But maybe later, when we've survived this madness. I can think of plenty of ways to... relax you."*

His words send a delicious pulse of anticipation down my spine, and my mind betrays me with a flash of imagery: his body beneath mine, the faint glow of his horn lighting our skin as I ri—

Nope. Not now. I slam the mental door on that thought so fast, it could've singed me. "File that under 'things to revisit when we're not on a queen's hit list.'"

His chuckle echoes warmly in my mind. "Filed. But for the record, you'd look stunning."

"Shut up," I say, though the warmth spreading in my chest makes it hard to sound annoyed.

Calythra's voice cuts through the moment like a whip, coming through the doorway of the building we're staying in tonight. "If you two are done flirting, some of us are trying to sleep before tomorrow's shit-show begins."

I stifle a groan, clambering to my feet and adjusting my jeans. "Right. Sleep."

Solan's smirk is pure mischief as he stands and leans in close, his voice a private murmur meant for my ears alone. "But remember, after this is over, *I'll be back.*"

I groan audibly this time, unable to help the laugh that bubbles out of me. "You're impossible."

"I'm yours," he counters simply, his eyes glinting with a promise that warms me to my core.

As we head inside, his hand brushes mine briefly, a touch meant to steady us both. Whatever happens next, I know one thing for sure: We'll face it together.

SOLAN

Trees groan and sway, their ancient roots clinging to soil that might soon be replaced by something other.

The merges have grown more frequent, chaotic. Each one feels like a ticking clock, its echoes in the distance warning of worse to come. My jaw clenches. It's only a matter of time before the queen's hunters come calling. And if they don't find what they're looking for?

I will. I'll have no choice if it's demanded of me—my price for a relatively quiet life.

The thought sends a growl rumbling low in my chest. Myra's Crossing depends on order, and enforcing it is my job. Not because I want it to be, but because the queen has her claws in me. I'm strong, dangerous. My fire makes sure of that. I've always known it's why she keeps me close: to hunt, judge, and carry out her will.

I have it easier, better than many others, but her rule stings all the same.

The light in the sky fractures, a jagged line splitting through it. My stomach tightens. Almost as soon as it began, the shaking ceases, the forest settling into an uneasy silence. The *suymi*, small birdlike creatures that live high in the canopy, shriek their displeasure before fleeing, leaving behind an oppressive stillness.

It's over.

Or it should be.

I feel the snap before my brain catches up to the sensation. Something primal roars to life in my chest, hot and untamed. My fire stirs, eager, ravenous, like it knows what I don't.

My fated is here. My bonded.

The realisation rocks me. My blood sings in a way it never has, a melody so consuming, it leaves no room for doubt. I stagger a step, fists clenched as the inferno inside me threatens to escape. Whoever they are, they've crossed into this world. And they're mine just as much as I'm theirs.

No hesitation. I act fast, grabbing a bow, a quiver of arrows, and my blades from the stash on my wall. They're crude weapons for someone like me, but if the sovereign's forces are nearby, I can't risk using fire openly. I attach my blades to my chest straps, my mind already racing ahead of my feet.

I follow the pull in my chest, an invisible thread drawing me forwards. Hours pass, each one stretching my nerves tighter. The trees blur into a haze of orange and green as I run. I refuse to think of what might happen if someone else finds them first.

The sound of crashing and shouting shatters the quiet. My heart lurches. It's close.

Then the scent of blood. Sweet, impossibly familiar. My fated's. The scent is unique and known despite me never smelling it before. They've been hurt.

I pick up speed, ignoring the burn in my muscles. The forest opens into a small clearing, and I spot it: a six-legged behemoth, its scaled body gleaming under Terrafeara's strange sun. It's a *klaustras* as large as a *takari* transport pod back home and twice as deadly. Its serrated fangs drip venom, its massive claws tearing through foliage as it searches for its prey.

For what's mine.

Not today.

I nock an arrow, aiming for the soft spot beneath its jaw. The string hums as I let the arrow fly, striking true. The *klaustras* screeches, its massive head swinging towards me, but I'm already moving, loosing another arrow that buries deep into its exposed throat.

That's when I see them. Him.

Through the trees, past the beast, a human man stands protectively in front of a small human on top of the Earth horses. His clothing is strange and unfamiliar, but there's no mistaking the fire in his gaze. He holds a weapon from Earth, his stance braced despite the tremor in his hands.

My heart slams against my ribs. He's beautiful.

He's mine.

The *klaustras* lunges towards them, bloodied but determined. My fire surges, demanding release. I let it. Flames race down my arms, engulfing the arrow I nock next. When I let it fly, it explodes on impact, the beast's screech cutting off as it collapses in a heap of charred flesh.

The man stares at the dead *klaustras*, wide-eyed and wary, the small human shaking.

"Come," I demand, my words deep and barely controlled. He could have died, been killed before I got the chance to even know his name. I latch onto the English words floating in my head, ones I've spent years deciphering. "There will be more. *Klaustras* hunt in packs. That will have been its scout."

The man hasn't seen me yet. With a hitch in my breath and a pounding heart, I step out of the cover of the dense forest.

"You and the human child, come with me if you want to live," I say, my words a little stilted. I've learned them from one of the human leader's moving pictures—the ones I watched on the TV I scavenged from a previous rift. They felt right to use.

For a moment, he doesn't move. His gaze flicks to the still-smoking corpse of the *klaustras*, then back to me. I don't breathe, waiting for his decision.

Finally, he steps forwards on the horse, the child within touching distance.

My heart fills, an overwhelming mix of relief and something deeper I can't name.

I lead the way, my senses on high alert as we navigate the forest. Every step feels like a victory, but I know the real battle has just begun.

He's here. He's mine.

Now I just have to keep him alive long enough to make him see it. But I will. As deeply and as completely as I know myself, I know I will not fail to make sure the human lives, becomes mine, and shares my fire, embracing it as if it's his own.

Once he has, we'll be forever. Because I am Solan, and he... he is my destiny, my flame, the reason my fire was ever born.

BONUS SCENE 1

Solan's grip is tight on my hips as I lower myself down, his massive frame tense beneath me. His golden eyes are locked onto me, glowing with arousal, his chest rising and falling in deep, measured breaths. The tip of his horn presses against me, smooth and warm, pulsing with his energy. The intrusion is perfect—stretching me just right, filling me so completely that I can feel every subtle pulse, every shift of his body vibrating through me. And then—

"Fuck," I groan, shivering as the thick ridge catches my prostate just right, sending a bolt of plea-sure up my spine. "That feels—"

"Intense?" Solan supplies, voice rough, his hair strands curling around my calf like he needs another point of contact. His tendrils shift, restless, brushing against my thighs and teasing the sensitive spots he's mapped out over the last few weeks.

I let out a shaky laugh, dragging my fingers down his chest, feeling the heat of his skin. "Yeah, baby. Intense is one way to put it."

Solan's fingers twitch against my hips. "We do not have to—"

"Nuh-uh." I cut him off, gripping his horns for balance and peering down so I can meet his gaze. "You're enjoying this as much as I am. Don't even try to play the noble mate routine now."

His lips twitch, but a shudder wracks through him when I shift, deliberately grinding gently down, his horn pressing deeper, snug against my prostate. A ragged breath stutters from him, and his eyes flicker molten gold before he recovers, fingers tightening like he's barely holding back.

"I am enjoying it," he admits, voice hoarse. "Too much, perhaps."

I grin, slowly rolling my hips just to see him clench his jaw. The sensation is mind-numbing—the firm, unyielding press inside me, rubbing in a way that has my entire body alight with pleasure. Each movement sparks something deep and visceral, pleasure tightening in my core like a vice.

"That's the point, Sol. Let me take care of you for once."

A guttural sound escapes him, his tendrils snapping around my waist, dragging me closer as his control frays. "You drive me to madness."

I bite my lip, feeling the heat coil tighter in my gut. "That's the idea."

His chest rumbles beneath me, his entire body taut like a bowstring as I find my rhythm, riding his horn in slow, deliberate movements. It's not just about the friction, though—it's the way Solan watches me, his expression somewhere between reverence and pure, unfiltered hunger. His hands tremble where they hold me, his fingers digging just enough to sting, grounding me in the best way.

"Jack," he growls, voice strained, like he's barely holding himself together.

I press a hand against his chest, feeling his rapid heartbeat that perfectly mirrors mine. "You're all right, big guy," I murmur. "Just let go."

His tendril tightens around my leg, his pupils blown wide, and when I lean down to lick his cock, bending in an Olympic-medal-worthy way, his control snaps. His arms wrap around me, pulling me flush against him as he groans, while another tendril wraps around my dick. The vibration, the firm grip, the feel of his ridged horn stretching me in perfect synchronisation—all of it becomes too much, setting off fireworks under my skin. The pleasure between us builds, amplified by our bond, until it's a heady, over-whelming force.

Then everything shatters.

Solan roars, his whole body locking up beneath me as pleasure crashes over him like a tidal wave. His hands clutch me close, trembling, tendrils flexing against my skin, coating me with his release as he rides it out. I follow a second later, gripping onto him as my own orgasm rips through me, leaving me breathless and shaking. The sensation is so raw, so consuming, that for a moment, I forget where I end and he begins.

"*I love you.*" My words filter through our bond and immediately I feel his emotions wrap around me.

"*You were made for me, and I you.*"

A soft sigh escapes me at his words, and I relax, trying to catch my breath, and honestly, kinda scared to pull off his horn. There's no way it's going to be graceful.

But for now, we just exist in the aftermath, tangled together, his horn still buried deep inside me, the echoes of pleasure pulsing between us. His breath is ragged, his hands gentle now as they rub soothing circles into my back.

Eventually, he huffs out a shaky laugh, tilting his head back against the pillows as he helps ease me off him. "You are dangerous."

I chuckle, only wincing slightly at the delicious ache in my arse as I nuzzle into his neck once he's helped reposition me. "You love it."

His arms tighten around me, voice filled with fond exasperation. "I do."

I grin, pressing a kiss to his jaw. "Told ya it'd be good."

Solan groans, covering his face with one massive hand. "You are insufferable."

I just laugh, utterly satisfied, and melt into his embrace, knowing full well he wouldn't have me any other way.

BONUS SCENE 2

Everything feels really fucking strange, but there's a legit pang in my heart when I see the tin roof of my home in the distance. It looks exactly the same: a little rust, a glare as it shines in the Terrafeara sun. It's just the green sky that makes the colour of the metal roof look different, tinted in a way that makes it crystal clear that my house doesn't belong in this world.

"There is no one around." Solan touches my shoulder, no doubt feeling the mixed bag of emotions that are coursing through my body. "We don't have to do this today."

It's kind of him to say, but it's taken us four days to get here, and as painful and weird as this is, I want to get in and out safely. The sooner we do, the quicker we can get back to Dathanor, where Jamie is being protected by Calythra. With a nod, I finally respond, "I'm good."

It doesn't take long to trek through the bush, but every step over the once-familiar red soil makes me swallow hard. The grass is dry and there's none of my cattle in sight. The knowledge sends a fresh jolt to my chest, but honestly, what did I expect?

I have no doubt that the queen has ordered for all living creatures to be taken.

"That is the entrance?" Solan points at the closed fly screen at the front of my old Queenslander.

"Yeah." I glance at the verandah, at the overgrown veggie boxes as we step closer. It's still here. There's not a drop of wind rustling the leaves on the collection of gum trees to the side of the house. I spot my abandoned car, my old tractor, my side by side—all had let me down during the rift.

I exhale through my nose, then take the first step onto the verandah. The wood creaks under my weight, and a thick film of dust coats the boards, but the disturbances in the dust tell me I haven't been the only visitor. It feels eerie—like my house is a time capsule, but one that has been tampered with.

Solan steps up behind me, his presence solid and grounding. His hand moves from my shoulder to the back of my neck, a warm, steady weight. "Are you sure you're okay?"

I swallow hard, then nod. "Yeah. Just feels weird, y'know?"

His fingers squeeze gently, reassuring. "You don't have to do this alone. I am here."

I manage a small smile and tilt my head slightly into his touch before stepping forward. "I know."

The fly screen squeaks as I push it open, and the heavier wooden door behind it groans when I turn the handle. It's unlocked, just as I left it. But as soon as I step inside, I know someone's definitely been here.

The air inside is stale, carrying the scent of dust, wood, and something faintly metallic. Sunlight filters through the blinds, casting long shadows over the lounge. My eyes sweep over the familiar space—old couch, coffee table, the TV stand where my busted flat screen still sits. But some things are missing—small items, some of my tools that I had lying around on a half-finished job, even a few of the framed photos that once sat on the shelf. The queen's forces have been here, thorough but not destructive. It's been searched, not ransacked.

Solan steps inside after me, ducking his head slightly to fit through the doorway. His hair flickers around him, and his glowing golden eyes scan the room with curiosity. "This is... cosy."

I huff a quiet laugh. "Yeah, well, it was home."

He pokes at a shelf lined with dusty trinkets and framed photos. His large fingers hesitate over one of me and Jamie at the beach, taken years ago. "You should take this."

I nod and grab the frame, tucking it under my arm. "Jamie'll like that."

Solan watches me carefully, his gaze lingering on my face. "This is difficult for you."

I shrug, trying to downplay it. "Yeah, but it's gotta be done."

Without a word, he steps closer, leans down, and presses his forehead against mine, a soft, grounding touch. His warmth seeps into me, steadying the ache in my chest. "We take what we need and leave the rest. Your past is here, but your future is with me."

My throat tightens, but I nod, stepping back with a deep breath. "Yeah. Let's get to it."

Moving further into the house, I head towards my old bedroom. The bed is still there, but the drawers have been opened, their contents slightly disturbed. I grab a duffel bag from the floor of the closet and start stuffing it with anything useful—some clothes, my old pocket knife, a few sentimental bits and pieces. Solan watches me, occasionally picking up something random and inspecting it. He lifts an ancient pair of board shorts, eyes narrowing. "What is this?"

I snort. "Boardies, mate. What, you reckon they won't suit you?"

He grumbles something under his breath and tosses them back onto the bed. "They look flimsy."

I shake my head and zip up the duffel. "C'mon, let's check out the kitchen."

We make our way down the hall, past the laundry and bathroom, until we step into the kitchen. The cupboards hold a few cans of food, which I shove into another bag, along with some old tools and a camping stove from the storage cupboard in here. Then my eyes land on something else—my DVD collection stacked haphazardly in a crate by the fridge.

A grin tugs at my lips. "Oh, now this... this is gold."

Solan tilts his head. "More movies?"

"More than just movies. Classics." I crouch and start sifting through them. "*Mad Max, Crocodile Dundee, The Castle*—oh, you've gotta see *The Castle*."

He crosses his arms. "Will it be better than *Terminator*?"

I bark out a laugh. "Very different vibe, but yeah, I reckon you'll love it."

He watches as I pull out a few more. "I have not yet managed to fix the television I found. It remains… stubborn."

I chuckle. "We'll figure it out. Even if we have to jury-rig some weird-arse generator, we're watching these."

His hair flickers again, thoughtful. Then, after a pause, he reaches out and pulls me into a firm, unexpected hug. I go stiff for a second before melting into it, letting his warmth sink in. "You have done well today," he murmurs. "I know this is not easy."

I let out an unsteady breath and squeeze him back. "Thanks, baby. You're a good bloke."

His tendrils of hair flick playfully against my back and shoulders. "I am the best *bloke*."

I snort and pull back, patting his chest. "All right, let's finish up."

Satisfied we've gotten what we can for now, I glance towards the back door. "Right. Let's check Jamie's place next."

Solan nods, and together we step back out into the strange, foreign sunlight, leaving the echoes of my old life behind—for now.

ABOUT THE AUTHOR

I live and breathe all things book related. Usually with at least three books being read and two WiPs being written at the same time, life is merrily hectic. I tend to do nothing by halves, so I happily seek the craziness and busyness life offers.

Living on my small property in Queensland with my human family as well as my animal family of cows, sheep, chooks, and dogs, I really do appreciate the beauty of the world around me and am a believer that love truly is love.

To check for updates head to my website:
HTTPS://BECCASEYMOUR.COM
HTTPS://LANDING.MAILERLITE.COM/
WEBFORMS/LANDING/R9F0I4
Plus, join my Facebook group, which I share with the awesome Louisa Masters here:
HTTPS://WWW.FACEBOOK.COM/GROUPS/
ROMMANCEWITHBECCALOUISA/

patreon.com/BeccaSeymour

facebook.com/beccaseymourauthor

instagram.com/authorbeccaseymour

bookbub.com/authors/becca-seymour

tiktok.com/@beccaseymourwrites

www.ingramcontent.com/pod-product-compliance
Lightning Source LLC
Chambersburg PA
CBHW032026180726
48283CB00008B/2829